RIGGED

ALSO BY D.P. LYLE

The Jake Longly Series
Deep Six
A-List
Sunshine State

The Cain/Harper Series
Skin in the Game

The Dub Walker Series
Stress Fracture
Hot Lights, Cold Steel
Run to Ground

The Samantha Cody Series
Original Sin
Devil's Playground
Double Blind

The Royal Pains Media Tie-In Series
Royal Pains: First, Do No Harm
Royal Pains: Sick Rich

Nonfiction
Murder and Mayhem
Forensics For Dummies
Forensics and Fiction
Howdunit: Forensics; A Guide For Writers
More Forensics and Fiction
ABA Fundamentals: Forensic Science

Anthologies
Thrillers: 100 Must-Reads (contributor); *Jules Verne, Mysterious
Island Thriller 3: Love Is Murder* (contributor); *Even Steven*;
For the Sake of the Game (contributor); *Bottom Line*

RIGGED

A JAKE LONGLY THRILLER

D.P. LYLE

OCEANVIEW⊚PUBLISHING
SARASOTA, FLORIDA

ISBN 978-1-60809-338-0

Published in the United States of America by Oceanview Publishing

Sarasota, Florida

www.oceanviewpub.com

10 9 8 7 6 5 4 3 2 1

PRINTED IN THE UNITED STATES OF AMERICA

ACKNOWLEDGEMENTS

To my wonderful agent and friend, Kimberley Cameron, of Kimberley Cameron & Associates. KC, you're the best.

To Bob and Pat Gussin and all the wonderfully dedicated people at Oceanview Publishing. Thanks for your friendship and always spot-on insights, making my writing the best it can be.

To my writers' group for helping make this story work. Thanks, Barbara, Terri, Craig, Donna, Sandy, and Laurie.

To Nancy Whitley, who always edits and proofreads my work.

To my friend and fraternity brother, Attorney Dag Rowe, for help navigating the legal intricacies of divorce in Alabama.

And, of course, Nan, for everything.

CHAPTER 1

LIFE RUNS IN odd circles. Creates circumstances you never see coming, could never predict. Makes for strange bedfellows.

As my grandfather was quick to say, "Life can park your butt in some unpleasant locales." Loved that guy. More so than my father, Ray, who could be a pain in the ass. Not that I didn't love him, just that he was a bit intense for my tastes. I think he and I tolerated each other as much as anything else. I often wished he was more like his father, but that train hit the rails decades ago.

Back to parking your butt in unpleasant places.

Right now, mine had found itself on an uncomfortably hard, wooden chair behind the defense table in the Gulf Shores Municipal Courthouse. I wasn't sure what caused the most unease—the seat, the fact that I was the defendant in the proceedings at hand, the stack of charges levied against me, or the sullenness of Judge Ruth Corvas. The woman was all decked out in her black robe, shoulders hunched forward, sharp eyes following my attorney as he walked back and forth before her, offering his closing argument. She looked like a hawk, eyeing prey. Maybe a turkey vulture sizing up carrion. Made me reconsider having waved my rights to a jury trial.

I was good with people. Always had been. That's one reason Captain Rocky's, my bar/restaurant, was so successful. I was the "face" of the operation. A jury might like me; Judge Corvas less so. She looked like she had eaten a bad taco. Or too many barbecued beans.

I could almost hear the rattle and clank of my cell door.

All that aside, the most uncomfortable situation here today was my lawyer. Walter Horton. Yeah, that Walter. The one that had sliced and diced my finances during a nasty divorce proceeding. Picture being stripped naked, sprayed with icy water, and slowly bleeding to death. That doesn't quite cover it, but you get the idea. And then, after my legal colonoscopy, dear old Walter had married my ex. Tammy the Insane, as I so affectionately call her. Not that the moniker was erroneous—she truly was deranged. Apparently, Walter didn't see her that way, which made me question his judgement.

But he was hands down the best attorney along the Gulf.

And now I was in his hands.

See, life can put your butt in some unpleasant locales.

"Your Honor, this entire case is a sham," Walter began. "It has no basis in reality, or in the law. The plaintiff, Mr. Edward Peck, has accused my client, Mr. Jake Longly, of kidnapping, auto theft, assault, and public humiliation and defamation."

Walter turned slightly and pointed toward Eddie Peck, who looked considerably different than he had that night. Blue suit, red tie, clean shaven, hair combed to perfection. Not sloppy, disheveled, hair matted with drunk sweat. All in all, he scrubbed up nicely.

"Mr. Peck should be thanking my client for saving his life." Walter turned back to the judge. "And potentially the lives of others."

Walter walked back to the table, squared up some papers, and gave me a wink. Walter winked at me? Like we were old buddies or in some mutual conspiracy? The truth was that after the plaintiff's attorney, a slick SOB if there ever was one, finished his final argument, I felt like I was headed for Kilby's death row. I came off

as an unrepentant master criminal who had unmercifully brutal-
ized poor Eddie. I swear Judge Corvas looked at me like I was a
serial killer.

Looking for moral support, I glanced back at Tommy Jeffers, aka
Pancake, and Nicole Jamison, who sat right behind me. Pancake,
my best friend and a witness in these proceedings, seemed unper-
turbed, but Nicole, my girlfriend, also a witness to all that went
down, had arranged her wonderful blue eyes in a wide stare that
only added to my discomfort. Maybe she was working on an escape
plan. A distraction of the guards while I bolted. She could do that
without even trying. Or maybe a saw in a cake. Problem with that
was that Nicole didn't cook. She possessed a multitude of skills, but
none included an oven. The kitchen wasn't her best room.

Walter continued. "The facts that we have presented before the
court tell the true story. Mr. Peck entered Mr. Longly's establishment, Captain Rocky's, just after 11:00 p.m. Several witnesses stated
that he was extremely intoxicated and belligerent. Private
Investigator Mr. Tommy Jeffers testified that his inquiries revealed
that Mr. Peck had just been expelled from another establishment,
Jimmy's Wharf, for similar behavior. Your Honor has several affida-
vits from witnesses who support these facts. He then drove the half
mile to Captain Rocky's in his severely inebriated state."

Walter looked at his shoes, gave a slight shake of his head. Waited.
Letting those facts sink in before resuming. He did so in a calmer,
softer voice that required the jury to lean forward. He had their
complete attention. He was good. Very good.

"Mr. Peck ordered a double scotch. Ms. Carla Martinez, the manager at Captain Rocky's, testified that when she saw Mr. Peck's state
of inebriation, she refused to serve him. Mr. Peck took offense.
Became angry, shouted, called her a few unrepeatable names. As he
reached for his car keys, which he had tossed on the bar before him,

Ms. Martinez secured the keys, saying he was in no condition to drive. My client, sensing the situation, approached. He offered to call Mr. Peck a cab. Even offered to pay for it. For his good-citizen concern, Mr. Longly was shoved, and a punch was thrown."

That's me. Concerned citizen. Knight in shining armor. White horse. Galahad. The whole enchilada. Unfortunately, Judge Corvas' hawkish eyes didn't soften. Could she really toss Dudley Do-Right in the slammer?

"Fortunately," Walter pressed forward, "the punch missed my client. At this point, Mr. Tommy Jeffers interceded, grabbing the plaintiff in a bear hug. Once order had been restored, a cab was indeed called, and Mr. Peck left for home."

Walter now looked back toward Peck.

"So, Your Honor, Mr. Longly did not kidnap Mr. Peck. He was free to go at any time. Just not behind the wheel of his car. He did not steal Mr. Peck's automobile. He merely kept the keys until the plaintiff could return the next day, sober, and retrieve them. He did not assault Mr. Peck and, in fact, was attacked himself. Only when Mr. Jeffers interceded was a truly physical altercation avoided."

Walter adjusted his tie. He looked sharp. Expensive, perfectly tailored three-piece gray suit, white shirt, red power tie. So Walter. He could afford fancy duds. Hell, I helped pay for them.

"So, here we are. Mr. Peck asking for fifty thousand dollars from my client. A ridiculous proposition. He should be grateful Mr. Longly and his staff interceded and prevented him from potential harm to himself and others. Mr. Longly didn't call the police and have Mr. Peck arrested for assault, or for DUI had he left in his vehicle. He took care of him. Got him safely home. Mr. Peck should be grateful, not vengeful." Walter walked toward the bench and faced the judge. "As for any public humiliation or character defamation, I think Mr. Peck took care of that himself. He needed no help from my client in that regard."

Judge Corvas didn't take a recess, or delay the proceedings for her consideration, or anything along those lines. She made her judgement right then and there. Weren't quick judgements bad for the defendant? Like the evidence was so overwhelming that the result was obvious? Or was that only in jury trials? Judge Corvas didn't look happy. Did she ever? She stared at me. Uh-oh. But then turned a glared at Eddie Peck.

I won.

She tossed the case, admonished Eddie Peck regarding frivolous lawsuits, and even approved my restraining order, Walter's idea, that prevented Peck from reentering Captain Rocky's. Peck was furious, tried to protest, but Judge Corvas gaveled him into silence, adding that if he continued his protestations he might find himself in contempt. Peck stormed from the courtroom.

I shook Walter's hand and thanked him.

My new buddy. Uh, probably not.

CHAPTER 2

HUNGER GNAWED AT Pancake. Not exactly earthshaking news. Truth be told, he couldn't remember many moments when he wasn't hungry. Maybe for half an hour or so after his mom's Thanksgiving dinner, but that's about it. But, come on. The three donuts—only three—he had eaten two hours earlier merely smoothed the edges. Got his juices flowing. Now, the feed-me beast had awakened and needed sustenance.

But his growling stomach wasn't the only reason he ambled around the corner from Bancroft Street, where he had parked his massive black Chevy dually, and on to Fairhope Avenue. Beautiful downtown Fairhope, Alabama. He hadn't been there in, what? Twenty years? Probably more. Not sure why. Cool, artsy, great restaurants, and right on the eastern edge of Mobile Bay, which added brilliant sunsets to the mix.

His destination was Mullins Bakery. A block and a half up the street. Where Emily worked. The fluttering in his stomach wasn't simply hunger.

Emily Rhodes. Now Emily Patterson. Been a long time since last he saw her. Not since she wore pigtails and had a gap in her front teeth. Would she remember him? He had her photo inside the gray canvas messenger bag that looped over his left shoulder. She had grown into a beautiful woman. No surprise there. She had been a beauty in the sixth grade. Prettiest girl in school. Even with a gapped-tooth smile, she won that prize. To Pancake anyway.

Inside the bakery, the rich aromas of butter, sugar, and coffee flavored the air. A woman stood behind the counter, ringing up a customer. She looked forty-ish, thin, fit. Not like she worked in a bakery. Dark hair with a few gray streaks, smile open and welcoming. She handed the customer a bag of something sweet and a to-go cup of coffee, saying, "Thanks for dropping in."

The customer left and Pancake stepped up to the counter.

The woman smiled. "What can I get you?"

"Is Emily in?" Pancake asked.

"She isn't here. Probably running late." She raised an eyebrow. "Who's asking?"

Pancake gave her a benevolent smile. "Sorry. I'm Tommy Jeffers."

"You? You're Tommy?"

Who was this woman? Why would she know him?

She apparently sensed his confusion. "Emily talks about you all the time. How you guys were sixth-grade sweethearts."

"We were."

"She speaks fondly of you."

"And I of her."

"I'm Allison." She wiped her hands on a counter towel and extended it toward him. They shook. "Allison Mullins. I own the place."

"Smells good."

"I do know my way around an oven."

"Looks that way." He nodded toward the glass display case. Croissants, donuts, cinnamon rolls, and an assortment of other gooey creations stared back at him. "What's your speciality?"

"Everything." She laughed. Pleasant and full. "You look like a ham and cheese croissant guy."

"I am. Maybe a couple of them."

"Heated?" Pancake nodded. Using tongs, she grabbed a pair and placed them on a paper plate and slid them into the toaster oven on the counter behind her. "Coffee?"

"That'd be nice."

She poured a large cup and slid it on the countertop. "Emily said you were a big guy, but I never imagined this." Another laugh. "She showed me a picture once. From school. I recognize the red hair, for sure."

Pancake remembered the picture. Those little ones that schools made each year. And kids traded with each other. He remembered swapping his for one of Emily's. Near her school locker, glancing over his shoulder, making sure no one was watching. He still had her photo in his top drawer at home. Inside the small wooden box where he kept such things.

"I haven't seen her since then," Pancake said. "Of course, back then she was Emily Rhodes. That summer her family moved up here."

"She still lives in the family home. A couple of miles north. Near Seacliff."

Pancake knew that. It was in the file he and Ray had built on Emily.

"So, she's not here?" he asked.

"No. She's supposed to be. Should've been here an hour ago."

"She late often?"

"Some." Her brow wrinkled. "Come to think of it, she said she had some meeting this morning. Not sure where so maybe that's where she is."

"The meeting was with me. Here."

"Oh? She didn't tell me you were coming. The one and only Tommy Jeffers."

"Folks call me Pancake."

"Pancake?"

He shrugged. "A name I got later. In high school."

"Let me guess. Football? Pancake blocks?"

"Very good," Pancake said. "Most folks think it's from eating."

"I have a son. He plays. Big guy, too. Not your size, but he's big enough to eat me out of house and home."

"My mom would've agreed with that."

The oven dinged. Allison retrieved the plate. "Let's sit." She ferried the steaming croissants to a table.

Pancake sat, snatched up one, and took a bite.

"These are great. You're my new favorite person."

She smiled. "Love to hear that." She seemed to examine him. "So you're the famous Tommy Jeffers?" She shook her head. "Never thought I'd get to meet you. But now that I have, I see what Emily was talking about."

"What's that?"

"Your eyes. Lively. Intelligent. She said that's what she liked most. You were smart."

Pancake shrugged. "I get by. But Emily was the smart one."

"She is that." She glanced toward the entry. "I wonder where she is? Can't imagine her being late for a meeting with you."

"She doesn't know the meeting's with me," Pancake said. "Just my firm." He smiled. "I wanted to surprise her."

"What's your business?"

"Private investigations."

"Oh. Does this have to do with her divorce?"

"It does."

She gazed toward the front windows, and the street beyond, unfocused. "She told me she'd finally filed it."

"A few days ago."

"You're from Gulf Shores? Right?"

Pancake took another bite, nodded. "I am."

"I know she hired some attorney from down there."

"And he hired us. Longly Investigations."

"To do what?"

"Mostly financial stuff."

"I'm glad she finally decided to move on. She's hemmed and hawed about it for months."

"Divorce is never an easy decision," Pancake said.

"That's true. For Emily particularly so. Made her feel like she'd failed. Or some such nonsense." She smiled. "Emily doesn't fail at anything. She's a smart cookie."

One croissant down. Pancake lifted the second one, took a bite. "I take it you know her husband?"

"I do. Sean's his name."

Pancake knew that, too. "What's his story?"

"He's okay. Not a bad guy." She gave a half smile. "Just not overly ambitious. Or attentive."

"Trouble in paradise?"

"Sort of. They get along fine. Most times. He just has a wandering eye."

"Seems to be a common state."

"They separated six months ago. Maybe a bit longer." She flattened one palm on the table, stared at the back of her hand. "I hope this doesn't become messy. I'd hate for her to have to go through a bunch of crap."

"Seems fairly low temperature," Pancake said. "At least from what we've managed to dig up."

"Good. Truth is, I think both of them are ready for it to end."

"I understand they were married for four years?"

"About that."

"And no kids," Pancake said, a statement. He knew.

"That's right. Early on they planned to but put it off until they were settled and more on their feet." She gave a half shrug. "Right now, that looks like a wise choice."

"Kids do make divorces more difficult. And a whole bunch messier."

She nodded, glanced at her watch. "I wonder where she is."

"Did you call her?" Pancake asked.

"Couple of times. No answer at home. Her cell went to voicemail."

"That unusual?"

"Yeah. She's usually pretty easy to locate."

Pancake finished the second croissant. "Let me pay up and then I'll head over to the bank to pick up some stuff. Maybe I'll swing by her place after that."

"She'll probably come in soon."

"If so, give me a call."

"Will do."

He refused her offer that the food was "on the house" and paid. He gave her his number and ventured back into the sunlight.

CHAPTER 3

PANCAKE SAT WITH bank manager Noah Hicks. He had called Hicks the day before to arrange a late morning appointment, figuring he'd be with Emily for a couple of hours at least. Going over everything. Maybe reminiscing about school days. But, with Emily a no-show, he called Hicks and moved the appointment forward. No problem. He could see why. The bank was essentially empty.

Hicks was a slight man, with thinning, combed-over hair. Wire-rim glasses made him look studious. Like, well, a banker. On a credenza behind him sat a gold-framed picture of him with an also slight woman and two girls, both in soccer uniforms.

After offering coffee, which Pancake declined, Hicks got right to it. He produced a letter from Walter Horton, stating that he was the attorney of record in these proceedings and that he had hired Longly Investigations as part of his team. He also had a signed statement from Emily that allowed him to discuss her financial matters.

"Looks like we have everything in order," Hicks said.

"Good."

Hicks gave a nod even as a look of pain, maybe even despair, fell over his face. "I hate to see young couples fall apart this way. Especially this one. I've known Emily since she was a teenager. Her family banked with us for many years. They were part of our family here."

"I knew her in grade school," Pancake said. "Down in Gulf Shores."

"You did?"

"We were an item in the sixth grade."

"So your inquiries have a personal angle?"

"On one level. But we were hired to look into the financials. Make sure everything is in order."

Hicks seemed to consider that briefly. "Seems like maybe too often married couples don't work it out. Give it a chance. Think ending it's the best option."

"Sometimes the writing on the wall is clear," Pancake said. "I've seen quite a few divorces in this business. Most turn into mud wrestling."

"I suppose that's true."

"From your perspective, any financial contentions in play here?"

Hicks flipped open the file folder in front of him. "Not really. I'm sure you know there's no such thing as community property in Alabama so the house won't be on the table."

"Because Emily inherited it from her parents?"

"Exactly. Their will passed it along to her and such property stays with the inheritor in that case." Hicks pushed a page toward him. "She received title to it when her father passed just over four years ago. Shortly before she and Sean married. Her mother had passed a year earlier. It was free and clear, but after she got married, she and Sean took out a mortgage for sixty thousand to do some remodeling. Been paying on that. The balance is around forty."

"So Emily's net is what?"

"The house is appraised for three-fifty, minus the forty, plus she has about twenty thousand in her savings and checking. A couple of CDs that currently are valued at another thirty. So around three sixty or so."

"The loan they took out? Could that be a sticking point?"

"It shouldn't. Since it's secured with the property, the debt would fall into the lap of the owner. So, that would be Emily's debt."

Pancake nodded. "And Sean Patterson? The soon-to-be ex?"

"He banks here, too. They each opened individual accounts six months ago. When they separated."

"He doing okay, too?"

Hicks leaned back, folded his hands over his abdomen. "Can't say. I don't have his permission to release that information yet."

"He reluctant to do so?"

"Not really. He works two jobs. One is over at the lumber supply. The other is out on the oil rigs. He'll go out there for two weeks, then back here for the same. I think he's out there monkeying around on a rig right now."

"I know assets acquired during the marriage," Pancake said, "minus the property we talked about, are considered pooled assets. So any issues there you see?"

Hicks shrugged. "I can't get into the details yet. Until Sean officially signs off. But it's my understanding that Emily's CD would remain hers. It was set up by her father in her name. I believe that would be considered inheritance. But the judge might feel otherwise."

"They often do."

"But, that aside, I can say that Sean's cash on hand and Emily's aren't that far apart so that should be a simple resolution."

Pancake nodded. "So, you don't see any financial storms brewing?"

"Sure don't. You can dig into the nuts and bolts once he gives permission. And I'm sure he will when he gets back onshore."

"Any idea when that might be?"

"I think in the next day or so. He always comes in to make a deposit when he returns to dry land."

"Hopefully he'll release his financials then."

"Don't see any reason he wouldn't." Hicks sat up, squared his shoulders. "I suspect if he doesn't, there'll be a court order issued."

Pancake nodded. "Usually goes that way. If necessary."

CHAPTER 4

AFTER GATHERING THE documents Hicks had prepped for him, Pancake headed north, toward Emily's place. Little traffic. Only took ten minutes. The property was in a sparsely populated area, just inland from the bayfront town of Seacliff. Looked to be around five acres, none of it plowed, or prepped, or planted. Emily apparently wasn't into farming. The house sat back a hundred feet from the road, up a gravel drive. White clapboard, two dormer windows, green tile roof. A blue Dodge Ram 3500 pickup sat at the end of the drive, nosed up to the garage door. He knew that wasn't Emily's car. His research showed she drove a three-year-old white Toyota Camry. Purchased used a year ago. And she hadn't acquired a new car. At least not since his last check, which was yesterday.

Did she have a visitor? Maybe an overnight guest? He hated that his mind went there. This was Emily. He still remembered the sixth-grade version. But she was separated, heading into a divorce, so companionship wouldn't be unexpected. Truth was, he couldn't remember a divorce where such liaisons weren't in the soup. Seemed folks always grabbed for something to soften the landing.

Gravel crunched beneath his tires. The dashboard temperature gauge said it was 84. And it was only ten in the morning. News had said it'd reach the mid-nineties. August in this part of the world tended to be overheated. Even though this entire area edged up against Mobile Bay, and the water moderated the heat somewhat, summers could still be a bitch.

Pancake rolled to a stop beside the truck and climbed out. Quiet and peaceful out here. Open fields, scattered with pines and gums and oaks. Crows fussing in the distance. The thought that it could have been him and Emily that lived here germinated in his brain but he squashed it. No need to play the what-if game.

Three steps led to the porch, the shade of the gallery welcome. A pair of wooden rockers to his left, a chain-suspended slat porch swing to his right. The screen door was closed, but the front door beyond was cracked open a few inches. Cool air spilled out.

He rapped a knuckle on the doorframe.

No answer.

Another rap, then, "Emily? You here?"

Silence.

He walked around the house to the backyard, most of the five acres beyond. No one there. Open land, more trees. Picnic table, fire pit, and a grill beneath a spreading oak. Cozy. The perfect place for a summer evening.

The back door was locked, the kitchen and dining area visible through the windows, empty. He completed his lap. The first two side windows curtained; the final offered a view between open drapes into the living room. He had seen that from the front. He returned to the front porch where he stood facing the door again.

If she had company, could they still be in bed? Maybe the shower? Why would they leave the door open and the AC running?

This time he banged on the doorframe with a fist. Hard enough to shake the walls. He shouted again, much louder than before.

Nothing.

Something was wrong. Even in the heat, his skin cooled, the hair on his neck and arms rose.

The screen door hinges creaked as he pulled it open. He nudged the front door back with one foot. Another shout.

He stepped inside. The air cool, bordering on cold.

The idea that he was essentially breaking and entering Emily's house crossed his mind. Was her friend armed? Hell, was Emily armed?

More shouting, moving through the living room, kitchen, hallway; a quick peek into a pair of open bathrooms and three bedrooms revealed nothing. Then the final bedroom. The door was closed.

He knocked, shouted her name. No response, no movement inside.

He closed his eyes, took a deep breath, murmured a soft, "Please," and opened the door.

No bodies, no blood. Nothing. He exhaled. Rein in your imagination, he told himself.

Back outside, he walked to the garage. Through the side-door window, he saw Emily's white Toyota Camry. He tried the knob. Locked. Next, he inspected the pickup. Also locked. He saw nothing of interest through the window.

He called Allison.

"Any word?"

"No."

"I'm here at her place," Pancake said. "The front door was open but there's no sign of her."

"If the door's open, she must be there."

"She isn't. I checked the house. Do you know who might own a blue Dodge Ram 3500?"

"Yeah. Jason Collins. Why?"

"It's here in the driveway."

"Emily's been seeing him."

"Her Toyota's in the garage. She have another car?"

"No."

"You think maybe they went for a walk or something?" Pancake asked.

"Not if she was supposed to be here for a meeting."

"Maybe she forgot."

"She wouldn't," Allison said. "And she wouldn't miss work without calling me. It's not her way. She's very reliable."

"I don't like it," Pancake said.

"Don't say that."

"Maybe I'm overreacting."

"What are you going to do?" Allison asked.

"Drive the neighborhood. See if I can find them."

And that's what he did. All of it. Back at the house, nothing had changed.

He called Ray. Ran the situation by him.

Ray took it all in. "I don't like it either. Maybe you should call the locals. Get them to sniff around."

"My thoughts exactly."

"Call Jake and Nicole. They can drive up and give you a hand."

"Why don't you?" Pancake asked.

"You know the answer to that. I'm the boss and shit flows downhill."

"So, I have to be the bearer of bad news?"

"That's how it works," Ray said.

"And babysit Jake and Nicole?"

"Just Jake. Nicole can take care of herself."

"True that."

"Besides," Ray said, "you don't want to eat lunch alone."

Pancake pondered that. He had eaten his two breakfasts all by his lonesome so company for the next meal wouldn't be bad. But that wasn't Ray's agenda. "Jake know anything about this case?"

"That's where you come in."

CHAPTER 5

I'M AN EX–MAJOR League baseball stud, restauranteur, defender of frivolous lawsuits, lover of women, well, one in particular, and for sure a world-class avoider of work. Something my father, Ray, has as yet failed to grasp. He probably never will. Actually, no probably about it. We have a difficult relationship. Ray seems to work endlessly. As a P.I. Multiple cases in process is his norm. Lots of phone calls, computer snooping, and occasionally some sneaky nighttime work. He continually tries to involve me, and often manages to, but I twist and turn and do all I can to avoid it. Work, that is.

Case in point: I was currently ensconced on the deck at Captain Rocky's, my bar/restaurant, at a table that overlooked the bright white sand of Gulf Shores. Across from me sat my manager, Carla Martinez. The one that actually runs the business. Also, the one that snatched Eddie Peck's car keys and began the cascade that landed me in court. Over the last few days I'd given her some grief about it, but she knew I was simply yanking her chain, that she had done exactly the right thing.

This morning, she had about a thousand pages spread over the teak tabletop and rambled on about this and that. Mostly purchase orders, I think. At least she mentioned seafood, ribs, and booze. Our staples here. I pretended to pay attention. I never liked the details of running a business. Too many numbers, too many moving parts. Which is why I have Carla. For years, she has kept me from neglectful bankruptcy.

Nicole Jamison sat at the next table. Reading through a screenplay she had in the works. I didn't know what it was about because she wouldn't show it to me. Or even tell me about it. She can be difficult. Gorgeous, fun, but at times difficult.

Earlier, she and I had completed our Krav Maga class. Yes, we're still participating in that insanity and I have the sore hands to prove it. Then here for breakfast. Egg and pulled pork burritos the guys in the kitchen whipped up.

Finally, Carla said, "So I should go ahead with all this?"

I had no idea what "all this" covered but was smart enough to know the right answer. "Yeah."

"I'm on it." She gathered her paperwork and headed toward the office.

I asked Nicole if she wanted more coffee, but she waved me away. Nose buried in her story. The one I knew nothing about.

I walked to the bar, refilled my cup, and returned to the deck, this time sitting across from Nicole. I gazed out over the beach, now teeming with people, catching the midmorning sun. August in Gulf Shores was one big traffic jam. Not only on the roads but also the beaches. If the folks stretched out on towels and slathered with suntan oil were smart, they'd head for shade by noon as it was supposed to reach the nineties by then. Most visitors to Gulf Shores weren't that smart, though. Drinking, partying, and sunburning the norm.

The good news was that many of them would wander in here for lunch. Hard to complain about that.

I watched Nicole read, those wonderous blue eyes moving back and forth, that sleek blond hair snaked to one side and draped over her shoulder. Quite a journey we'd been on. Now for what? A year. Amazing.

"Quit staring at me," she said.

"I'm not."

"You are. And you look like a wolf."

"I am."

"You wish."

"I'm admiring your beauty."

She glanced up. "Do you think such flattery will get you anywhere?"

"It did last night."

Boy had it. Well, that and a bottle of tequila.

"That was all me," she said. "If memory serves, you wanted to crash early. I was the one that diverted your attention from sleep."

"You mean when you took your clothes off and jumped on me?"

"My signature move."

Along with a bunch of others.

"Wonder where Pancake is?" I asked.

There weren't many mornings he didn't show up for food, hunger being his major driving force.

She shrugged. "I know he has some case he's working on."

"Ever seen that interfere with food?"

"No."

She melted back into her writing, and I watched two teenage dudes negotiate their boogie boards down the face of a three-foot wave. "Has he seemed off the past couple of days?" I asked.

"What do you mean?"

"A little too quiet. Not like him."

She looked at me, tapped the red pen she held against one cheek. "Now that you mention it, maybe so." She glanced out toward the water. "Ray's probably working him too hard. Maybe it's this new case."

"You know anything about it?"

She shook her head. "I asked, but he said it was nothing."

"See, that's what I mean. He usually rattles on about that kind of stuff."

"Maybe it's a boring case."

"Nothing is boring to Pancake."

"You have a point."

"What do you want to do today?" I asked.

She placed her pen on the table. She stretched, arms up, some of her best parts nearly ripping through her tank top, and gave a half yawn. "Maybe drive over to Orange Beach. Have lunch at that cute little diner."

"Sounds like a plan."

"Maybe go by your place for a quick shower."

I lived nearby, just up the beach. Nice place. On the sand. She lived at her uncle Charles' mega-mansion out at The Point. That's Uncle Charles the big-time movie producer. His place is nicer. But farther away.

"I like that plan even better."

"Don't get any ideas." She smiled. "Unless you want to."

"I do."

Amazing how the simple chirp of a cell phone can trash even the most carefully concocted plans. And I was working on a couple of good ones. That involved soap and hot water and, well, slippery fun.

The tone in question came from Nicole's phone.

Here's the side of the conversation I heard:

"Hey there. What's up?"

"I see. So, why didn't you call Jake?"

A laugh. Then: "Got it."

"He's right here. Maybe you should tell him."

She punched on the speakerphone and said, "It's Pancake."

"What were you afraid to tell me?" I asked.

"Ray was, too. That's why I got stuck with being the messenger."

"So, what is it?"

"Need your help with a job," Pancake said.

"I don't work for Ray."

"Are we going to go through that again?"

That again was me refusing, him reminding me that Nicole did sorta, kinda, work for Ray, and that wherever she went I'd follow.

"I guess not," I said. Some battles you can't win so why bother?

"You remember Emily Rhodes?"

"I do. You wanted to marry her in the sixth grade."

"She did get married. Guy named Sean Patterson. And now, after four years, they're getting a divorce."

"I'm sorry to hear that. I liked her."

"Yeah, well, we're looking into things for her. Financial stuff mostly."

"Who's her attorney?"

"That's the reason neither me nor Ray wanted to call you."

"That doesn't make sense," I said.

"Your new buddy Walter Horton."

Did I hear him correctly? Walter? Spending the better part of a day sitting in a courtroom with him was more than enough Walter-time for me. Okay, he did save my bacon, but still. And now Walter pops up in this.

"Walter hired Ray?" I asked.

"Sure did."

"Does Tammy know? She hates Ray."

"Compared to you, she loves Ray. Likes me a whole lot better than both of you."

Nicole laughed. I looked at her. "You think that's funny?" I asked.

She gave a half shrug. "Hysterical would be my choice."

"Me, too," Pancake said. "Anyway, Walter liked the work we did on your behalf and hired us."

"My behalf?"

Pancake grunted.

"So what do you need from us?" Nicole asked.

Pancake told the tale. Emily not showing up for a meeting with him, or for work, what he found at her house. Said he'd called the police and was waiting for them and that everything was getting complicated and he needed some extra eyes and ears and footwork.

"Okay, we're on it," Nicole said.

I never liked it when she said, "We're on it." Nothing pleasant ever followed. Rather, it erupted into things like a middle-of-the-night swan dive into the Gulf from the back of a hundred-foot yacht, or whacking some angry gator with a baseball bat, or smacking a cop in the face with a snow globe. All in the name of truth, justice, and the American way, was Ray's take.

"I suspect I'll be here at her place for a while," Pancake said. "Either answering questions for the police or hopefully she'll come home from wherever she is."

"You want us to meet you there?" she asked.

"Yeah. I'll text you the address."

Nicole disconnected the call and smiled at me.

Now she looked like the wolf.

CHAPTER 6

FAIRHOPE, ALABAMA, IS considered the jewel of Mobile Bay. Seated on the east side, facing west, its water-reflected sunsets are spectacular. The permanent population is around twenty thousand, but the tourists who roam the streets each year dwarf that. Downtown is small, quaint, artsy, and loaded with fun coffee shops and restaurants. To the north is the equally quaint town of Daphne and to the south Point Clear, home to another bayside jewel, the Grand Hotel.

Only thirty miles separates Fairhope from Gulf Shores. But getting there could take anywhere from forty minutes to an hour and a half. Such is Gulf Coast summertime traffic. Probably why I hadn't been there in years, though that seemed like a flimsy excuse. Nicole had never seen the town.

We sailed up State Highway 59 aimed toward Foley. Nicole in her element. Dissecting the traffic, maneuvering her white Mercedes 550SL through the moderately dense traffic.

"I'm excited to see Fairhope," Nicole said.

"No, you're not," I said. "You're eager to get your teeth in a new case."

"If there is one." She glanced at me. "She and that guy she's seeing might have simply gone somewhere. Visit friends, a romantic getaway."

"Maybe."

"You don't think so?"

"I don't."

"Based on what exactly?"

"Something in Pancake's voice. He thinks things are out of whack. And his instincts are always on the button."

"I guess we'll see soon."

"Especially at this rate."

"Wimp."

My cell buzzed. The ID read "Tammy." My ex. I don't know why, but she calls me at least once a week. With some problem she thinks I can solve, or even cared about, but always with another stack of complaints about my behavior while we still shared matrimonial bliss. Which was years ago. She was now Walter Horton's problem. Yet, she continued to wage psychological warfare against me. Or so it seemed.

I angled my phone toward Nicole.

"Oh, this should be fun. Put it on speaker. I don't want to miss anything."

Of course she didn't. Not that she and Tammy were friendly. Not even close. Cordial wouldn't work either. A common rift between exes and current girlfriends. For Nicole, these episodic calls from Tammy supplied facts, real or imagined, that Nicole could use to give me grief. I was sure it was some sort of feminine conspiracy. One that even enemies shared. Some kind of XX chromosomal connection us guys weren't privy to. Me, paranoid? It's not paranoia if they're actually shooting at you.

I briefly considered ignoring the call, but that never worked with Tammy. She'd keep hammering until I relented. A war of attrition. Better to get whatever today's issue was over with. I answered, activating the speaker function. Didn't get a word out. Not even hello.

"Jake, what the hell are you doing?"

"Trying to decide why I answered your call."

"What's that noise? Are your driving?"

"No. Nicole is."

"She hasn't put you on the road yet?"

"We are on the road," I said.

"So, you dragged her into this business?"

"What business?"

I could hear an exasperated sigh hiss through the phone. Mission accomplished.

"You know very well what I'm talking about. Walter hired Ray and now he's got you involved?"

"I'm simply a passenger. I don't work for Ray."

"Yet you always seem to land right in the middle of everything."

She did have a point. Regardless of how much I dodged and weaved, struggled to avoid it, I repeatedly got swept into Ray's world. Not by my own doing, but Pancake and Nicole are impossible to resist. Pancake because we'd been brothers in arms since childhood, and Nicole because, well, she's Nicole. I mean, take a gander.

Tammy wasn't finished. Was she ever? "You create chaos everywhere you go. I don't want you nosing into Walter's business."

"I'm not."

"And after he pulled your ass out of the fire last week."

"I'm sure that made you happy," I said.

She tossed out a disgusted snort. "It's the attorney's creed. They have to defend everyone. Even snakes."

"Cobras are cool." I could almost hear her teeth grinding. This was actually bordering on fun. So, I continued. "And tell Walter I said thanks for the discount."

Walter had done nothing of the sort. Wasn't in his nature. And for me, not a chance. But I knew what was coming. I know, I know, evil for sure. But this is Tammy we're taking about. Nicole gave me a look, a slight headshake. She knew what was coming, too.

"What? Walter gave you a break?"

"A much appreciated one."

"Well, I'll fix that. You can expect a bill."

"I don't usually open junk mail."

More teeth grinding. I think she fractured a molar.

"Look," I said, "Nicole and I are headed up to Fairhope to meet Pancake for lunch. He was lonely. Wanted the company."

"Jake, don't screw this up."

"How could I? I'm not even involved."

"Right. This is Walter's case. His reputation is on the line. I don't want you goofing around and making a mess of it."

"I'll leave that to you."

"Jake, I swear."

"You shouldn't swear."

"Fuck you."

"That's better."

My iPhone felt hot. As if Tammy's anger had somehow flashed through the ionosphere and scorched it.

"Please don't mess up Walter's case."

"That's up to Ray and Pancake. We're simply offering moral support."

"You have no morals."

"Goodbye, Tammy." I disconnected the call.

Nicole merged onto US 98, toward Magnolia Springs. Less traffic, so she cranked up the RPMs. My cell phone buzzed three more times over the next five minutes. Each from Tammy. She had more to say. Each punched over to voicemail. I didn't.

"Did Walter really give you a discount?" Nicole asked.

"No."

She stared at me. I hate that she does that while hurtling down a highway at Warp Factor 4. Closing in on a massive SUV.

"You're evil," she said.

She whipped around the Suburban, my heart flipping and flopping and banging around in my chest. Once my breath returned, I managed to say, "I work at it."

"Poor Walter."

Now I stared at her. "There's nothing poor about Walter."

"True. But I do love it when Tammy calls," Nicole said.

"Why on earth?"

"Entertainment." She smiled at me. "And to see you squirm."

"I didn't squirm. Not once."

"Right."

CHAPTER 7

THE GPS GUIDED us north on Section Street through downtown Fairhope. Nicole actually went with the flow, no whipping around slower traffic, no impatiently tapping the steering wheel, no muttering or sighing. She seemed to be taking everything in. The relaxed pace of the town, the eclectic assortment of buildings, the tree-lined side streets that seemed to melt into quiet neighborhoods.

As the town fell away, the scenery became decidedly more rural. A right turn onto State Highway 104 plugged us into farm country. Another mile, Emily's driveway appeared on the left. At the end of the gravel strip, near the garage, sat Pancake's black truck, a metallic-blue Dodge Ram 3500 pickup, and a black Fairhope PD cruiser. Pancake and a uniformed officer stood near the patrol unit. They turned our way. Nicole parked and we stepped out.

Pancake introduced us to Officer Burton Moody. Forty-ish, maybe five-nine, one-forty tops. A thick, bushy mustache hid his upper lip and appeared too substantial for his thin face. The service weapon on his right hip likewise seemed bulky, listing his body that way.

"Jake and Nicole work for the firm," Pancake said.

I wanted to say that WE didn't but I let it ride.

"I understand you're looking into Emily's divorce," Moody said.

"That's right," Nicole said.

Moody gave a brief nod but said nothing.

"Anything new?" I asked Pancake.

"Nope. She's still a no-show."

I glanced at Moody, who was examining Nicole. All of Nicole. "What's your take on it?" I asked him.

"Not sure." He tugged one edge of his mustache. "Nothing looks out of place. No signs of a struggle or anything like that." He looked back at me. "Like they walked away, leaving the door open."

"They didn't," Pancake said.

"We don't know that," Moody said.

"It doesn't feel right. Something's off kilter here."

Moody glanced toward the house, hooked a thumb in his service belt. "Maybe."

"You are going to explore that possibility, aren't you?" I asked.

"That'll be up to the chief. She's on the way."

Good timing. I heard tires crunch gravel and turned. A black and white SUV lumbered toward us. It jerked to a stop and a woman stepped out. Jeans and a dark-blue short-sleeved shirt, the Fairhope PD logo on the breast pocket.

"This is Chief Billie Warren," Moody said. "This is Tommy Jeffers."

"Folks call me Pancake."

One corner of Warren's lips elevated slightly. She got it.

I introduced Nicole and me, shook her hand. She was medium height and build, fit, obviously no stranger to the gym. Handshake firm, almost painful.

"Which one of you showed up here first?" Warren asked.

"That's me," Pancake said.

"I take it you know Emily?"

"Long time ago. We went to school together. Through the sixth grade anyway."

"And you dropped by to get reacquainted?"

"I had a meeting with her. Over at the bakery where she works. She didn't show."

A frown settled over Warren's face. "A meeting about what?"

"They're private investigators," Moody said.

Warren eyed Pancake. "Investigating what?"

"We're from Longly Investigations in Gulf Shores," Pancake said. "Gathering information for her impending divorce."

Warren nodded. "I heard rumors they were headed that way."

"She filed a few days ago," I said.

Warren took a couple of steps toward the house, seemed to study it, then shot over her shoulder, "You go inside?"

"I did," Pancake said. "Front door was open. No one answered. I figured I'd better make sure everything was okay."

"Nothing looks disturbed," Moody said.

Warren nodded. "Maybe she went somewhere?"

"Her car's in the garage," Pancake said. "The Ram belongs to Jason Collins."

Warren turned back toward him. "How do you know that?"

He smiled. "We're investigators. We find out stuff."

Warren stared at him but said nothing.

"You know him?" Pancake asked. "Jason Collins?"

"Sure do."

"Anything there?"

"Anything like what?"

Pancake shrugged. "Like anything."

"Seems to be an okay guy. Never had any trouble with him."

"Before I called you guys, I drove the neighborhood. Thinking they might've gone out for a walk or something. Nothing."

Warren's brow furrowed. "This divorce? Any issues that would require a P.I.?"

Pancake shook his head. "Pretty routine from what we've seen so far. Mainly came up to chat with Emily. Get some financial information. Noah Hicks over at the bank gave me all that."

"You talk with her husband, Sean, yet?" Warren asked.

"No. I understand he's out on a Gulf drilling platform."

Warren nodded. "That boy does work a lot. Two jobs."

"Any issues with him?" I asked.

"Not that I know. At least nothing that ever reached my desk." She rubbed her neck. Her biceps strained against the sleeve of her shirt. "I better take a look."

Pancake said he needed to call Ray, so Nicole and I followed Warren. I expected her to object, but she didn't. Nice house. Clean, well decorated. Emily Rhodes, now Patterson, seemed to live well. And indeed, everything seemed normal.

Back outside, I asked Warren, "What's your plan?"

"Not sure. I don't see any evidence of a crime."

"Except she and this Jason dude are missing."

"Maybe." She sighed. "I'll try to track them down."

"Anything we can do to help?" Nicole asked.

"I think we can handle it." She examined Nicole, then me. "I suspect they're off somewhere and will be back before long."

"Their cars are here," I said.

"Sure are." She gave the Ram a look. "Maybe someone picked them up for lunch. Or to go down to the beach in Gulf Shores. That sort of thing."

"And they left the house unlocked?" Nicole asked.

"Folks around here don't lock up all that often." She rotated her neck as if working out a kink. "Don't really need to." She gave a half smile. "At least they think they don't."

CHAPTER 8

CARL FLETCHER LOVED to walk his property. Smell the rich soil, the pungent aroma of the pines that wrapped much of his acreage, and, of course, the sweetness of the honeysuckle that clung to his tool shed and tractor barn. His farmhouse squatted along Highway 104 and occupied one corner of the eighty acres he called Fletcher Farms. The land supported two growing seasons. He was a week away from planting his fall crops—pumpkins, squash, cucumbers, and melons. Another month the chick peas would go in. The soil had been turned, fertilized, and the irrigation lines stacked and ready to lay out.

He rambled along the dirt road that circled his property, a straw reed angling from the corner of his mouth. Forest to his left, his fields to his right. Quiet now, just the way he liked it. Another week and it'd be chaotic. Plantings always were.

He dropped on one knee to re-tie a boot lace, then used the bandana from his back pocket to mop his face and neck. One hand shielded his eyes from the noon sun as he looked over the section that would soon hold rows of pumpkins.

The weatherman had said the temperature would drop a good ten degrees over the next two weeks. A blessing. If it happened. Those guys were more wrong than right. But any relief from the August heat was welcome.

He continued along the back side of his acreage, satisfied that everything was in order. Even though he had worked this land for over twenty years, this was always an anxious time for him. The quiet time between spring harvest and late summer planting. He was a workingman, and this down time invariably proved stressful. Better to work than think on stuff you couldn't do nothing about. All that worry that something needed doing, or was overlooked, or hadn't been prepped properly. That was never the case, but that familiar unease resurfaced every year. And every year he chided himself. Didn't help. His wife constantly reminded him that if he didn't have the soil, the weather, or the crops to fret over, he'd find something. The woman had a heap of wisdom, and knew him all too well.

The dirt track bent to the right directing him along the far side of the field, his home just visible across the way. He mopped his face again.

That's when he saw what appeared to be a pile of discarded clothing. A hundred feet away, near a stand of pines. Maybe left by some of those kids who seemed to gravitate to that spot near the tree line to smoke dope. Wouldn't be the first time. He saw no one and no activity so he left the road and marched through the ankle-high grass to get a closer look.

It wasn't discarded clothing. Not even close.

He recoiled. Stared. His stomach lurched as he fought the urge to vomit. He backpedaled a few steps, nearly stumbling over a wad of Johnson's grass, then turned and rushed across the field toward his house, wobbling to his knees twice along the way.

CHAPTER 9

CHIEF BILLIE WARREN watched Nicole's Mercedes and Pancake's truck turn on the road back toward town. She scanned the area, the house, the blue Ram in the drive. She wasn't sure what to make of the situation. Nothing really pinged her radar. At least not loudly. Sure, the front door was ajar, and that was a bit odd, but otherwise all seemed normal. Getting all amped up didn't seem the right response. Had there been something out of place, a broken window or damaged door jamb, or, God forbid, blood, she'd for sure have a different sense of things. But the fact was that nothing clanged the alarm bells.

Warren told Burton Moody that she had to see the mayor for a minute and then get to the paperwork on her desk. She tasked him with tracking down Emily and Jason, saying maybe go chat with Jason's boss and any of their friends he could locate.

She had just gotten settled in her office after a brief visit with the mayor, budget crap, when she got the call. Carl Fletcher barely managed to gasp out something about finding two bodies. Before she could even slide her service weapon back into its holster, she connected the dots. Two bodies, Emily Patterson and Jason Collins missing, Emily's place not far from Carl's.

Please don't let that be true. Let it be one of those coincidences she didn't believe in.

She found Carl sitting on the gallery that stretched across his white clapboard farmhouse. On the steps, a half-filled glass of iced tea sweating next to him. He looked up, face pale and drawn. She climbed out of her SUV. Lila, his wife, came through the screen door.

"You okay?" Warren asked Carl.

"No. He ain't," Lila said. "He just threw up his lunch. I made him some sweet tea—" she nodded toward the glass—"but it hasn't done much good."

Carl looked up. "I'm fine."

He didn't look fine.

"Tell me about it," Warren said.

He took a sip of tea, but seemed to have difficulty swallowing it. "I was up walking the plots. We'll be planting next week and I wanted to make sure we were all set. Across the way I saw what I thought was a pile of clothes. Thinking it might be something those kids left behind."

Warren had been out here a couple of times in the past year to shoo away a group of teens who liked the seclusion to smoke marijuana, use meth, have sex, whatever they did. Last time was four months ago. She had impressed on them, clearly and forcefully, that one more incident like that and she'd lock them up for drug possession and trespassing. Clear?

She knew from looking at Carl that this had nothing to do with kids. He confirmed it.

"What I saw, I don't ever want to see again."

"Let's head over there and you can show me what you found," Warren said.

Carl stood; his legs unsteady. He grabbed the galley's support column for balance.

"Tell you what," Warren said. "You stay here. I think I can find them on my own."

Carl didn't argue. After telling her where to look, he made his way to the porch glider and sat down heavily. Lila sat next to him, clasping his hands in hers.

Warren eased her SUV forward and continued along the dirt road that lapped the freshly plowed fields, slowing when she reached the far side. She let the vehicle lope forward while she scoured the grassy strip between the road and a stand of pines. A flash of yellow caught her eye. She jerked to a stop and climbed out, tugging on a pair of latex gloves. She approached the bodies. Male, female, face-down, side by side. Entry wounds in the back of each head. She knelt and carefully rolled the female corpse over, rigor resisting her.

Emily Patterson's exit wound had blown out the right side of her forehead. A hank of her hair, stiffened with dried blood, angled out oddly. Warren's stomach knotted. Jason Collins' exit wound had taken out his left eye. Only a ragged, gaping hole remained. Blood and brain matter matted the nearby grass above their heads and shoulders. Now dried and brownish in color.

She stood, circled the bodies, scanned the area. Didn't take a lot of investigative skills or years of experience to know what had happened.

This had been an execution. Pure and simple.

She peeled off her gloves, tugged out her phone, and made two calls. The first to Burton Moody, telling him to call off his search for Emily and Jason and get his butt out to Carl Fletcher's place; the second to Baldwin County Coroner Melissa Goddard over in nearby Robertsdale.

She retreated to the shade of her SUV, where she sat, gripping the steering wheel and trying to make sense of this. Who would do this? Why?

Took twenty minutes for Moody to arrive and another fifteen for two coroner's techs to show up. Warren turned the scene over to them and drove toward town.

CHAPTER 10

AFTER WE LEFT Chief Warren and Officer Moody at Emily's, we followed Pancake back into Fairhope. Found a pair of parking slots just off Section Street. He led the way, saying we were headed to Mullins Bakery. I thought he was hungry, but he actually wanted to introduce us to the owner, Allison. Said that Emily worked there and that she and Allison were best friends.

The bakery was small, neat, and filled with the aroma of butter and sugar. Made me hungry. After introductions, Allison said she still hadn't heard from Emily. She had called several more times; each diverted to voicemail.

"I drove the neighborhood, but saw no sign of her," Pancake said. "Of course, I don't know her usual haunts or friends. That would be the next step. Chief Warren and an Officer Moody came out. They're on it now, too."

"Makes no sense," Allison said. "Emily's never out of touch like this."

"Is it possible she and Jason headed down to the the shore for a day at the beach?" Pancake asked. "Or off to some friend's place?"

Allison gave an emphatic headshake. "Not without calling." She wadded the small towel she held, knuckles whitening. "I'm worried something's happened."

Me, too. I didn't know the current version of Emily, not having seen her since we were twelve, but I can sense tension. In Allison, and in Warren and Moody. Pancake, definitely. Something wasn't right. The question was what.

Had the couple simply driven somewhere to visit friends? Maybe for something as bland as lunch? There were several small towns within a thirty-minute radius and each had its share of restaurants and bars. Good food, flowing conversion, and time becomes a lost commodity. Appointments forgotten. It happens.

Would she do that without calling Allison? According to what Allison said, and the conviction with which she said it, I believed that would be out of character. An unscripted road trip for two lovers? Day at the beach? That didn't seem likely either with both cars left behind.

Which brought up darker possibilities. A kidnapping? Who, and to what end? A passion murder and Jason now on the run? No evidence of that at the house. Jason's truck still in Emily's drive. That was the joker in the deck. Both cars there but no Emily or Jason.

"Any problems between her and Jason?" I asked.

"No," Allison said. "And I'd know. Emily's a very open person. With me, anyway."

"Anyone else in her life?" Pancake asked. "Other than Jason and her husband?"

Allison nodded. "She's seeing another guy. Charlie Martin."

"What's his story?" I asked.

"Nice enough." Allison massaged one temple. "I know this all looks bad. Like Emily is some tramp or something. But that's simply not true. She and Sean are separated. Heading for a divorce. Why wouldn't she see other guys?"

"No judgement here," Nicole said. "We understand. What about Jason and this Charlie guy? Any trouble between them?"

"Emily sees Jason mostly. I think they have a real connection. She only sees Charlie rarely."

"How does he feel about that?" Pancake asked.

"Not happy, from what she told me. Wanted something more serious was her take. But she said she made it very clear that she wasn't looking for that." She shrugged. "With him, anyway."

"Do you know where we could find Charlie?" Pancake asked.

"He works over at the garden center. Copeland's Nursery." She gave a half headshake. "If you're thinking something bad has happened and that maybe Charlie is involved, I'd find that hard to believe. He's quiet, even shy. If you talk to him, you'll see."

"We probably will," Pancake said. "After we grab something to eat."

"Pancake doesn't miss many meals," I said.

Allison smiled. First time I'd seen that. It was a bit strained but a smile nonetheless.

"Look," I said, "we're creating all kinds of unpleasant scenarios, and there's no evidence of anything like that. I don't know why Emily's out of pocket, but I'm sure there's an innocent explanation."

"You're probably right," Allison said.

Nicole jumped in. "We do investigations so we always assume the worst."

"I suppose that's true. Maybe this is all an overreaction."

Allison put on a confident face, another thin smile, but she didn't appear convinced to me. Since she knew Emily better than anyone, my own unease didn't diminish an ounce.

"It's probably exactly that," I said.

Pancake redirected the discussion back toward lunch options. Allison recommended a café just down the street. Stella's Bistro. We headed that way. Of course, since it was an entire half a block away, Pancake bought a triple chocolate cupcake to tide him over during the journey.

Stella's turned out be pleasant. Soft music, white tablecloths, a single red rose in a white ceramic vase centering each table. The food flawless. I think Pancake ate half the menu. Plus, two desserts—key lime pie, followed by pecan pie with vanilla ice cream.

Our plan was to drop back by the bakery, see if there was any news, and, if not, head over to chat with Charlie Martin. That all changed when we walked through the bakery door.

Chief Billie Warren stood at the counter, facing Allison, whose face blared red, as were her eyes, tear tracks glistening her cheeks. Warren apparently heard us and turned our way. Her grim expression stopped us in our tracks.

"What is it?" I asked.

"We found Emily and Jason," Warren said. "Murdered."

Nicole released an audible moan. Pancake a grunt.

"What happened?" I asked.

Warren took a couple of steps toward us. "Shot. Both of them."

"Where?" Pancake asked.

"Out on Carl Fletcher's farm. Lives about a mile on down the road from Emily's place."

I looked at Allison. "I'm so sorry."

She broke. Turned and scurried through a door toward the kitchen. Nicole followed.

"Any idea who?" I asked.

"Not yet."

"Her husband's still out on an oil platform, right?"

"He is. Got a call in to him. Communication out there isn't the best." She sighed. "Speaking of which, I now get the pleasure of calling her brother and breaking this to him."

Daniel Rhodes. Emily's younger brother. By four years. I remembered him mostly as a pain in the ass. Smart, mischievous, but mostly annoying. But, to be fair, we were twelve, him eight. Little brothers were always a pain.

"Daniel," I said.

"You know him?" Warren asked.

"Not since we were kids. He was four years younger. Sort of a brat."

"Not anymore, he isn't."

"He live nearby?" Pancake asked.

"He's on deployment, the last I heard. He's a Marine."

So, little snot-nosed Danny made it all the way to the U.S. Marine Corps. Never saw that coming. I remembered the last time I saw him. The party Ray and my mom threw for Emily's going away. When her family left Gulf Shores for Fairhope the summer after sixth grade. Scrawny, hair flopped over one eye, that goofy grin he always had.

"A Marine?" Pancake said. "Can't say I would've predicted that."

"He's a bit of a local hero," Warren said.

Pancake hurt. I could see it in his face. Feel it radiating from his body. Emily dead. Murdered. A lot to grasp. When he spoke, his voice came out thin, weak. Not Pancake at all.

"You've got no idea who could've done this?" he asked.

She shook her head. "Two young people? Good people? Makes no sense. None at all."

"You know about Charlie Martin?" I asked.

She gave me a look. "What about him?"

"Allison said Emily was seeing him, too. Said he was somewhat infatuated with her and wasn't thrilled about her relationship with Jason."

She nodded, one eyebrow elevated. "I suspect I'd better have a chat with him."

"That's where we were headed," Pancake said.

"Why?"

"To see what his story is."

Warren's eyes narrowed. "You're here to dig up divorce dirt. I'd say that's off the table now. This is now a double homicide. That's on my table."

"Maybe we can help," I said.

"Maybe not. Seems to me your work here's done." She looked at me, Pancake, back to me. "Am I clear?" She squared her shoulders, pushed past us, and marched out the door.

Guess that settled that.

I could hear Allison's moans and sobs from the back room. My instinct was to go check on her, but decided Nicole could handle it better.

Pancake called Ray, placing it on speaker. Told him the story. After listening, Ray came down on Warren's side. We no longer had a client so best not to meddle in an investigation.

Pancake argued, saying, "Come on. It's Emily. We need to do something."

"What we need to do," Ray said, "is back away. Let the locals handle this."

"Don't seem right," Pancake said.

"I understand. We'll watch it from afar. If something comes up and we need to step in, we will. But right now, it's best to not stir the waters." Ray sighed. "I'll give Walter a call."

Nicole and I almost made it back to Gulf Shores before the circle of life, or in this case death, completed its turn, proving the old cliché that bad news travels fast. This is particularly true in Tammy's domain. It took a mere thirty minutes for Ray's call to Walter to be passed on to Tammy and for her to call me. Did she have my number on speed dial?

"What is it now?" I asked.

"I knew you'd screw this up," she said.

"Screw what up?"

"Everything. But this time it's Walter's case."

"What are you talking about?"

"Walter's divorce case."

Tammy's logic always baffled me, but this was one of her best ever. "Tammy, Emily was murdered."

"See? That's what I mean. Every time you get involved in something, this is what happens."

"Someone gets killed?"

"No, not that. It's just that it messes up my life."

"I don't see how any of this affects you. You weren't the victim."

"I am, too. Walter's upset. And that makes me upset."

"A young woman was killed. Someone we knew from grammar school. So, you'll have to excuse my lack of interest in your problems."

"See? That's why we got divorced." She disconnected the call.

Welcome to Tammy's world.

"And here I thought your divorce was due to your escapades and not your lack of interest in her problems."

I glanced at her. Her grin brighter than the sun.

"Tammy's problems, both real and imagined, aren't of this world. I have rarely been able to find any rational thought in that tangle of linguini she calls a brain."

"I have to agree; this one is a little convoluted."

"A little? To answer your question though, I didn't run around. I ran away. You can only stand close to that level of insanity for so long before your own synapses begin to fray and sputter."

She reached over and mussed my hair. "Hold on, cowboy. When we get home, I'm going to sputter a few of your synapses."

I smiled. "Drive faster."

She did.

CHAPTER 11

WARREN SAT IN her office. It was just after 9:00 p.m. She had earlier contacted Sean Patterson's boss, told him of the murder, no details, of course. He said he'd arrange to get Sean back onshore as soon as he could. No easy task. Not like they had hourly shuttles out there. Finally, he called back. Supply copter was headed back, and he'd put Sean onboard.

Once onshore, Sean called and said he'd head straight to Warren's office. Probably be there by nine.

Warren tried to clean some of the paperwork off her desk but couldn't stay with it. Images of Emily Patterson and Jason Collins kept intruding. She had done some of her training and worked a couple of years in Birmingham. Not exactly Atlanta, or New York, or Chicago, but still she'd seen some dreadful stuff. Even as disturbing as this. But that was in the big city. Where bad things happened. Where drugs and gangs were part of the subculture. Where the victims were almost universally anonymous. Names, case numbers, autopsy reports. Still tragic, still with family and community ripples, but with a certain degree of buffering.

Here, in this tiny community, these things carried extra baggage. Created deeper, longer-lasting ripples. She hadn't known Jason well, maybe ran into him once or twice, but Emily she knew well. Saw her several times a week at the bakery where she treated herself to a blueberry muffin after her gym visit. She knew Sean, too. Part of the community.

This killing, this execution, reminded her of a few of those over in Mobile. Mostly drug and gang related. Could that be in play here? Fairhope had no real gang presence. Drugs were small-time and could be traced to only a handful of people. And they mostly kept their noggins down.

Could some unexpected drug conflict have raised its head? Here? Nothing along those lines had tickled her radar. Emily or Jason? She didn't see either connected to such activities. Could she be wrong? Just last week she had been thinking about how pleasant her job was and her good fortune to be in a place where folks said please and thank you. Amazing how quickly things could veer off course.

"Chief?"

She glanced up. Sean Patterson. He looked like warmed-over hell.

"Come on in. Have a seat." She waved at the chair across her desk.

He sat. "Sorry for my appearance. And smell. Didn't want to take the time to stop by home and clean up."

"No apology needed."

He had the look of a rig worker. One down the food chain that had to do the dirty work. Grime, dried sweat, three-day-old beard, smudged blue shirt, grease-stained cuticles, chipped fingernails. Warren had seen it more than a few times. Out there on the water life was no vacation. Dirty, backbreaking work. Constant noise from generators and pipes and drills and pumps. And if the weather turned sour, a whole other batch of problems. Sleep was sporadic and restless. It took a toll. Sean showed all the signs.

"I'm so sorry for your loss," she said.

"It's a big shock."

"You okay?" Warren asked.

"I don't know. I honestly don't. Been out on the rig for nearly two weeks. Bad food, lots of racket, no real sleep." He sighed. "You'd think I'd be used to it by now, but I'm not sure that's even possible. Always takes a couple of days to get my system back in order." He shrugged. "Now, this. About now I don't know nothing about nothing."

"I imagine so. But I appreciate you coming in to talk with me." She tapped a pen on her desk. "Time is important here."

"I suspect that's true." He forked back his oily hair.

"I don't want to make it any more difficult than it already is but I do need to ask a few questions."

He nodded. "Sure. But first tell me what happened. I don't really know nothing."

She told him what she could. Both shot. Apparently abducted from Emily's house. Both their cars still there. Door open. Killed out on Fletcher's Farm. She left out the execution part.

"You got any idea who might've done it?" Sean asked.

"That's what I'm asking you. You know anyone who had an issue with Emily, or Jason?"

"Not Emily. That's for sure. Everybody liked her. She made friends, not enemies."

"And Jason?"

"I don't know him real well," Sean said. "Seemed like a good enough guy."

"Tell me about your divorce. Any issues?"

He stared at her. "Guess there won't be one now." He shook his head. "But no. Everything was going okay there." He stared at the floor, spoke to it. "Truth was, we knew right about a year ago it'd come to this. Sort of drifted apart."

"Did you know she had filed this week?"

He looked up. "No. Did she?"

"She did."

"We been talking about it for months. I told her it was up to her. Whatever she wanted to do."

"You were happy to stay married? If that was her decision?"

He seemed to consider that. "No. Not Emily either. We knew it was going to happen. It was the timing that never lined up." He shrugged. "I told her to go ahead whenever it felt right to her. There wasn't any real urgency as far as I could tell."

"You had no problems with Jason and Emily dating?"

"Look, Chief, I know you got to ask these questions. Me and her heading into a divorce. The husband is always the prime suspect." He scratched one ear. "I watch those TV shows. But the truth is we were over. We each moved on. To me, her seeing Jason was a good thing. I know she liked him a lot."

"That's a very adult approach," Warren said.

He smiled. Half-hearted but a smile. "We actually laughed about that a few times. Seemed like most folks felt that one or the other of us should be mad. Or angry, or something. We weren't. Sort of made people wonder if we were serious about it or not, I suspect."

"Any financial issues with the divorce?"

"None. We cut all that up months back. She had her money and I have mine. Seemed to work okay."

"What about the house?"

"That's hers. From what I understand, it would legally go to her." He extended and then flexed his right knee as if it were stiff. "And rightly so. Been in her family a long time."

"So you weren't going to make a claim on it. Community property?"

"Couldn't according to the law. And wouldn't. Like I said, it's hers." He sighed. "Was hers."

"And now it's yours," Warren said.

He stared at her. "I suspect that's true. I hadn't thought of it that way." Gaze back toward the floor. "There's just too much to all this. I have no idea what I'm going to do."

"About the house?"

He looked up. His eyes moist. "About any of it. I mean that, and all her stuff, and a funeral, and calling her brother, and . . ." He stared toward the window. "And all of it."

"It will be a lot. But take it one thing at a time. Don't let it overwhelm you."

"It's funny. While I was riding the copter in, you know what crossed my mind?"

"What?"

"What was I going to do with all the things she had collected? All kinds of glass doodads? Her family china?" He sighed. "She loved those things. And her clothes? I don't even know where to start." He looked at Warren. "Ain't that some stupid crap to be thinking about?"

"Not really. There isn't a manual for how to handle these things."

"Wish there was."

"Friends will help. You'll be fine."

"I suppose." He fell silent for a few seconds, then said, "Chief, do you have any idea who would've done this? You must have some suspect or the other?"

"I wish we did." She dropped the pen on her desk.

"Well, I guess I better get home and knock the grime off."

"One more thing," Warren said. "What about a drug angle?"

"What do you mean?"

"Two people shot. In a rural area. I have to at least consider that."

"Makes sense, I guess. But I'll tell you this for sure. Emily wouldn't use anything and wouldn't be around anyone who did."

"Voice of experience?"

Sean seemed to consider his answer for a few seconds. "Back then, when we first started dating, I smoked a little. But she put an end to that in short order. Wasn't even open for discussion."

CHAPTER 12

THREE DAYS LATER we were back on the road to Fairhope. This time for Emily's funeral. Nicole followed Pancake's truck, Ray ensconced at shotgun. Good news since that kept Nicole closer to the speed limit. Something she handled poorly. Impatient, fingers tapping the steering wheel.

"Makes you crazy, doesn't it?" I asked.

"What does?"

"Being trapped behind Pancake."

"I could pass. I know where we're going." She glanced at me. "I'm just being polite."

"I'm sure that's it."

"Don't be a dick."

"Me? Never."

She passed Pancake's truck.

The three days between the murders and Emily's funeral hadn't been stagnant. Pancake had become obsessed with looking into what had happened. Even when Ray suggested they had plenty of other things on their plate, Pancake wouldn't be deterred. The boy could be a bulldog. I understood. Emily had been his first love. Maybe the puppy variety, but those are often the most powerful. Last a lifetime. Her name had come up off and on over the years, and each time, Pancake had become wistful, played the what-if game. Yet, in all the years, he, we, never sought her out. Fairhope might only be thirty miles up the road from Gulf Shores, but it was worlds apart. By the time Pancake and I could drive, life had moved on. School, sports, other friends and girlfriends, and grammar school memories faded.

And now Emily was gone.

No way to rewind the clock.

Woulda, shoulda, coulda.

So, despite Ray's complaints, Pancake dug. He uncovered a host of interesting facts about the players. He always did. Enough to fill a large three-ring binder. He made a copy for Nicole and me.

Last night, after Nicole had used me for her pleasure, really, she had, and then rudely fell asleep, I read through Pancake's research. Now I related the highlights to Nicole.

She was excellent at multitasking. She could terrorize other motorists, check her hair, nails, and makeup—what little she used—for flaws—finding none, of course—this is Nicole we're talking about here—and listen to my ramblings all at the same time.

After Emily's family moved to the Fairhope area, to the house where Emily had slept her last night on Earth, she finished high school and then attended the Fairhope campus of Coastal Alabama Community College. Majored in English. Stellar grades. No surprise there. Pancake and I had often copied her test answers. That tidbit drew a smile, a nod, and an "Of course" from Nicole.

Pancake made good grades, me average, but neither of us were thrilled with the classroom. More a nuisance than anything else. Our focus had been sports, girls, and stealing beer from Ray.

After completing two years at Coastal, also with stellar grades, Emily snagged a job at the library. A year later, she moved on to Mullins Bakery. That's where she met her husband, Sean Patterson.

Sean decided high school was enough formal education so as soon as he strolled out the schoolhouse door, diploma in hand, he took a job at Watkins' Lumber Supply. Been there ever since. A couple of years later he added Chevron to his employer list and worked the offshore rigs. Two weeks on and two off. No legal issues that Pancake could find.

Jason Collins was fairly new to the area. Originally from Laurel, Mississippi. Two years earlier, he had moved to Fairhope and took a job at Sharp's Used Cars. Just north of town. He did fairly well, earning salesman of the month honors three times. He had had no run-ins with the law, but otherwise Pancake had found little on him. His photo revealed light brown hair, blue eyes, and a pleasant smile. Seemed like an ordinary guy.

The cemetery sat along Highway 98 just north of Fairhope High School. Nicole swerved around the entry monument, white with maroon lettering that read "Memorial Gardens of Fairhope." It squatted in a grassy oval planted with shrubs and flowers. An American flag hung limply above it. Noon, ninety degrees, and no breeze. Didn't bode well for a funeral ceremony. She parked and we waited for Pancake and Ray. Ten minutes. She had left them that far behind.

We stepped out into the stifling heat. The suit I wore seemed to melt to my flesh. I'm not a suit guy. Never had been. Neither was Pancake. He tugged at his collar as if to let in more air, maybe release heat. Ray was Ray. Nothing fazed him. Nicole, her black dress sleek and crisp, showed no signs of wilting. How does she do that?

Expansive, mostly open, sparsely dotted with trees and head-stones, the cemetery had ample plots remaining for future inhabitants. The grave sites of Emily Patterson and Jason Collins were toward the middle of the property, maybe a hundred feet apart. A casket suspended over each rectangular opening. I guessed a hundred and fifty people had showed up, most loitering near Emily's site. The four of us headed that way.

I saw a preacher, Bible tucked beneath one arm, chatting with Emily's brother, Danny Rhodes, who wore his Marine blues. My how he had grown. Tall, fit, he looked like the poster boy for the Marine Corps. The preacher moved along to chat with who I recognized as Sean Patterson. The grieving husband.

Sean did appear grief-stricken. His face drawn and pale. Maybe five-ten, thin, his suit oversized, collar limp from the humidity. Medium-length brown hair, dark, deep-set eyes. He mopped his forehead with a handkerchief while he talked with the preacher, who laid a fatherly hand on his shoulder.

Danny saw us and walked our way.

"Danny," I said.

"Jake. Tommy. Mr. Longly."

We shook hands. I introduced Nicole.

"Sorry for your loss," I said.

He nodded. "I'm still in shock."

"We all are," Pancake said.

"Glad you came," Danny said.

The preacher moved to the grave site, indicating the ceremony was about to begin.

"Let's talk afterwards," Pancake said.

Danny nodded. "I'd like that."

The ceremony was short. Tears flowed, Danny spoke of his sister, of all he had learned from her, of how much she had meant to him growing up. Allison followed, saying how she and Emily had become close through their work together, and how she would miss her humor and "gentle nature." Finally, the librarian, whose name I didn't catch, told of how valuable Emily had been during her brief stint at the library. How everyone liked her, particularly the kids.

Of how she inspired so many of them to put away the electronics and read. The preacher concluded with a prayer and the casket descended into the ground.

Many of the mourners expressed condolences to Danny, thanked him for his service, and then the preacher and most of the crowd moved over to Jason's burial site.

"Want to grab some lunch?" Ray asked Danny.

"Sure. I've been in the air the past twenty-four hours and haven't had much to eat. Military transports aren't known for their cuisine." He managed a weak smile.

CHAPTER 13

LUNCH WAS AGAIN at Stella's Bistro. Pancake insisted. Said there were things on the menu he didn't get to last time. The aroma of the day's special, spaghetti with meatballs, thickened the air and smelled too enticing to pass up. We each ordered it. Pancake added a massive plate of fried calamari topped with jalapeños and a side of polenta with marinara.

The conversation was casual, mostly about old times, until the food arrived. Danny ate with little enthusiasm. He cleaned his plate, but more like he needed the calories rather than relished the food. He had a long flight with only military rations ahead of him. Soldiers in combat zones learn to tank up whenever the chance arises.

Pancake, on the other hand, demolished the calamari and polenta, scoured his plate, and then marched through two-thirds of mine, which was fine as I had little appetite. He also ate an entire basket of garlic bread. Little interfered with his appetite. And today, he needed to soothe his pain.

Danny addressed Pancake. "Emily brought up your name not infrequently. Tommy this, and Tommy that."

"Folks call me Pancake now."

Danny nodded. "Football?"

"You got it. Did you play?"

"Yeah. High school."

"What position?" I asked.

"Receiver."

He was tall enough. An inch under my six-three and near my one-ninety. Of course, he seemed in better shape. The difference between a Marine and a bar owner. Even though I had been taking Krav Maga classes with Nicole.

"I wasn't good enough for college ball so the Marine Corps seemed a logical step," Danny said.

"How long have you been in?" Nicole asked.

"Since the week after I finished high school. Ten years now."

"You must like it."

"It's a good career. Scary as hell sometimes, boring others, but overall, it was the right choice for me." He glanced at me. "I followed your career. You were something else."

"Long time ago," I said.

Danny caught Ray's gaze. "Mr. Longly, I have to say you were part of the reason I joined the Marines."

"Call me Ray."

Danny nodded. "Ray."

"What did I have to do with your career?" Ray asked.

"I always looked up to you. You seemed to have an answer, a fix, for everything. And you were a Marine."

Ray shrugged. "Sort of."

"What does that mean?"

"I was a Marine, for sure. But my career was mostly in the darker areas."

Danny smiled. "Things you never talk about, right?"

Ray nodded. "What about you?"

"Just a grunt."

"Where are you stationed now?"

"Here and there. Lately in Saudi Arabia. That's where I was when I got the call about Emily." He stared at his empty plate for a few seconds. "My CO got me a pass. Flew into Quantico, then to the Pensacola Naval Air Station. Drove up here." He took a sip of tea. "It's been a crazy seventy-two hours."

"I imagine so," Ray said.

"I still can't quite grasp it." He looked at Ray. "I understand you guys were looking into Emily's divorce? For her attorney?"

"That's right."

"Took her a long time to get to that point. She'd been thinking about it for the last year or so."

"She say why?" Ray asked. "Any issues?"

"Not happy. And I think Sean did a little roaming. Fact is, I'm sure he did. She always forgave him, but it added up."

"As things like that do," Pancake said.

"Don't they though." Danny shrugged, then to Ray said, "You find anything else in your investigation?"

"Not really. Of course, we were just beginning our research when this happened."

We were seated at a table near the front window. Danny's gaze moved that way, toward the street. "Any idea who could've done this?"

"None," Ray said.

"Isn't it usually the spouse?" Nicole asked.

Danny looked at her. "Usually. But I understand he was out on a rig at the time."

"He was," I said.

"I wish I could stay here and figure it out. But I don't think my CO would go for it." He looked at Ray. "What about you?"

"We were asked to look into the financials of the divorce. Make sure everything was on the up and up."

"So, your work is done?"

"Looks that way."

"I wish I could hire you," Danny said. "To find out who did this. But Uncle Sam doesn't pay me that kind of money."

Ray mulled that for a beat. "You got a dollar on you?"

"Sure."

Ray made a gimme sign with his fingers.

Danny pulled some folded bills from his pocket, peeled off a single, and handed it to Ray.

"Now we work for you," Ray said.

"For a dollar?"

"Let's call it a brothers-in-arms discount."

"Really?" Danny asked.

"Really."

His jaw squared. "I can't tell you what that means to me."

"We'll find the dude," Pancake said. "And it won't go well for him."

"I don't think the local chief will be happy," I said. "Based on our last chat with her anyway."

"Billie Warren?" Danny said.

I nodded. "She didn't seem thrilled with us being here in the first place. And if we start snooping into this, she'll be less so."

Did I actually say *we*? Had I been roped into Ray's world again? Nicole thought so. She gave me a discreet smile and a raised eyebrow. Truth time. I was all in. This was Emily. This was Pancake's pain. Walking away wasn't an option. My head-butting match with Ray would have to take the back seat on this one.

"Don't worry about Billie," Danny said. "I'll have a sit-down with her before I head back to Pensacola."

"You know her?" I asked.

"For years. In fact, during high school, my summer job was at the police department. Mostly running errands and cleaning up.

Sometimes I'd go out on patrol with her. She wasn't the chief back then." He glanced toward the window again. "In fact, I considered law enforcement, but the Corps won out."

"A word would help," Ray said. "But since you're now the client, we'll be able to sniff around anyway."

"One of the things I always admired about you, Ray, even as a kid, is that you never hesitated to jump in and straighten things out." He nodded toward Pancake and me. "Even with these two."

"A full-time job," Ray said. "If you can get Chief Warren to at least tolerate us, that'll make things smoother."

As if on cue, Chief Warren and Officer Moody walked by the window. They saw us and detoured through the front door.

"Danny," Warren said. "I'm sorry we didn't make the funeral."

"We've been a bit busy," Moody added.

"I suspect that's true," Danny said.

I introduced Ray to Warren and Moody.

"Anything new on the case?" Ray asked.

Warren hesitated.

"I've hired them to help find out who did this," Danny said.

Warren's jaw tightened. "I see."

"Look, Billie," Danny said. "I don't want to step on your toes or anything like that, but I can't stay here and do it myself."

"And you don't think we're capable?" Warren asked.

"You know that's not the case. It's just that the more eyes looking into this the better."

Warren didn't seem convinced.

"We're here to help," Ray said. "Not get in the way."

Warren shrugged. "But will it work out that way?"

"I hope so." Ray twisted in his chair to face her more directly. "We can do things you can't. Don't have to follow all the rules, so to speak." Ray smiled. "And we're pretty good at what we do."

"Which is?"

"Gathering intel. Looking in dark corners and under rugs. We—" he waved a hand toward Pancake—"have certain skills in that arena. And friends if need be."

Warren raised an eyebrow. "What does that mean?"

"Like Danny, I was a Marine. Unlike him, my career isn't part of the public record. The skills I learned during that part of my life, and the friends I acquired, often come in handy in situations such as this."

Warren listened, said nothing.

Ray continued. "Pancake has crazy computer skills and can rummage in places most folks don't even know exist."

Warren nodded toward Nicole and me. "And you two?"

Before I could answer, Ray jumped in. "Nicole's smart and good with people. Jake's pretty and has a nice smile."

My father speaking.

Warren smiled. "So all that boyish charm draws people to him?"

"Exactly." Ray glanced at me. "And he does have his moments."

Okay, that was good, but being the topic of this table conversation was getting uncomfortable.

"He has lots of good moments," Nicole said. She mussed my hair. "Most we can't talk about."

Warren actually laughed.

"Tell us more," Pancake said.

Nicole shook her head, her blond ponytail wagging behind her. "I don't kiss and tell."

Warren's expression became serious again. "I did a little of my own research. Longly Investigations is well known down in Gulf Shores, it seems. And expensive." She looked at Danny. "I assume you can afford these guys."

"We have an arrangement." Danny looked at Ray. "A very generous and greatly appreciated one." Then to Warren, "All I'm asking is that you work together. Find out who did this to my sister. Isn't that the important thing here?"

Warren nodded. "It is." She sighed, gave a quick nod. "I hope I don't regret this, but okay." Back to Ray. "But the rules are mine. Clear?"

"Crystal," Ray said.

CHAPTER 14

DANNY'S RELUCTANCE TO leave was evident. I saw it in his bowed head, shuffling feet, the sagging of his military-erect posture. We were a block from Stella's, at the curb where he had parked his rental.

Danny looked up the street, unfocused. His face revealed his pain, through an almost lost little boy expression. Here he was, heading to the other side of the planet, while his sister lay in the ground. Not that he had a choice. Staying wasn't an option.

He finally took a deep breath. "I feel like I'm abandoning her."

"You're not," Ray said. "You've done the best thing you could do. You hired us."

"Sort of," Danny said.

"No. You did. It's not always about the money."

Danny nodded. "I meant what I said. It's greatly appreciated."

"We'd do it for free," Ray said. "Look, you get back on station. Do your job. We'll take care of everything."

Pancake laid a hand on Danny's shoulder. "You know what Emily meant to me. To Jake and Ray, too. I promise we'll find who did this."

Danny looked up. His eyes glistened. "I have this urge to say 'Fuck it,' and go AWOL."

"You won't," Ray said. "You're a Marine. You'll slap on the back-pack and move forward. Leave this to us."

Danny gave a half nod, then each of us a hug, climbed in his car, and drove away.

Nicole wiped a tear from her eye. "I feel sorry for him. And I'm sure he does feel like he's running away. Leaving behind unfinished business."

"Finishing this business is on us," Ray said.

"What's the next move?" Nicole asked.

"That's what we need to work out. Pancake and I. We'll head back to Gulf Shores and put a game plan together."

"And us?" I asked.

"This is a small town. Folks know each other fairly well. We need to tread lightly. At least initially. The first order of business is to make sure Chief Warren is truly onboard. Drop by and see her. See what she'll give up. How comfortable she is with us being here. Whether she was being truthful about collaboration or was simply blowing smoke up our asses."

"Jake can charm her," Nicole said.

"If he doesn't piss her off first," Ray said.

"I'll keep his leash short."

Was I going to get a pat on the head and a treat for this? I made a mental note to ask Nicole about the treat later.

"Then we'll need to get a read on Sean Patterson," Ray said. He fell silent as an older couple walked by. They nodded, said "Hello," and moved on. "Stop by and see him. Low key. Don't press him on any facts. More to get a feel for where his head's at. Is he the heart-broken ex he seemed to be at the funeral, or is he a good actor?"

"I can handle that," Nicole said.

Ray smiled. "Of that I'm sure."

And that was the initial plan.

Ray and Pancake left. Nicole and I walked the short distance to the Police Department. We found Warren in her office. She directed us to a pair of wooden ladder-back chairs and sat behind her desk.

"I still have reservations about this," Warren said.

"I'm sure you do," I said. "I'd be surprised if you didn't."

She gave a half smile. "So, reassure me."

"What Ray said was true," I said. "He and Pancake are very good at finding what's hidden."

"He's your father, yet you call him Ray. Interesting."

"Long story."

"I have the time."

"Ray and I don't always see eye to eye. Not sure we ever have."

"Yet you work for him?"

"Not really." I nodded toward Nicole. "I think she does."

"You think?"

"I do," Nicole said. "And Jake does, too. He just won't admit it."

"You're not inspiring a lot of confidence here," Warren said.

"Don't worry," Nicole said. "We're focused on helping. That's it."

"And share with me everything you uncover?"

"Absolutely."

Warren looked at me. "You onboard with that?"

"I am." I scooted forward to the edge of the chair. "This isn't just another case. It's personal. We, Pancake and I, went to school with Emily. Down in Gulf Shores. Pancake and Emily were sixth-grade sweethearts."

Warren absorbed that. "First love kind of stuff?"

I nodded. "Until her family moved here the summer after sixth grade. Neither of us had seen her since."

Warren stared at her desktop for a beat, then looked back up. "Okay. Both Emily and Jason were murdered out on Carl Fletcher's place. About a mile on down the road from Emily's house. He found the bodies."

"You thinking they were dumped there?" I asked.

"The blood spatter says otherwise. They were shot where they were found."

"Any suspects?" Nicole asked.

Warren shook her head. "Truth is, we've got nothing. No stray fingerprint at her home. No usable tire impressions at the scene. No rain lately and the road's fairly compacted up there."

"Anyone with a grudge, or any motive?" I asked.

"Not that we know." She picked up a pen from her desk, examined it. "The husband's always the first look. Particularly with a divorce in the works. But he has a pretty solid alibi."

"Out in the Gulf?" I asked.

"Yep. His foreman verified that. Plus, they had to put him on a supply copter to get him back onshore after I called."

"What about that other guy Emily was seeing?" Nicole asked. "Martin? Isn't that right?"

"Charlie Martin. I talked with him. He has a pretty good alibi, too. He was over at his cousin's place. Helping prep his fields for planting. Over near Magnolia Springs. Apparently, he was there until midnight. Maybe a bit later."

"The time of death?" I asked.

"The coroner says between 10:00 p.m. and 2:00 a.m. Thereabouts."

"That would give him time to drive back," I said. "It isn't that far."

"I suppose. Still doubt he's the guy. Doesn't seem the angry, jealous type."

"You never know about people though."

Warren clicked the pen a couple of times. "That's true."

"Can we see the scene?" I asked.

"Don't see why not."

Ten minutes later, we rolled past Emily's house, Nicole riding shotgun in Warren's SUV, me in the back. I noticed an older, street-worn, metallic-gray Chevy sedan in the drive. Sean's ride? If so, had he moved back in? Seemed odd if that was the case. I knew he had an apartment back toward town. I started to ask Warren, but felt she might stop by to see him. I wanted to have a chat with him but not with Warren present. Less confrontational. More casual.

Warren rolled on down the blacktop road. I saw a sign that read "Fletcher's Farm."

"This is Carl's place," Warren said. "I'll let him know we're on his property."

She turned onto a gravel drive that led to a white clapboard farmhouse. A man in jeans and a blue work shirt came through a screen door and on to the porch. Warren lowered the window. A blast of hot air invaded the air-conditioned interior.

"Carl?" Warren said. "You doing okay?"

"More or less."

"Got a couple of investigators. Want to see the scene. That okay?"

He stood at the top of the steps, looking down. "Of course."

"Want to go over with us?"

He shook his head. "Seen more than enough the other day."

"Ain't that the truth," Warren said. "Just wanted to let you know we're on your property."

"I appreciate it."

The window slid up; the vehicle moved forward. Around a bend in the hard-packed dirt road that circled the back of a plowed field, and then another turn along the far side. She came to a stop and we stepped out. Warren led us into a grassy area about halfway between the dirt road and a stand of pines.

"The bodies were found right here." The grass was still bent and flattened and matted with dark stains. "Lying side by side. Facedown."

I walked around the area. Looked back across the field toward the house. Maybe two hundred yards away. "You're sure they were shot here?"

She nodded. "Blood and brain tissue all over the place."

"Mr. Fletcher didn't hear anything?" Nicole asked.

"Nope."

"Were they bound?" I asked. "Anything like that?"

"Nope. And no rope marks or tape residue that would suggest that." She looked at me. "They were executed. On their knees. Back of the head. Close range based on the charring of the hair around the entry wounds."

I stared at her. This wasn't where my mind was going. Not close. Not sure what I had expected, but this wasn't it. A domestic situation, sure. A robbery, possible. A kidnapping, maybe. But a full-on execution?

"Who would do that?" I asked.

"That's the million-dollar question."

"Sure changes things," Nicole said.

Warren nodded. She hesitated as if considering something. Like she had more to say but wasn't sure how to say it. Or maybe say it at all.

"There's something else?" I asked.

She glanced at her feet, then across the field toward Carl Fletcher's home. She looked back at me. "Can I trust you guys?"

"Of course."

"This isn't for public consumption."

"We understand," Nicole said.

"There is one more thing. The ME said that when they removed Jason Collins' clothing, they found two small bags of meth."

"Really?" Nicole said.

"Was he a known user?" I asked.

Warren gave a quick headshake. "Not that we know. And the people we've talked to said he wasn't and he never had."

"Could be a closet user."

"Maybe. The other odd thing is that they found no prints on the bags. They were plastic and should hold prints okay, but these were clean."

"If he had them in his pocket, couldn't the prints have been wiped away?" Nicole asked. "While he walked or moved?"

"Sure. He was found facedown. Shot in the back of the head. The two bags were in his back pocket. Seems an odd place to carry them." She shrugged. "To me, anyway."

"You think they might've been planted?" I asked.

"It does beg the question."

CHAPTER 15

THE IDEA THAT Emily and Jason had been hauled out to a rural area and executed did indeed change things. The killing field was not truly rural but isolated enough that no one, not Carl Fletcher for sure, saw or heard anything.

Why do it there? Why do it that way? Efficient if nothing else. Two shots done. But, why not right there at Emily's home? Transporting two bodies would be much easier, and much less risky, than ferrying an alive and well couple down a public road. So many things could go wrong. A fight, a flat tire, an accident, a minor traffic violation involving the police, a random citizen witnessing what was going down. Seemed dicey. According to Warren, the two were shot where they were found, but were they incapacitated in some way? That would make the transfer easier for sure. Warren had said they weren't restrained. Maybe drugs? I suspected the coroner would be able to determine that.

Another question: Why do it on Carl Fletcher's property? A couple of hundred yards from his home? Why not deep in one of the wooded areas? More isolated. Less likely anyone would see. Or hear.

Why not hide the bodies? Why leave them where they would be easily found? Or was their being found a necessary part of the crime?

A message? See what happens if you cross me, us.

Did either Emily or Jason, or both, step on someone's toes and that person used them to warn others of the consequences of such decisions? Gangs and drug dealers do that all too often. The U.S.-Mexico border was littered with such corpses.

Fairhope wasn't exactly a hot bed of gang activity. Did the cartels reach this far? Of course they did. Their arms were long. We had seen some of their activities down around Gulf Shores so why should Fairhope be left off their radar? The cartels aside, we didn't yet know much about the local drug culture. On the surface, this area seemed too normal, too idyllic for that to be a big issue. I knew better. Even perfect little towns had warts. More than once I had tossed someone from Captain Rocky's for selling drugs. Even permanently banned a couple of dudes.

Could drugs be the glue that held this together? Jason had meth in his pocket, and this sure smelled like a drug hit. Pop, pop, done. No fuss, no muss. Message delivered.

But it didn't fit what we knew about Emily. Jason? Didn't know much about him yet. Could he have been the real target and Emily merely collateral damage?

Too many questions. Too many directions this could go.

We were in Nicole's car headed back north after leaving Warren at the station and thanking her for the information. She had reminded us of our promise to share anything we uncovered.

I told Nicole what I was thinking.

"I guess it could be a drug deal gone bad," she said. "Or maybe one of them got in debt to a dealer."

"Wouldn't be the first time."

"Fairhope doesn't seem to be a major drug hub."

"True," I said. "But that's a problem everywhere."

"That would complicate things," Nicole said.

"And up the ante considerably. If some really bad guys are involved, it makes our job a shade more tricky. And dangerous."

She glanced at me. "You mean, like if we start digging into someone's business, they might push back?"

"Exactly."

Nicole whipped past a slow-moving pickup. "You're just full of good news."

I had another thought. Don't know where it came from but there it was.

"It wasn't just one guy," I said.

"Who wasn't?"

"The killers."

"Why would you think that?" she asked.

"How does one guy control two people? Without binding them."

She thought about that for a couple of seconds. "The trunk?"

"I guess that's possible."

"Or they were drugged?"

"Also possible."

"Or make them drive, the guy sits in the back, gun on them. Or maybe they met him there."

Each of those were possible. Except the latter. Who could've driven either Emily's or Jason's car back home? Two or more guys made the most sense. To me anyway. I told her that.

"You're getting good at this," she said.

"I am."

"Ray would be proud."

"Not likely."

We approached Emily's house. Her former house anyway. The Chevy sedan still in the drive.

"You're thinking that's Sean's car?" Nicole asked.

"Don't know who else would be here."

To answer the question, Sean came through the front door. He stopped at the foot of the steps when he saw Nicole turn into the drive. We climbed out. He eyed us suspiciously, then looked at Nicole. His expression softened. She had that effect.

"Sean?" I asked.

"Yeah."

I made the introductions. "We're sorry for your loss."

"Thanks." He glanced at Nicole. "I saw you guys at the funeral. With Tommy Jeffers."

"I didn't know you knew him."

"I don't. Never met him. But Emily talked about him from time to time."

"We all went to school together," I said. "A long time ago."

"That's what I heard."

"We're private investigators," Nicole said. "We were hired to gather some information on the divorce."

Sean hesitated. "I just found out she'd filed it. I didn't know until after I got back on dry land."

"Unexpected?" I asked.

He kicked at some loose gravel. "Not really. She said she was going to." He gave a half shrug. "I just didn't know exactly when that might be."

"How did you feel about it?" Nicole asked.

"The truth? It was time. We'd separated. Six months now. It was inevitable."

I nodded.

"We simply drifted apart." He looked off in the distance, unfocused. "I mean, I think we still loved each other. Or maybe cared a good deal about each other would be a better way of putting it." He shook his head and looked back toward me. "But, sometimes that ain't enough." A deep sigh. "We'd each moved on."

"So her filing wasn't a surprise?" Nicole asked.

He shook his head. "Maybe three months ago now, we sat down and decided that was best. For both of us. It'd sort of let us both roll on down the road." He shoved his hands in his jeans pockets. "Anyway, I told her it was up to her. That she could make the move whenever it felt right for her. I actually expected it sooner."

"Those decisions are never easy," Nicole said.

"That's the truth of it. Even the right decisions ain't always easy."

I was impressed with Sean. He seemed—I'm not sure what the word was—maybe resigned. Dumped into a situation that couldn't be unwound. Sad, for sure, in the face of what had happened, but through all that, he revealed no anger or resentment. Felt that way to me, anyway.

"She was seeing Jason, we understand," I said.

"Yeah."

"That okay with you?"

"Jason was a good guy. I was happy for her."

I smiled. "That's a very mature attitude."

"I've been seeing someone, too. And Emily was okay with that."

"From what you've said," Nicole said, "it sounds like the divorce wasn't going to be contentious."

"That's a fact. I didn't even have no attorney. Figured why spend all that money for no good reason?" He rubbed his nose with the heel of one hand. "She had that guy down in Gulf Shores. Expensive dude. I figured that was about enough to fork over to lawyers."

Amen to that. Walter Horton was indeed expensive. I know. I had written him checks for some big numbers during my divorce from Tammy. Painful. But then dear old Walter ended up marrying her, so I got off easy. Of course, Walter had gotten back in my pocket just last week. Thanks to the oh-so-pleasant Eddie Peck. I felt like I was becoming an annuity for Walter.

"Were you going to pay part of her legal fees?" I asked.

He nodded. "Seemed fair we'd split all that."

The more Sean talked, the more normal he seemed. I know when someone is murdered, the spouse is always the first person looked at, but the guy standing before me didn't seem the type. I didn't yet know that to be true, but I found myself hoping it was. But then Pancake often said, "Don't focus on the shiny thing. Watch the magician's other hand." Pancake was definitely smarter than the average bear, but was there a shiny thing in play here?

"How much do you know about what happened?" I asked. "How they were killed?"

He scratched his cheek. "Too much." He looked up toward the sky. "Still hard to believe."

"Any idea who could've done this?" Nicole asked.

His gaze moved to her. "For the life of me, I can't even imagine who could've." He took a deep breath. "Emily? She didn't have an enemy in the world."

"And Jason?" I asked.

"I don't know him all that well. He's only lived here a couple of years. Seemed an easygoing guy. Worked hard for sure."

"But no enemies?"

"Not that I ever heard. And, for sure, no one who would've done this."

"Let me ask you something," I said. "And I don't mean to cast stones at anyone." Sean looked my way. "With how they were killed. And left where they would easily be found. Looks to me like someone was sending a message."

"A message?" Sean said. "That don't make no sense."

"Any way Emily, or Jason, was involved in anything criminal?"

His head jerked upright. "No way. Not Emily, for sure."

"Drugs?"

"I'm not sure I like this," Sean said.

"We're just trying to look into everything," Nicole said. "Drug dealers aren't often bashful about killing anyone who had crossed them."

"Emily didn't use drugs. Ever. Wouldn't have anything to do with them. She barely even drank. Wine every now and again, but even that wasn't a big deal for her." He shook his head. "So, no way." He looked at me. "Why are you interested in this? I mean, there isn't going to be no divorce now. And you said that's what you was looking into."

"We were," I said. "But things have obviously changed. We have a different client now. Her brother, Danny, asked us to look into Emily's murder."

Sean seemed to mull that over. "Wonder what Chief Warren thinks about that?"

"Actually, she's onboard," Nicole said. "Maybe not at first, but she seems to welcome any help she can get."

"She showed us the scene," I said. "Where the bodies were found. Shared what she knows so far."

"Which is?" Sean asked.

"Just about nothing."

"Where is Danny anyway?" Sean asked.

"Headed back to his deployment," I said. "They only gave him a couple of days to come to the funeral."

Sean nodded. "He's the real deal, I'll tell you that. So if he thinks you guys can help, I'm all for it."

"What about you?" Nicole asked. "What are you going to do?"

"I don't know. It's a bit overwhelming. Seems like every time I think of all the stuff that needs doing, I want to crawl in bed and forget it all." He glanced toward the house. "The big thing is what to do with the property." He looked back toward me. "Emily would've kept it, of course. Been in her family a long time. But now that it's in my lap? I just don't know."

"The mortgage she took out?" I said. "Would that have been a joint debt?"

His brow furrowed. "You know, I don't know. I guess it would've gone with the property."

"So it would have been her issue?" Nicole said.

"Maybe." He shrugged. "Though that don't seem right. I think I'd've had to pony up half of it. Maybe not legally, but that'd've been the right thing, I think."

"It's a moot point," I said. "The house, the mortgage, they're yours now."

He nodded. "Part of me wants to keep it and another part can't see myself living here." A deep sigh. "I guess I'll sell it. Don't know what else to do." He shook his head. "This past month hasn't been a great one."

I watched him. Waited for him to continue.

He pointed toward his car. "Several weeks ago, a gasket blew. Took a couple of weeks to track down the parts and get it fixed. Cost a bunch to do. Then the place where I work got robbed. Then, this." He took a deep breath and exhaled, puffing out his cheeks. "I'm about ready for some good news."

"The oil company got robbed?" Nicole asked.

"No." He offered a weak smile. "I got two jobs. Out there on the rigs and then I work over at Watkins' Lumber when I'm here. Two weeks here, two out there on the Gulf."

"And you were robbed?" I asked.

"Sure was. Two guys came in with guns. Emptied the safe. Scary as hell. Me and Becky Woodley, she's the bookkeeper for Mr. Watkins. It was a Saturday. We were closing up when they came in."

"Who?"

He shook his head. "Don't know. They had on ski masks. And guns."

"Sounds scary," Nicole said.

"I honestly thought they'd shoot us both."

"How much did they take?" I asked.

Sean shook his head. "I don't really know. Whatever was in there."

"I take it that it's still unsolved?" I asked.

"Far as I know that's true. I'm not sure Chief Warren even has any suspects."

"They say bad news comes in threes," I said. "So maybe all that's behind you now."

"That'd be welcome."

"Thanks for talking with us," Nicole said.

He gave a quick head bob. "Hope you guys, and the chief, can find out who did this. Emily didn't deserve none of it."

CHAPTER 16

THE NEXT MORNING, I woke up with a hangover. Harsh sunlight angled through Nicole's bedroom window and sandpapered my eyes. My temples throbbed; my stomach felt like I'd been punched. Lower ribs, left side. Tender when I touched them. I didn't remember bumping into anything, or falling. Did Nicole hit me? Hard to remember but she does do that sometimes. Woman had a mean hook. And all that Krav Maga crap made her even more dangerous.

The sound of the shower hissed through the open bathroom door, carrying a faint steam cloud with it. I swung out of bed. The room swayed. I saw the tee shirt Nicole had worn to bed on the floor. When I stepped into the shower, Nicole made her move. She wanted sex. I didn't. Okay, okay, that was a lie. But after last night, it wasn't my first thought. Until Nicole got all touchy feely. Truth was, she always wanted sex. It was sort of her main hobby.

Last night. Mostly a blur. After we returned from Fairhope, we stopped by Captain Rocky's, drank tequila with Carla and a couple of the regulars, ate some fried oysters, and then headed to Nicole's. More tequila, the hot tub, and lots of Nicole.

By the time we finished our shower, and a few acrobatics, the water was cold. We dried quickly and retreated to the bedroom to dress for the day. I rubbed my stomach.

"Did you slug me last night?" I asked.

"I did."

"Why?"

"You were being an ass."

"I was?"

"You were. At the bar."

I racked my brain but came up empty. "What did I do?"

She pulled on a pair of jeans and a tank top. Pink and tight. Oh, yeah. "You don't remember?"

"No."

She smiled. "I'm not the keeper of your feeble memory."

Feeble? "You're not going to tell me?"

She sat on the bed and slipped on a pair of sandals. "Why should I?"

"So I won't do it again."

"You will. Whether I tell you or not. It's in your nature." She stood. "Besides, it'll give me an excuse to whack you again."

"I should report you to the police."

"Child protective services might be more appropriate." She punched my arm. Lightly this time. "Let's go."

Off to Ray's for our scheduled 9:00 a.m. meeting. We swung by Captain Rocky's on the way. Not for some hair of the dog, though that might have relieved some of the throbbing behind my eyes, but rather for a half dozen breakfast burritos. Three for Pancake, of course.

At Ray's place, Nicole and I grabbed some coffee from the kitchen before joining Ray and Pancake in Longly Investigation's main office. The round teak table on the deck. I dropped the bag in front of Pancake. He ripped it open, literally, unwrapped a burrito, and took a bite before grunting out, "Thanks. I was starving."

Of course he was.

"Ray ain't got shit to eat in this place."

"There's fruit and yogurt in the fridge," Ray said.

Another massive bite of his burrito and Pancake said, "My point."

While we ate, I told Ray about our chats with Chief Warren and Sean.

"Warren's okay with us sniffing round?" Ray asked.

"I think so," I said. "She showed us the scene, told us what she had so far."

"Which was basically nothing," Nicole added. "She has no suspects and doesn't really have a line on anyone."

Pancake chimed in. He had dug into the career of Chief Billie Warren and offered up his findings. Trained at the Birmingham Police Academy. Near the top of her class. Followed by two years on patrol. Involved in one officer-involved shooting.

Harrowing tale, according to Pancake. Serving as backup for the drug unit and SWAT team, she and her partner manned a back road that just might serve as an escape route for a crew of dealers. Rural farmhouse, perfect for meth cooking. The raid went well, but indeed, a pair of skinhead brothers blasted their pickup through a rear wooden gate and climbed on the two-lane blacktop that led them toward Warren. She stood in the road. They gunned the engine. She took out the driver, the truck sailing into a field landing on its roof and skidding into a tree. He showed the picture he had downloaded. Mangled would be the word. The driver didn't make it, a head injury, not Warren's bullet, doing him in. The brother vowed vengeance. Which would be delayed twenty years while he was a guest of the State. She was not only cleared, a good shoot it seemed, but she also received a commendation. Then she moved on down I-65 to Fairhope where she worked under the previous chief, ascending to his position when he retired.

"Seems like she's a good, tough cop," Pancake said.

That was my take from the little I had seen her.

"We'll still need to tread lightly," Ray said. "It's her turf, and I suspect she defends it tenaciously. Keeping her as an ally will make our job easier."

"Kid gloves all the way," I said.

Ray gave a quick nod. "You capable of that?"

"I'll handle him," Nicole said.

My father; my girlfriend.

"Jake did have a thought," Nicole said.

"Really?" Pancake said. "Where'd that come from?"

My friend.

"He thinks every now and then," Nicole said.

Pancake grunted. "Just with the wrong head."

Nicole laughed. "No complaints here."

That's me. Longly, Jake Longly. Super lover.

"But you're right," Nicole said. "Too much real thinking does give him a headache. But he's cute."

"So, what's your big idea?" Ray asked, bringing everyone back to reality.

"I think there must have been more than one killer," I said.

"Based on?"

"One person would've had a hard time controlling two people."

"That's what guns are for," Ray said.

"Yeah, but transporting and keeping an eye on them wouldn't be easy. Warren said that according to the ME there was no evidence they had been restrained in any way. No bruises or tape residue."

"Trunk," Pancake said. "Or he sat in the back with his weapon on them."

"That's what I said," Nicole added.

"Great minds." Pancake unwrapped his third burrito, took a bite. "But I agree with Jake. Two guys would make more sense."

"He came up with that on his own," Nicole said. She ruffled my hair. "He's such a clever child."

Good Lord.

"If that's the case, it changes things," Ray said. "Executed. By two hitters. Very pro. The question now is who? And why?"

"Jake has some thoughts on that, too," Nicole said.

"You're on a roll," Pancake said. He finished the burrito and wadded the wrapper.

"This sounds like it could be a drug thing," I said. I told them what Warren had said. Jason had a pair of small bags of meth in his back pocket.

Ray stared at me. "Didn't expect that."

"Both Allison and Sean said Emily would never be involved in drugs," I said. "And they knew her better than anyone, I suspect. Jason, no one really knows for sure. But secrets are secrets. Maybe Emily or Jason or both used on the sly. Got themselves into a bad situation."

"Maybe they owed money," Nicole said.

Pancake's eyes narrowed. He didn't want to hear that, to think that. He said, "Warren have any evidence of that?"

I shook my head. "None. But drugs found on Jason, execution-style murders. It's an interesting combination."

"And one we have to consider," Ray said. "Something we should chat with Warren about. She would know the players in her domain."

"We're on it," Nicole said.

On it? I was really beginning to dread those words. But she was now in full P.I. mode.

"But, let's say it isn't that," Ray said. "Where are we?"

"Besides drug dealers and gangs, who else does this kind of thing?" I asked.

"Maybe they were hired," Nicole said. "By Sean. Or someone with issues with Jason."

"I dug into Sean's finances," Pancake said. "While this was still a divorce."

"I didn't think he ever signed off on that," I said.

Pancake gave me a look. One that said permission wasn't needed. That he could access whatever he needed. Which was true.

"His bank accounts aren't exactly flush," Pancake said. "A few weeks ago, he took out fifteen hundred in cash, but other than that, I didn't see any large amounts moved around."

"Fifteen hundred?" Nicole asked. "Would that be enough?" She scanned each of our faces. "What would it cost to have two people killed?"

"More than a six-pack," Pancake said. "Probably a few thousand."

"Or fifteen hundred?" I asked.

Pancake shrugged. "You never know. I suspect they're some guys who'll do it for the price of the ammo." He scribbled on the notepad that lay before him.

"Sean said he had some car trouble," I said. "A gasket or something. Maybe that money was to pay for the repairs?"

"Could be," Pancake said. "I'll also take a peek at Jason's situation. See if his finances were in order."

"If you're thinking he might be dealing, or something like that, I don't think he'd drop any proceeds into his bank," Ray said.

"But, if he got in over his head, he might've had to raid his bank accounts to pay off any debts." Pancake shrugged. "Worth a look."

"Or he has a stash of cash," Ray said. "Most dealers do."

"That'll be harder to track," Pancake said. "Not impossible though."

"Okay," Ray said. "Let's build a list of the people we need to talk with. Then you three head that way and begin your interviews."

"What about you?" I asked.

"Got to run over to Biloxi for a couple of days. Another case." He nodded toward Pancake. "We were both going, but he won't now."

"Emily takes priority," Pancake said. "I want the guy, or guys, that did this."

"It would be good to see them in cuffs," Nicole said.

"They won't be needing any cuffs," Pancake said. "Maybe a neurosurgeon."

CHAPTER 17

We decided bouncing back and forth between Gulf Shores and Fairhope wasn't the shrewdest strategy. The thirty miles could be slam, bang, done or, depending on the time of day, day of the week, and luck, the brutal traffic could quadruple the time and wear you out. Ray booked us rooms at the Grand Hotel in Point Clear, just a few miles south of Fairhope. Nicole and I packed up a few things and headed north. We made good time so by eleven thirty we were settled in our room and met Pancake in the lobby.

The plan: Nicole and I would track down Charlie Martin, the other guy Emily was seeing, while Pancake sniffed around Jason's world. Of course, we had to stop by Mullins Bakery to feed Pancake. Me, too. We sat with Allison while Pancake demolished three ham and cheese croissants. Nicole had a plain one, me a cinnamon roll. Lots of coffee.

"Anything new?" Allison asked.

Was there ever. A couple of little baggies in Jason's pocket changed the flavor of everything. But Chief Warren had revealed that fact only because, on some level, she trusted us. And, we had promised to keep it under wraps. Anything we did to fracture what seemed to be a collaborative relationship with her would have serious blowback and could gum up our investigation. Yet, Allison and Emily had been very close and she might have some useful insights. I knew we had to tread carefully. Like tightrope walking on a windy day. But we had to cross that bridge, so to speak, sooner or later, and sooner seemed best. I put on my best casual face.

"Not really," I said. "But let me ask you something. Did anyone here, Emily, Jason, or Sean, use drugs of any kind?"

The question surprised her. She actually recoiled slightly. Shoulders straight, eyes wider. I guess my casual face wasn't casual enough. Pancake gave me a glance.

"No," Allison said. "For sure, Emily didn't. Why are you asking that?"

Pancake jumped in. "When two people are murdered the way Emily and Jason were, it often points to some underlying criminal activity. Drugs are sometimes involved."

"Not for Emily. No way. Jason, I don't know all that well, but every time I was around him, he seemed—normal. Not stoned or hyped up or anything like that."

"Sean?" I asked.

"No." She took a sip of her coffee. "Emily told me that back when she and Sean started dating, he smoked a little from time to time. At first, she ignored it, but when things got serious between them, she put her foot down. No weed or she would break it off."

"Did he?" Nicole asked. "Stop?"

"He did. Emily said he didn't even protest." Allison's eyes glistened with moisture. "I hate this. All of this." She dabbed her eyes with a wadded napkin. "I haven't slept much lately. I keep replaying every conversation Emily and I ever had. Trying to make some sense of it."

"Some things don't make sense," Pancake said. "That's the truth of it."

Nicole gave Allison a comforting hug, and we left her to her work. Pancake headed toward his truck. Nicole and I to Copeland's Nursery for a chat with Charlie Martin.

The young lady behind the counter, her name tag revealing she was Megan, told us that Martin was out on a delivery. When we asked about Mr. Copeland, she pointed toward the rear of the store, saying, "He's out back helping a customer."

Out back was an explosion of greenery. Rows of trees and shrubs to the left, long raised bins of potted flowers and plants to the right, some shaded by a ten-foot-high mesh canopy that filtered the sun.

I saw Carl Copeland near the far end of the shaded flower bins. I recognized him from the photos Pancake had gathered. He stood with a woman who wore jeans and a dirt-stained, aqua-blue shirt. She held a pair of six-inch pots that sported red pepper plants.

While we waited for him to spring free, we roamed through the foliage. Nicole seemed to know the names of everything. Many I couldn't pronounce, and spelling them was out of the question.

"How do you know all this?" I asked.

"I had a summer job during high school at a place very much like this."

She constantly amazed.

Copeland helped his customer ferry a pair of plant trays inside and then came back out, walking toward us. "Megan said you wanted to see me," he said.

"We're actually looking for Charlie Martin, but we hear he's out on a delivery."

"He is. Should be back in a few minutes." He gave a quick nod. "Anything I can help with?"

"We're private investigators," Nicole said. "Looking into the murders of Emily Patterson and Jason Collins."

He stiffened slightly. "I see."

"Emily's brother, Daniel, hired us," I said.

"Chief Warren onboard with this?"

"She is," Nicole said.

"I grew up with Emily," I said. "Daniel, too. Down in Gulf Shores. Before their family moved up this way."

Copeland nodded, shoulders relaxing. "So this is more than a professional inquiry?"

"It is. My friend Tommy Jeffers and Emily were sixth-grade sweethearts."

"Pancake—that's what folks call Tommy—is part of our firm," Nicole said. "Longly Investigations."

Copeland gave a half smile. "Heard of them." He looked at me. "You're the baseball player?"

"I was."

"Can we ask you a few questions?" Nicole said.

"Sure."

"Charlie Martin? What kind of guy is he?"

Copeland's brow furrowed. "He's not a suspect, is he?"

"Not likely," I said. "Truth is, we, Chief Warren, too, for that matter, are dead in the water. No real suspects. No leads at all. We're trying to get a handle on all the folks in Emily's life. See if anyone can point us in the right direction."

"That would definitely include Charlie," Copeland said. "I suspect you know they were dating."

"We do," Nicole said. "She was seeing Jason, too. How did Charlie feel about that?"

"Not good. He was in love with Emily. No doubt about that. What happened to her really tore him up." He sighed. "He's been more or less a zombie since then. Not able to concentrate on his work, or anything else it seems."

"Is that a problem?" I asked.

Copeland shook his head. "Charlie's a good man. Good worker. Been with me awhile. I guess I can cut him some slack. Given the circumstances."

I liked Copeland. His sun-tanned, creased face, lean muscular build, and rough hands revealed a man who worked for a living. One of those guys with a kind, soft-spoken demeanor. I suspected he was a good boss.

"I hear they were basically executed," he said.

"Where'd you hear that?" I asked.

"From several people. Over at the coffee shop I stop by every morning for breakfast."

Small-town news never sits still. Spreads like a bad flu. I knew Warren wanted to keep that detail under wraps. I wondered who leaked it. And what Warren would do if she found out. I suspected it wouldn't be pretty.

I decided to neither confirm nor deny that fact. Instead, I asked, "Any idea who might've done something like that?"

"Not Charlie, for sure. No way. Ain't in his nature."

"That's what we hear."

"Bet on it. Look, Charlie's a quiet guy. Shy even. The boy ain't got a mean bone in his body." He looked at his feet. "He loved Emily. He'd never bring her any harm."

"From what we know so far, we agree," Nicole said. "We're hoping Charlie might give us some insight into Emily. Maybe Jason, too."

The sound of tires on gravel drew my attention. A white van, "Copeland's Nursery" printed in black script on the side, crunched to a stop near a group of shrubs.

"There he is now," Copeland said.

CHAPTER 18

PANCAKE'S RESEARCH INTO Ira Sharp Jr. revealed he was forty-four and had worked at Sharp's Used Cars since graduating from high school. He had taken over the operation eight years earlier on the death of his father, who had created the business on an expansive plot of land near the north end of town. Sharp's had pumped out used cars for over thee decades. Financials showed the enterprise was profitable and stable. It enjoyed ninety-percent positive posts on the various online rating sites. For a used car dealer, that seemed amazing. Sure, there was the occasional "crooked," "dishonest," and "liars" sprinkled through the evaluations, but those were the outliers.

Pancake parked next to a clean-looking, white Toyota 4-Runner with "$2499 As Is" in red paint on the windshield. Thirty other similarly decorated vehicles filled the lot. Overhead, alternating red, yellow, and blue triangular flags hung from sagging lines that stretched between light standards and flapped in the onshore breeze.

As soon as he stepped from his truck, a salesman appeared. Young, looked high-school-age, short-sleeved, blue-checked shirt, clip-on navy tie, and a pleasant smile.

"How you doing today?" he asked.

"Fine. You?"

"Good. Good. Can I show you anything? We have some very clean vehicles in stock."

Pancake scanned the lot. "Looks that way." He turned back to the young man. The name tag on his shirt indicated he was Gregory. "I'm here to see Mr. Sharp."

"Oh." He looked disappointed. "He's in his office." He pointed toward the building.

Pancake entered a small showroom. Three cars sat at angles in the main, glass-enclosed space. To the left, a middle-aged woman looked up from behind a counter. She smiled.

"I'm looking for Mr. Sharp," Pancake said.

"And you are?"

"Tommy Jeffers. From Longly Investigations."

"Oh?"

"I need to chat with him about Jason Collins."

"I see."

Ira Sharp Jr. came through the door behind her. He looked a little older, and a couple of biscuits heavier, than his photo on the website. "Did I hear you mention Jason?" he asked.

"I did," Pancake said. He repeated his name and affiliation.

Sharp hesitated, then said, "Come on in my office."

"Thanks for seeing me," Pancake said, taking the seat that faced Sharp's desk.

"Mr. Jeffers? Right?"

"Folks call me Pancake."

Sharp smiled. "I like it. What can I do for you?"

Pancake went through who he was, yet again, and that they had been hired by Emily's brother, and that, yes, Chief Warren had given her blessing, and that they were looking into the murders of Jason and Emily.

Sharp leaned back in his swivel chair. It creaked under his weight. "I'm here to tell you that Jason's murder shocked everyone here. It don't make much sense."

"Murder often doesn't," Pancake said. "You have any thoughts on it?"

"You mean like who might've done it?"

Pancake nodded.

"None. Jason was a good kid. Been with us a couple of years. Hard worker. Good salesman. Never had no problems."

"I take it you knew he and Emily were dating?"

"Sure. She'd drop by from time to time. And, of course, I'd see her over at the bakery." He patted his belly. "Maybe too often. Very nice young lady as far as I could see."

"Any thoughts on their relationship? Emily and Jason?"

Sharp slid aside a stack of papers and folded his hands on his desk. "Jason was smitten. I can tell you that. My impression is she was, too."

"She was seeing someone else though."

"You mean Charlie Martin?"

"I do. Any issues there as far as you know?"

"Jason wasn't happy about it. I mean, who would be?" He shrugged. "But Jason told me once, recently, in fact, that Charlie and Emily were just friends."

"Do you think he really believed that?"

A sigh. "Not really. I could tell it hurt him."

"He ever say anything that led you to believe Charlie could be a threat?"

"Charlie?" He actually laughed. "Do you know him?"

"Not yet."

"You plan on paying him a visit?"

"We do."

"Then you'll see for yourself. He's a bit of a wimp." Now he tapped a finger on the desktop. "I guess that wasn't very nice. What I mean is that he's very quiet and very passive as far as I know. He works over for Gene Copeland. At the nursery. Gene says he's a good boy and a hard worker."

"That's what we've heard."

Sharp glanced down toward his hands, then back up. "Look, I watch all those cop shows on TV. I know these love triangles can lead to some bad behavior. And I know the quiet ones are sometimes the worst ones. But, truly? Charlie Martin? I'm afraid I don't see it."

"What about Emily's ex? Sean Patterson?"

"I don't know him all that well. He dropped by a few weeks ago now. Something like that. Looked at some trucks. I think he had some issues with his car. Maybe a gasket thing. Don't remember. So he was maybe interested in buying something. I think in the end he got his car fixed and that was that."

"Did Jason ever express any opinions on Sean?"

"Just that he was Emily's ex. Well, almost ex. I guess legally they were still married."

"Did that bother Jason?"

"Not that he ever said. I suspect it must've. I mean, he and Emily were getting a might serious." He scratched the back of one hand. "You know, a week or so ago he did mention that Emily was finally going to file for a divorce. Make it all official."

"She did."

"Oh." Sharp's eyes narrowed. "You think that had anything to do with this?"

"Maybe."

"Sort of like a couple decides to separate? Everything is copasetic? Then one of them moves to make it real and the other one ain't so happy about turning the page? That sort of thing?"

Pancake nodded.

"Well, I don't know nothing about that. All's I can say is that Jason and Emily seemed happy with one another."

CHAPTER 19

TO SAY THAT Charlie Martin was shy didn't quite do it justice. He was painfully so. Nice-looking kid, light brown hair that flopped over his forehead and partially hid his left eye. His jeans seemed a size too large, pale, skinny arms fell from a baggy navy tee shirt.

After Copeland waved him over, introduced us, and with a brief nod retreated back inside, Charlie, Nicole, and I walked into the parking lot, away from the customers that roamed among the plants. Charlie tugged a pack of Pall Malls from his jeans pocket, shook one out, and lit it with a Zippo. He leaned against the front of the Copeland's van he had been driving.

His gaze bounced up from the gravel toward me for a beat, then back down. When he spoke, his voice was soft. "So, you want to talk about Emily?"

"We do," I said. "We're sorry for your loss. We know you and Emily were close."

Another brief glance, a slight head nod.

"You want to tell us about it?" Nicole asked. "You and Emily?"

He puffed on the cigarette, the smoke swirling around his head. "Still hard to believe." Now he looked up. His eyes glistened.

Nicole moved closer, touched his arm. "You loved her, didn't you?"

A sharp sob escaped him.

"I can see it," she continued.

"I did. I do." He took a deep ragged breath. "I always will."

Charlie Martin was broken. That was evident in the tug of gravity on his face, his stooped shoulders. He looked as if he might collapse and disintegrate into dust. He appeared just that fragile. Nicole sensed it, too.

"Look, Charlie," she said. "We know this is hard. We know that talking about her hurts. Deeply. And we're sorry we have to add to your pain. But we need to find out who did this."

He sniffed, wiped the back of one hand across his nose. "I know. I'm sorry." He looked up at the sky. "It's just so unfair." He looked back at Nicole. "She was so very special."

"She was," I said. "I grew up with her."

His head snapped toward me. "You did?"

I nodded. "Her and her brother, Danny. He's the one that hired us. We went to school together until her family moved from Gulf Shores to here."

That seemed to relax him a little. He took a puff, inhaled, let it out. "Emily didn't like my smoking. I didn't around her."

"How long did you guys date?" Nicole asked.

"Six, no, eight months."

"What kinds of things did you do?"

"Movies, dinners, sometimes just watch TV. With popcorn. Emily liked popcorn." He smiled. Weak and unenthusiastic, but a smile anyway. "And chocolate."

Nicole laughed. "All us girls like chocolate."

That drew a warmer smile from Charlie.

I hated to break the mood, but we needed info.

"We know Emily was also seeing Jason Collins. How'd you feel about that?"

"I didn't like it. But there wasn't anything I could do about it."

"Did that make you mad?"

He pulled out another cigarette and lit it with the remnant of the first one. He crushed that butt against the bumper and dropped it onto the gravel.

"Look, I know where this is going," he said. "Chief Warren asked me all this. So let me make it clear—I had nothing to do with what happened to Emily and Jason. Nothing. I couldn't. I loved her."

Well, well, Charlie Martin did have balls. When he felt backed in a corner, his spine stiffened. Made me feel good that it did.

Charlie continued, "I wanted Jason to simply go away. Move to another state. Get a job in Alaska. Or get abducted by space aliens." He tapped a cigarette ash away. "Maybe then I'd have a chance with Emily. But that wasn't going to happen. As long as he was around, he had the inside track. She felt things for him she didn't with me. I knew that."

"Some could see that as a motive," I said.

"Maybe for Jason," he said. "But Emily? Not possible. All I can say is that I don't know anything about it. If I did, I'd be down at the police station telling everything I did know."

"What was your plan?" I asked. "To make this play out in your favor?"

"Didn't really have one. Except wait. Most relationships fall apart sooner or later. I figured that might happen and I'd be there." He sighed. "Not very smart probably, but I didn't see any other way."

"And if it didn't fall apart?"

"I guess I'd have to live with it, wouldn't I?"

"How did you hear about the murders?" Nicole asked.

"Chief Warren came by here. Late that afternoon. Told me. Asked me all these same questions." He took a deep breath and let it out slowly. Gaze downward, slight headshake. "At the time I didn't realize she considered me a suspect. I was in shock, I guess.

Fact is, I don't remember much about that conversation. Time sort of froze when she said Emily had been murdered."

"A natural reaction," Nicole said.

He glanced at her. "I remember feeling numb. Cold. As if the world had turned into an ice box or something."

"Where were you when it happened?" I asked. "That night?"

"I had been over at my cousin's place. In Magnolia Springs. I took the day off here to help him clear a field for planting."

"You spent the night?"

"No. I had to work the next day, so after we had dinner and watched some TV, I drove home. Left there around midnight."

Which didn't exactly clear him. According to Warren, the ME determined the time of death to be between 10:00 p.m. and 2:00 a.m. Granted Magnolia Springs was a few miles east and Emily's place and Fletcher's Farm a few more north of Fairhope, it wasn't that much out of the way. Especially that time of night. The towns around here rolled up the sidewalks long before midnight. The drive time was doable and there would be few folks to randomly witness his movements. Shy Charlie had the motive, at least partially, and the opportunity. But did he have the means? Could this beaten-down soul before me actually do that?

"As far as you know, did either Emily or Jason have issues with anyone?" I asked. "Problems? Disputes?"

Charlie shook his head. "I don't know for sure about Jason, but Emily never said anything like that. And she would've. We talked. A lot. She was very open." He sniffed. "Like she would be with a brother." He glanced up, shrugged.

And there it was. Charlie was the personification of unrequited love. He loved her; Emily viewed him as a brother.

"One last question," I said. "Drugs? Did either Emily or Jason use drugs?"

"No." The answer came out quick and sharp. "Emily for sure. She barely even drank. And drugs would be out of the question."

"And Jason?" Nicole asked.

"I can't say for sure, but I suspect no. I don't think Emily would be around him if he did."

"What about Sean?" I asked. "He use?"

"Not that I know." He looked up at me, brushed his hair back from his eyes. "Why all these questions about drugs?"

"The way they were killed. Makes you think it could've been a hit."

His eyes widened. "I never thought of that."

"Probably not the case," I said. "We just have to consider all possibilities."

Charlie seemed to consider that. "I guess that makes sense."

"Did Emily say she was having any problems with Sean?" Nicole asked.

"Other than the divorce, not that she ever saw." He hesitated a beat. "That sounds strange, doesn't it? *Other than the divorce?* The truth is, it seemed they'd settled any issues they had and were ready to move on."

"Sean, too?"

"It's what he said. He's got a girlfriend. You know that?"

"We heard. A waitress around here?"

"Yeah. Whitney Meyer. Works over at The Rib Shack." He crushed the second cigarette against the bumper. "You don't think Sean had anything to do with this, do you?"

"Do you?" I asked.

He sighed. "I guess anything's possible. But I'd surely doubt it. Don't see any reason he would."

"Maybe the house?" Nicole said.

Charlie's brow furrowed. "Never thought of that."

CHAPTER 20

"YOU GUYS WERE going to get married?" Chief Billie Warren asked.

"Had it all planned out," Pancake replied. "Three kids. Tommy Jr., Little Emily, and Jake."

"Ahhh. For your charming friend?"

"He ain't all that charming once you get to know him. More a pain in the ass."

"I'm sorry," Warren said.

"For Jake?"

"No. For Emily. First loves are always lasting."

"True that. Her murder sort of ripped out a piece of my soul."

They were standing in line at Latte Da, the coffee counter inside Page and Palette, a combination bookstore, bar, and coffee shop on South Section Street. A very cool place was Pancake's assessment.

The person in front of them gathered up three tall cups and moved away.

"What can I get you?" the young lady behind the counter asked. She was short with light-brown curly hair, a row of jewels along the edge of her left ear, and a bright smile. She eyed Pancake.

Pancake waved to Warren who ordered a coffee, black. Pancake the same, plus a blueberry muffin.

Out on the street, Warren said, "I think you have a new fan." She laughed.

Pancake grunted, took a bite of muffin, and spoke around the mouthful. "Women love me."

That drew a smile from Warren. "So it seems."

Pancake had called Warren ten minutes earlier and asked to see her. She had said she was downtown, searching for some coffee. After he said he was buying, she suggested meeting at Page and Palette.

Now they walked back north on Section Street. More small talk during the journey to Warren's office.

Once inside and seated, she asked, "I've got to ask, did any of you tell anyone that they were executed?"

"No." Pancake shook his head. "Not a chance. Why?"

"It's out there. On the streets."

"Wasn't us. Maybe someone in your department?"

She raised an eyebrow. "Better not be. I've been known to take scalps."

"Bet that's true."

"Might've been from the ME's office. Those folks like to talk."

"Voice of experience?" Pancake asked.

"You might say. So, what'd you want to chat about?"

"Drugs."

"Okay. In what context?"

"Up front, I don't think Emily and Jason getting murdered had anything to do with drugs. I think they were planted to make it look that way."

"Can't say I disagree."

"But we could be wrong." Pancake opened his palms toward her.

"We could."

"More to the point, whoever planted the meth must have access to it. Means they're a user, a dealer, or they know someone who is."

"I agree. That's why I had a chat with Clive and Reba Mack."

"Who are?"

"A couple. Local dealers. Mostly marijuana, but they've been known to step up their game. Meth, cocaine, bigger stuff."

"What'd they say?"

"Nothing. They know nothing about the murders."

"Could be lying."

"Of course they're lying. Every word out of their collective mouths is a lie. Still doesn't mean they were mixed up in murder."

"Would they be capable?"

"They're drug dealers. I know this won't be news to you, but drugs, guns, and murder are common bedfellows."

"They carry much weight or are they small-time?"

"Both," Warren said. "They're not big-time like the cartel-connected thugs in Mobile and over in Biloxi, but for here, not much happens in the drug world without their knowledge. Maybe even consent, or involvement."

"They keep their fingers on the pulse?"

"So to speak."

"Have you busted them before?" Pancake asked.

"I've tried. They're pretty clever. I did tag Clive once with some Oxy. About a year ago. The judge let him plead it down to simple possession and not dealing so he got thirty days and two years probation. He's still on probie so I have easy access to him."

"And the wife?"

"Reba? She's tougher than he is. And more dangerous. At least that's my take. She's not a wilting flower. Not even close. Some guy grabbed her tit in a bar once, and she knocked out two teeth and stomped him in the face. She broke a pool cue and was going to go all vampire-hunter on him when a couple of guys pulled her off."

"She sounds pleasant."

"Actually, she doesn't look the part. Blond, attractive, not very big. Short, wiry. Then again, so are rattlesnakes."

"You mind if we take a run at them?"

"Be my guest. Run over them if you want. Lord knows, I've tried."

Pancake laughed. "We can do that."

"One word of advice."

"Yeah?"

"Don't touch her tits."

CHAPTER 21

Bobby Taylor, Charlie Martin's cousin, owned and farmed a plot of land just south of Highway 98 near Magnolia Springs. According to the satellite image I pulled up on my iPhone, its western edge was demarcated by the Magnolia River, which itself continued west and dumped into Weeks Bay, an out-pouching of the larger Mobile Bay. The other three sides of Taylor's slice of Baldwin County were embraced by pine forests.

Nicole turned onto a gravel road and aimed us toward a light-gray house with a green slanted metal roof. A covered gallery extended its entire length. A large sun-bleached red barn loomed just beyond. She slowed, but I touched her arm, pointed ahead.

"Keep going," I said.

In the distance, a man sat astride a tractor, its wheels churning into the dirt. A long chain extended rearward, taunt, buckling, ripping a tree stump from the ground.

"You think that's Bobby Taylor?"

"Probably."

"What's he doing?"

"Pulling up stumps. Clearing the land for planting, it looks like."

"Which fits with what Martin told us."

Nicole angled past the house and along the edge of the field. The gravel gave way to rutted dirt. Nicole stopped and we climbed out.

Taylor looked our way. We waved. He shut down the tractor and jumped to the ground. A handkerchief appeared from his rear pocket, and he mopped his face and neck, walking toward us. He looked familiar, but I couldn't remember where I might have seen him.

"Bobby Taylor?" I asked.

He eyed the Mercedes, then Nicole, finally back to me. "Yeah. And who are you?"

"Jake Longly. This is Nicole Jamison."

"You were at Emily Patterson's funeral," Taylor said.

That was it. I could picture him now. Standing toward the back of the gathering.

"We were. I grew up with Emily and her brother, Daniel. Down in Gulf Shores."

"What can I do for you?"

"We're looking into the murders of Emily and Jason Collins," Nicole said.

His brow furrowed. "And you want to talk to me?"

I nodded.

"About what exactly?"

I explained that we had been hired by Daniel to look into the murders of Emily and Jason Collins. I added that Chief Warren was onboard with our efforts. "We're gathering as much information on Emily and Jason as we can, and since your cousin Charlie Martin was seeing her, we thought you might have some helpful information."

"Don't see how. Didn't really know her all that well. Charlie brought her out here for dinner a couple of times. Me and the wife met them in town for dinner or a movie a few other occasions."

I explained that we had just left the nursery where we had talked with Charlie. "Charlie said he was here helping you clear land and then stayed for dinner on the day of the murders."

His shoulders straightened. "Are you trying to say that Charlie's a suspect?"

"No, we're not," Nicole said. "But everyone who knew Emily or had any connection to her might have some information that'll lead us in the right direction."

"Well, I can tell you for damn sure, if you're thinking Charlie did any of this, you're wrong. Dead wrong."

"I agree," I said. "He seems like a nice, quiet guy. Not the kind that would do something like this."

"He is nice and quiet. And shy. Sometimes too much so."

That was my take.

Taylor continued. "To answer your question, he was here all day. Helped me take down all these trees and chop them into firewood."

He waved toward a swath of land that was pocked with tree stumps and ragged holes where others had been removed. Near the corner of the field sat a neat stack or firewood and an unruly tangle of stumps, long roots like Medusa's snakes projecting from each.

He went on. "He stayed for dinner and didn't head out for home until near midnight."

"What about him and Emily?" Nicole asked. "How did he feel about her?"

Taylor sighed. "He loved her. Her death tore him up. That's for sure." He looked down, kicked at a clod of dirt. "That's why there's no way he could've harmed her."

"What about Jason? Any issues there?"

"I don't know Jason. Never met him. Charlie, of course, knew Emily was seeing him, too. Wasn't happy about it, but Charlie's the kind that stays the course. I think he felt that all he needed to do was hang steady and that, eventually, Jason would move on and he and Emily just might have a future."

"No real animosity against Jason as far as you know?" I asked.

"That ain't Charlie," he said. He gave a weak smile. "Ain't in his makeup. Sometimes I wish he would get angry—at something, anything—but he never does. He just smiles and carries on. Someone might slight him, and he basically ignores it. Been that way his whole life. Even when we were kids."

"Do you have any idea who might have done this?" Nicole asked.

"None. Except I suspect that you should start with the husband. Sean. You talked to him yet?"

"We have," I said.

"We watch those cop shows all the time. Seems like it's always the spouse."

"That's true," I said. "But he's got a pretty good alibi."

"I heard. Out on an oil rig, wasn't it?"

"That's right."

CHAPTER 22

NICOLE WHEELED INTO the gravel parking area at Watkins' Lumber. It buzzed with activity. Two flatbed trucks were backed into a loading area where three men lifted two-by-fours and Sheetrock panels onto the bed of each. Another man stood nearby with a clipboard, apparently checking off the materials loaded on each truck.

Reminded me of the summer Pancake and I had worked at such a place. Hot days of lifting, stacking, carrying, and loading wood and other materials only to drive them somewhere and lift, and carry, and unload them for a customer. Mostly DIY types, but some true construction sites.

I watched as one of the men balanced a Sheetrock panel and carefully lowered it onto a stack of others. Of all the things we had done that summer, by far the most grueling was handling Sheetrock. Heavy, awkward to handle, and easily fractured, which would render it useless.

Backbreaking. For me, anyway. Pancake, less so. He handled even three-quarter-inch panels with ease.

The man with the clipboard turned out to be Fred Watkins. He wore a red shirt with "Watkins' Lumber" stitched over the breast pocket, tan khakis, and work boots, brown with red laces. He peered at us over the half glasses. I introduced Nicole and me, adding that we were with Longly Investigations. Man, I hated saying that. Made me feel like I sold out. That Ray had won our years-long battle. Nicole had no such reservations. She shook Watkins' hand firmly, flashed that wonderful smile of hers.

"Investigators, huh?" Watkins said. A frown creased his brow. "Investigating what?"

"The murders of Emily Patterson and Jason Collins," I said.

He hesitated, his frown deepening. "And you think I can tell you what?"

Watkins was lean and wiry. Fit. And right now, his shoulders were erect, his back straight, and his expression hard-edged.

"Just so you know," Nicole said, "Chief Warren is onboard with our enquiries."

He gave a half nod, seemed to relax a notch.

Nicole continued. "We're helping her gather information. Trying to look into Emily's world. See if anything shakes loose."

"So, you're interested in Sean?" Watkins asked.

"Exactly."

"Why?" His back stiffened again. "He a suspect?"

"Not really," I said. "He wasn't even around at the time of the murders."

"True." Watkins nodded. He glanced back over one shoulder. "Let's go to my office. It's cooler there."

It was. Watkins had the AC cranked up. Coming in from the heat, it felt like a meat locker. He sat behind his desk, we in the chairs across from him.

"Have you talked with Sean?" Watkins asked.

"We did," I said. "He seemed pretty shaken by all this."

"That's true. So much so that the rig operator where he works didn't want him to come back for a while. I guess he figured Sean would be too distracted. Maybe be a hazard. That sort of thing." He shrugged. "But things changed. Apparently, he had a couple of guys go out sick, so he called in Sean."

"He's out there in the Gulf now?" Nicole asked.

Watkins nodded. "Just for a couple of days. I think he'll be back tomorrow. Maybe the next day."

Sean hadn't mentioned that when we talked to him the other day. Maybe he didn't yet know he was going to be called in.

"Tell us about Sean," Nicole said.

Watkins scratched one side of his nose. "I didn't think he was a suspect."

"But his soon-to-be ex-wife was one of the victims," I said. "Maybe he was the target."

"You mean like someone went over there to kill him and Emily was collateral damage as they say?"

"Maybe."

"But they didn't live together anymore."

"Maybe the killer didn't know that," Nicole said.

He sighed. "I can't imagine anyone having that kind of issue with Sean. He's a good guy. Hard worker. When he's here."

"So you're okay with him only being here part-time?" I asked.

"Sure. He's worked here since he was in high school. Of course, I wish he was here every day, but he loves that rig work and so we make an accommodation." He tapped a finger on his desk. "I don't know why he likes it. It takes a toll."

"He had no issues with anyone as far as you know?" Nicole asked.

"Sure didn't. Even his divorce was going smoothly. From what he told me. I think he and Emily had reconciled everything and were comfortable with ending it."

"That's what we hear," I said. "He told us you got robbed not too long ago."

"Sure did. Sean and Becky Woodley were here. Becky keeps our books."

"What happened?" Nicole asked.

"It was a Saturday. We had just closed. Fact is, I had left an hour earlier. Me and the wife had to go to her cousin's place for some get-together. Over in Mobile." He offered a half smile. "Anyway, they were getting ready to close up. Two guys came in with masks and guns. Forced Becky to open the safe. She—Sean, too, for that matter—tried to convince them they didn't know the combination. Truth was, only Becky did. They must've sensed that. Put a gun to her head is what she said. She opened the safe. Then they tied them up with duct tape. Took the cash out of the safe."

"How much?" I asked.

"A shade over eighteen grand."

"You keep that kind of money around often?"

He nodded. "Most of the time. A lot of our customers pay cash." He bit one lip. "That's why we have the safe." He nodded over his shoulder.

A large black safe sat in the corner. It looked substantial. Hard to crack. Unless you had the combination. Or someone at the business end of your gun did.

"Who would know you kept cash on hand?" I asked.

"Besides me?" Another half smile. "Becky, of course. A couple of other folks."

"Sean?"

He nodded. "Yeah. He helped with inventory. And often took the cash over to the bank."

"Is eighteen K typical for you?" I asked.

"Mostly. Sometimes more, sometimes less, but I suspect that's in the average ballpark."

"You have any idea who the two robbers might've been?"

He shook his head. "Sean and Becky said they wore ski-type masks. They only saw their eyes and mouth. Far as I know, Chief Warren doesn't have any leads either. Last I heard anyway."

"She doesn't," I said.

He shrugged. "Probably never know." He gave a quick headshake. "I got insurance that'll cover the loss, but the invasion, the shear audacity of it all, there's no rectifying that."

Isn't that the truth? Many years ago, Captain Rocky's was robbed. More like burglarized. Someone walked away with a pair of tables and half a dozen chairs from my deck. Never found out who, never saw the furniture again. I figured it had to have been several people and they were now enjoying them on a patio somewhere.

It wasn't eighteen thousand, maybe eight hundred, but the sense of violation was real and it lingered.

CHAPTER 23

THE HOUSE SAT on a rural stretch of County Highway 27, State Highway 181, a shade over three miles from downtown Fairhope. Rich farmland, stands of pines, cedars, and gum trees. Houses scattered here and there across the terrain. Quiet, not much traffic. Made snooping around a problem. Pancake knew his truck would ping everyone's radar.

He imagined that since Clive and Reba Mack were the major local dealers, and that fact didn't seem to be a secret to anyone in the county, their neighbors were used to having strangers in their midst. He was also sure that everyone who visited the Macks was considered a drug buyer. A stain on their God-fearing community. Someone to keep an eye on.

Meant that folks paid attention to who came and went. Not just to the Macks' door but up and down the rural roads. Especially strangers in strange vehicles. You just never knew when remembering something like that might be important.

Warren had given him the address, scribbling it on a scrap of paper. Pancake then swung down by the Grand Hotel and picked up Ray, who was still unpacking. He had bounced over to Biloxi, finished his business, and headed back to the Grand Hotel. After

Pancake said they had a mission, Ray grabbed his surveillance bag, and they were off.

Pancake rolled past the house. It was late afternoon, the sun low. The two large oaks in the front yard laid long shadows over the roof. Three vehicles in the drive: a metallic gold Lexus SUV, a white BMW X5, and a red Ford F150 truck, camper shell on the back. Ray aimed his camera, long telephoto lens, through the lowered passenger window. Click, click, click.

"See anybody?" Pancake asked.

"Looks quiet."

Pancake continued a quarter of a mile and tuned off the highway onto a dirt road.

"You think all those vehicles are theirs, or do they have visitors?" Pancake asked.

Ray shrugged.

Pancake found a flat shoulder and made a U-turn, coming to a stop. "What now?"

"Let's do another drive-by. I think I saw another road just beyond the house. Like this one except it looked like it went into a stand of trees. Maybe we can get in there and get a closer look."

That's what they did. Driving by, the house appeared unchanged; the spur road did indeed melt into the trees. Pancake jerked to a stop and they climbed out. They pushed through the pines and squatted near the edge, the house fifty yards away.

Pancake examined it through a pair of binoculars. "I got something," he said. "That left-most window. Looks like the living room."

Ray leveled his long-lensed camera toward the house. Click, click. He saw two people beyond the window. A man and a woman. Now a third. Another man. The woman facing the pair—hand gestures indicated she was talking. Then they moved from view.

"They're coming out," Ray said.

Pancake watched the three step onto the porch, followed by another man. Ray snapped dozens of pictures, then switched to movie mode, capturing the unfolding scene. Pancake adjusted the focus of his field glasses. The quartet chatted for a minute, and then two of the men descended from the porch and walked to the red pickup. One tall, thin, the other shorter, thicker. The tall dude wore jeans, a black tee shirt, his hair long, stringy, a blue backpack slung over one shoulder. The shorter one's hair was longer, shoulder length, and also stringy. Jeans and a black tee. The uniform of the day apparently. They climbed in, spun a turn through the yard, and then headed south on the highway. The couple stood and watched, then went back inside.

"What do you think?" Pancake asked.

"Probably a couple of their dealers. Picking up more product and laying off some cash."

"Yep," Pancake said. "What now?"

"Let's get back on the road. I'll call Jake and see what they're up to. Then let's go have some dinner and compare notes."

"Dinner sounds good to me."

"Of course it does."

CHAPTER 24

THE RIB SHACK seemed to be a hot spot. It was just past five and the after-work crowd had descended. Music pumped from overhead speakers; chatter and laughter hung in air thick with the aroma of barbecue. My stomach grumbled. I think we had missed lunch. Last thing I remembered was breakfast. Oh, and that cinnamon roll at Mullins Bakery. And that Blue Belle ice cream Nicole and I had grabbed a few hours ago. Still, it felt like I hadn't eaten all day.

"Smells good," Nicole said.

"True. Seems it would have attracted Pancake by now."

"The night is young."

"And his food radar net is extensive."

We grabbed a pair of stools at the bar. Two young ladies sat to my left. They turned, smiled. I returned their smiles.

One of them mumbled, "Sorry," as she moved her purse down the bar and out of my face.

"No problem."

Nicole leaned over and said, "Looks like you have new admirers."

"That's because I'm so charming."

"Dream on, little broomstick cowboy." She nudged me with an elbow. "You're not that charming, but you are hot."

"As are you." I gave a slight nod toward the end of the bar. "And I'm not the only one who thinks so."

The bartender was mixing some concoction, but his attention was definitely on Nicole. She gave him a quick glance.

"He's cute," she said.

"In a puppy dog kind of way."

"Are you jealous?"

"Of course."

She shook her head. "No, you're not. You don't do jealousy."

"I'm not the only one."

"You mean Pancake?"

"Yeah. That's who I was thinking."

It was true. My attitude had always been that people should be where they want to be, and if they want to be somewhere else, then that's best for all concerned. I had my heart broken in junior high when my first love left me for anther guy. I hung on to that jealousy for months. It was a painful time. Sort of broke me from that need. With Pancake, it had been earlier. With Emily. After she left town, he moped for a few months. But once he surfaced from that, I never saw him in those dark waters again.

Nicole was the same. She didn't hold tightly, didn't demand much. Seemed content with letting things be what they were. Of course, with a mere nod of her head, or one of those wondrous smiles, she could have any man she wanted. Like Mike the bartender.

That turned out to be his name. He appeared, big grin, gaze devouring Nicole.

"What can I get you folks?" he asked.

He never looked at me so I figured Nicole was the folks he had in mind.

"I'll have a Makers Mark," Nicole said. "Neat."

Mike the bartender recoiled slightly. "A bourbon lady?" He smiled. "I like that."

He started to turn but then seemed to remember me.

"The same," I said.

My phone buzzed. Ray. When I answered, he was on speaker. I could hear the rumble of Pancake's truck engine in the background.

"What's up?" I asked.

"We're headed back to the hotel. We can hook up there, grab a bite, and compare notes."

"We have a better plan," I said. "We're at The Rib Shack."

"Ribs?" It was Pancake. "I'm all over that."

"Sounds like we're headed your way," Ray said.

"It's on Fairhope Avenue. Just north of downtown."

"Later." Ray was gone.

Mike the bartender returned. "Get you guys anything else?" Again, to Nicole.

"We're looking for Whitney Meyer," Nicole said. "Is she here today?"

"She is." He scanned the restaurant. "Over there."

I turned and looked the way he indicated. She stood next to a table about twenty feet away, scribbling an order on a pad. Attractive. Fit. Short, sculpted black hair, one side shaved. Jeans, green tank top, a small rose tattoo on her right shoulder.

"I'll let her know," he said.

A couple of minutes later, she walked up. "You wanted to see me?"

"Yes," I said and introduced Nicole and me. "Just need to ask a few questions."

She hesitated. "About what?"

"Maybe a table," Nicole said. "We have two more joining us."

She pointed to a four-top in the corner. A busboy was wiping it with a cloth. "That's one of mine."

I laid three tens on the bar, nodded to Mike, and we headed that way. The busboy placed four water glasses and napkin-wrapped utensil sets on the table. Whitney appeared.

"Get you anything?" she asked.

"We're good right now." We had brought our drinks with us. "We want to ask about Sean Patterson."

Her brow creased. "What's this about?"

"Nothing sinister," I said. I offered her my most charming smile. See, I am charming? I explained to her who we were and why we were asking. Looking into Emily's life.

She nodded, said she had a break coming and would get someone to cover her tables for a few minutes. She left, chatted with one of the other waitresses, and returned, taking a seat opposite me.

"We understand you've been dating Sean," I said.

"That's right. For a few months."

"How's he doing?" Nicole asked. "With all this?"

"Mostly okay. He does have his down moments."

"Which is what you're there for," Nicole said. A soft smile. "We talked to him a few days ago. Seems like a nice guy."

"He is. He's been good to me, for sure."

"Did you know Emily?" I asked.

"Sure. She worked over at the bakery. Came in here frequently."

"What did you think of her?"

"Very nice. Always a pleasant smile. Very smart. We talked about books a lot. We both like to read."

"No friction between you two?" Nicole asked.

She shook her head. "No. Sort of amazing, isn't it? I mean, the wife and the new girlfriend getting along?"

"Very adult," I said.

I should have her talk to Tammy. Maybe not. Tammy and Nicole being chummy would be a disaster for me. Absolutely nothing good could come from it. I strangled the thought.

Whitney laughed. "I've never been much of an adult. Probably afraid I'd turn into my parents."

"I understand," I said. Boy, did I. My fear was becoming Ray. I didn't see a way that could ever happen, but then again, here I sat, doing Ray's work.

"It's just so sad," Whitney said.

I told her that I had known Emily in an earlier life, went to school with her.

"So this investigation, or whatever it is you're doing, is personal?"

"It is. We were hired by her brother, Daniel, to find out who killed her and Jason."

"Daniel? Our local hero."

"I remember him as a bratty kid," I said. "But he sure grew up."

"Oh, yeah."

"Did you know Jason Collins?" Nicole asked.

"Not well. He and Emily were in here a few times. So just to say hello."

"How did Sean feel about them dating?" I asked.

"He was okay with it." She looked at Nicole, back to me. "You know she had just filed for divorce?"

"We do," I said.

"We understand Sean was happy about that," Nicole said. "Or maybe happy isn't the right word."

"Sean and I talked about it. A lot over the last month or so. I think he wanted it over with so he was good with the whole thing."

"Maybe so you guys could move forward?" Nicole said.

She smiled, shrugged. "I hope so."

"You guys are serious I take it?"

"Getting that way." She traced a circle on the table with an index finger. "Even talked about moving in together."

"Into the house?" I asked. "Emily's house?"

"I don't think so. I wouldn't feel comfortable."

"Did you tell Sean that?" Nicole asked.

"Sure. Before—" she hesitated a beat. "Before, it wouldn't have been an issue anyway. Sean said that after the divorce the house would remain Emily's. Something about inheritance laws. I don't really understand all that."

"That's true. The house would have gone to her."

"And now it's his." She sighed. "Regardless, he feels uncomfortable with it, too. He goes back and forth, but I think he's decided to sell it."

I nodded. "Makes sense."

"He said it never was his house. It was always in her family. So he doesn't really have a strong tie to it."

"Probably worth a good bit," Nicole said.

Whitney considered that. "I don't know. He never said." She stared at the tabletop, unfocused. "Hell of a way to inherit a property."

We sat in silence for a full half a minute.

"Do you know Charlie Martin?" I asked.

"Sure. Not well. I know Emily was seeing him, too. Seems like a nice guy."

"That's our take."

She looked at me. "You don't think he had anything to do with this, do you?"

"Do you?"

"Not really."

"That's a qualified no," I said.

"All I know is that Sean felt Charlie was jealous of Jason. He apparently loved Emily." She looked up at me. "Love triangles can make even the most passive person do stupid stuff."

Ain't it so.

CHAPTER 25

RAY NIXED TALKING things over in the restaurant. Too many people around, tables tightly packed. So, after Pancake marched through half of The Rib Shack menu—scorched earth was the term that came to mind—we headed to the Grand Hotel and gathered in the bar. Ray had suggested his room, but Pancake said Ray didn't have any food except that "whiney-ass stuff" in the mini-fridge, so the 1847 Bar it was.

Nicole and I continued with whiskey, Ray joining us, but Pancake went the beer route. The 1847 had a full-menu dinner so Pancake added a shrimp cocktail and fries. Good Lord, where did he put it? It wasn't like I hadn't witnessed this many times, but it still amazed. And he never gained an ounce. Of course, an ounce, even ten pounds, would be the proverbial spit in the ocean to Pancake.

The way I see it," Ray said, "is we have three avenues to pursue. The drug world, Charlie Martin, and Sean the husband."

"Unless it was simply random," I said.

"Doesn't smell that way. The house wasn't disturbed, other than the front door being left open. Nothing stolen or vandalized. The victims were taken away and executed in a more remote location. If it were a home invasion, or something like that, why take the risk? Kill everyone right there. Take what you want. Leave."

"Makes sense," I said.

"I do agree that there must've been more than one of them," Ray added. "Unless Emily and Jason knew their killer and willingly went out to that field with him. Not knowing what was going to happen until it was too late."

"So we got those three paths to follow," Pancake said. "Let's start with Charlie Martin. What'd you guys find out?"

I told him and Ray of our visit to Copeland's Nursery and our talk with Gene Copeland. How Copeland said that Charlie was a good and loyal worker. A bit shy. Definitely in love with Emily and not happy with her seeing Jason. But in the end, he saw no way that Charlie could be involved in a double murder. And particularly if one of the victims was Emily.

"How long has he worked for Copeland?" Pancake asked.

"Awhile now. Copeland said he was a hard worker. He did say that, since the murders, Charlie has been a bit off his game."

"A zombie," Nicole said. "He said Charlie was dazed like a zombie."

I nodded. "Copeland said that he wouldn't blame him. Something like this happens to someone you love and being off balance would be expected."

"No problems as far as Copeland is concerned?" Ray asked.

"None. I got the impression that he was very fond of Charlie and felt for him."

"What else?"

I told him of our talk with Charlie.

"He's truly damaged by all this," Nicole said. "He loved Emily. A lot. He resented Jason."

"A motive," Pancake said.

Nicole tapped a fingernail on the tabletop. "Maybe. But I think Mr. Copeland was right. Charlie seems like a quiet, passive guy. Hurt for sure, but I didn't sense any anger."

"Maybe he let it all out when he killed them," Pancake said. "He's now dealing with the empty aftermath."

"What else?" Ray asked.

I recounted our drive over to Magnolia Springs to see Martin's cousin Bobby Taylor. How Taylor corroborated Martin's story about that day. That the logs and stumps we saw piled up on Taylor's property indicated that they had done a full day's work. "He said Martin left there around midnight."

"Which gives him just enough time to do the dirty," Pancake said.

"That's true," I said. "The time of death was as late as 2:00 a.m. The drive time between Magnolia Springs and Emily's place at midnight, with everyone tucked in for the night, would have been thirty minutes, tops."

"I still can't get around the fact that he doesn't seem the type," Nicole said.

Pancake shoved a wad of fries in his mouth and spoke around them. "It's the quiet ones that are most dangerous." A slug of beer. "But Ira Sharp over at the used car lot where Jason worked agrees with you. He knows Martin and he says he sees no way he could do something like this."

"See," Nicole said, crossing her arms over her chest.

Pancake bounced an eyebrow. "I'm still going to dig into his world."

"Of course you are."

"Anything new on Sean?" Ray asked.

I went through our chats with Fred Watkins and Whitney Meyer. Both saying Sean was cool with the impending divorce. I finished with Watkins' description of the robbery.

"They were lucky," Pancake said. "Eighteen grand is adult money. Enough for the robbers to whack any witnesses. Even with them wearing masks."

"Sean did say he thought that might happen," Nicole said.

"What about the drug angle?" I asked.

"Had a chat with Chief Warren," Pancake said. "She said all things drug related in Baldwin County run through the Mack household. Clive and Reba."

"We did a drive-by," Ray added. "Snapped a few photos. Made a video."

"Any connection between them and Sean or Martin? Jason?"

"Don't know yet," Pancake said. "Haven't got into them yet."

"Looks like they deal from their house," Ray said. "We saw a couple of guys. Looked like they were either delivering money or scoring new supplies."

"Probably both," Pancake added.

"You saw the exchange?" Nicole asked.

"Nope. But it smelled that way. Couple of losers. Bright red pickup. F-one-fifty. Camper shell." Pancake shrugged. "Looked like dealers to me."

"What's the plan?" I asked.

"Pancake'll do some digging," Ray said. "Tomorrow morning I think we should have a powwow with Warren. Bring her up to date on what little we have. Maybe pick her brain."

"And keep her in the fold," I said.

"Exactly."

"So, we're free tonight?" Nicole asked.

Ray nodded. "Seems so."

"Great." She looked a me. "You ready, cowboy?"

Was I ever.

CHAPTER 26

"IT'S GOOD TO finally put a face with the name," Chief Billie Warren said as she shook Ray's hand.

We were gathered in her office. We took seats, as did Warren. Behind her desk.

She went on. "Of course, I'd heard about you before, but you're a bona fide celebrity lately. What with Victor Borkov, Kirk Ford, and then Billy Wayne Baker. See you in the papers more than the Kardashians, it seems."

"They get paid better," Ray said, offering a half smile.

"They get paid better than anyone. Still haven't figured that one out."

"Some things defy description."

"Which brings up a question," Warren said. "How does Daniel afford you? Even at the discount you mentioned."

"We gave him the family rate," Ray said. "All of a buck."

She flattened her palms on her desk. "So, this really is personal?"

"Emily and Daniel have a history with us," I said. "And she broke Pancake's heart in the sixth grade by leaving town."

Pancake grunted.

"To what do I owe the pleasure of the entire crew from Longly Investigations?" Warren asked.

"Thought we might compare notes," Ray said.

"Really?" She looked at me. "When Jake said you'd give me everything you turned up, I thought he was simply blowing smoke up my skirt." She smiled. "If I wore skirts."

"Afraid we don't have much," I said. "Hopefully, you do."

"So far I got nothing. Of all the folks in Emily's and Jason's world, I don't see any of them good for it." She cracked her knuckles, her muscular forearms tightening into bands. "Sean has a pretty iron-clad alibi, Charlie Martin just doesn't seem capable, and the drug connection hasn't offered any breadcrumbs."

"We're on the same page," Ray said. "Those are the avenues we think are most relevant."

"Charlie Martin had the opportunity, at least," I said. Warren started to say something, but I raised my hands. "I know, I know. Nicole and I talked with him. He doesn't seem the type for sure. And his cousin Bobby Taylor agreed. Charlie loved Emily. No doubt about that. Taylor said Charlie was the patient type. He felt Emily and Jason would probably fall apart at some time and he'd be there."

"Sort of a Steady Eddie?" Warren asked.

"Exactly. But sometimes those frustrations grow and fester, become intolerable. Even for someone like Charlie Martin."

"And if so," Pancake said, "things could go sideways in a hurry. Let's say Charlie finally decided to confront the couple. Maybe even do something to Jason. Things got crazy, both ended up dead."

"You believe that?" Warren asked.

"No." Pancake gave an emphatic headshake. "I don't. But it's at least possible."

"Let me ask you something," Warren said. "You think there's any way Sean could've hired someone to do it? I mean, it's most often the spouse that's involved. Money and property being valuable."

"I went deep into his finances," Pancake said. "Other than fifteen hundred he took out to apparently pay for a car repair, there's nothing."

"How'd you do that?"

Pancake smiled.

"Probably better I don't know," Warren said.

"Chief, you're a genius." The voice came from the hallway. Burton Moody rounded the doorjamb. Put on the brakes. "Sorry. I thought you were alone."

"Come on in."

Pancake, Nicole, and I already knew Moody so I introduced him to Ray.

"Don't know why you sound so shocked that I'm brilliant," Warren said, "but what are you talking about?"

"You wanted me to dig a little more on Jason Collins and his family. And I did."

"You going to tell us, or is it a mystery?"

"His parents passed, but he had a brother. Brett. Over in Pascagoula. Did a couple of years for meth possession. Now works odd jobs over there."

"Meth?" I asked. "Any connection between that and his brother?"

"You mean besides finding a couple of packets in Jason's back pocket?" Warren said.

"Maybe they weren't planted?" Pancake said. "Maybe he was holding?"

Warren gave a half nod. "That sure would open up that line of thought to further scrutiny."

"If so, don't you think Emily would've known?" Nicole asked.

"Maybe she did."

"Everyone we talked to said she was completely opposed to drugs of any kind."

"People wear masks," Ray said. "Users are often adept at hiding it. From family, friends, lovers, everyone."

"And then they're the enablers," Pancake said. "Even those that are most opposed will cover for family and loved ones. Even help them get fixed."

"I've seen it," Warren said. "Don't always understand it, but I've definitely seen it."

"I think we need to visit Allison again," I said. "Maybe she held it back. Didn't want to harm Emily's reputation."

"Or she didn't know," Nicole said. "Or even suspect."

I nodded.

"Back to the brother," Warren said. She nodded toward Moody. "Did you talk to him?"

"Nope. But that's my next step."

"May I offer a suggestion?" Ray said.

"Go ahead," Warren said.

"Let me and Pancake drop in on him. Unannounced. See what he says."

"You're thinking that he'd try to protect his brother?"

Ray nodded. "Maybe. I also want to look in his face when we open that can of worms. If Jason has, or ever had, a history of meth use, that would change things."

Warren waved a hand. "Have at it. Pascagoula's a little out of our jurisdiction anyway."

"Which brings up this," Ray said. He pulled out his cell. "We visited the Mack place yesterday."

"What'd you think of them?" Warren asked.

"They didn't know we visited," Pancake said.

Ray thumbed to the images he had taken at the Macks' place. He had earlier transferred them from his camera to his phone. He handed the cell to Warren. She swiped through the pics, examining each.

"Looks like you guys did a little creepy crawling."

"We did," Pancake said.

"The guys with them?" Ray asked. "You know them?"

She smiled. "Sure do. A pair of losers. They sell for the Macks'. Jack Reed is the taller one. Reavis Whitt the other."

"And?"

"They deal. Popped Reed once, but all he had was a few crumbs of marijuana. Didn't charge him for that. But they deal the whole palate. Meth, coke, oxy."

"So they've been slippery?" I asked.

"More like luck. Neither one of them could pass the SAT. So they aren't exactly criminal masterminds."

"Lucky is the right word," Moody said. "We know they deal. I've pulled them over a couple of times. The chief has, too. Minor stuff like rolling through a stop sign. But enough to search them and their vehicle. You know? For weapons and such? Officer safety? Never found anything."

"I think I know the answer to this," Ray said. "But you've never connected them, or the Macks, to Jason Collins?"

"No. Never even suspected such a thing."

Out on the street, Ray said, "We're off to Pascagoula. You guys chat with Allison. We'll see what turns up and go from there."

Pancake was already buried in his iPhone. No doubt thumbing through all the places he goes when he's digging for information, or dirt.

CHAPTER 27

PANCAKE AND RAY followed us to Mullins Bakery. Pancake's take was that if he had to travel the sixty miles to Pascagoula, he needed nourishment. Of course he did. The massive breakfast he had had at the hotel before we all ventured up to Fairhope a distant memory. It had been a couple of hours, and feeding the beast—as he called it— was more or less a full-time job.

Fully stocked with ham and cheese croissants and bear claws, they hit the road. Nicole and I grabbed coffee and settled at a corner table while Allison served several customers. She then came over and sat with us.

"Anything new?" she asked.

"Maybe," I said.

She gave me an expectant look.

I knew we had to tiptoe here, but you can't make an omelet without breaking a few eggs. Discussing the evidence would be betraying our promise to Chief Warren to keep certain things undercover. But the revelation that Jason's brother had done a couple years for possessing the same drugs found on Jason made the risk necessary. To me anyway. My assessment of Allison was that she was straightforward, honest, trustworthy. I hoped us driving out of our lane didn't put us in a ditch. I took a breath and pressed forward.

"One of the avenues we've been exploring to explain Emily's and Jason's murders is a drug connection."

She shook her head. "I told you. Emily would never, ever be involved in that world."

"I remember. What I want to ask is more about Jason. Is there anything you ever saw, or even suspected, that would suggest he was a user?"

"No. If he were, Emily would've dumped him flat."

Nicole shrugged. "If she knew."

Allison's shoulders straightened. "Are you saying he did? That you found something?"

"We didn't tell you earlier," I said. "And this is not for public consumption. Okay?"

"What does that mean?"

"It means this goes no further than this table."

She clasped her hands together in her lap and looked at us. Now, her shoulders sagged. "Okay."

I looked around, made sure the family of four two tables away wasn't eavesdropping. They weren't. Hands full with two wiggly and giggly boys, maybe four and five. I leaned forward, spoke low. "Warren found two bags of meth at the scene. In Jason's pocket."

She looked up, eyes wide, a hint of moisture. "I don't believe this."

"Our best guess is that they were planted," Nicole said.

"What? By who?"

"The killer," I said.

"Why would they do that?"

"To make the killings look like something they weren't."

She snatched a napkin from the decorative holder on the table and touched each eye. "That makes no sense. Who? Why?"

"We don't know," Nicole said. "And that might not be the case."

"Back to my question," I said. "Did you ever suspect Jason was using?"

"No. Neither did Emily. If she had, like I said, he'd be gone, and she would've told me."

"I believe that," I said. "The truth is that a lot of users are able to hide that fact from even those closest to them. Kids do it all the time. Spouses and friends, too. If Jason was a closet user, and if he got sideways with his dealer, the result could be exactly what we saw in the field."

Allison sat quietly. Obviously processing everything. She sighed. "I never suspected anything like that."

"Not even the merest hint?" Nicole asked.

Allison shook her head.

"Did you ever meet Jason's brother?" I asked.

"Brother? I didn't know he had one."

"He never mentioned him?"

"No. Does he have anything to do with this?"

After reiterating that this must be kept private, I told her about Jason's brother. What little I knew.

She spoke to the napkin wadded by white knuckles in her lap. "This keeps getting crazier."

Nicole reached over, clasped her hand. "We're sorry we had to talk about this. The last thing we wanted was to bring any more pain to you."

Allison nodded. "I wouldn't want your job. I'd rather remain naive about things like this."

Me, too, I thought.

CHAPTER 28

RAY DROVE. PANCAKE shotgun working his iPhone. After a search of the databases and services he used, he pulled the shades back on Brett Collins. Four years older than Jason, left their Laurel, Mississippi, birthplace at age eighteen. Right after he was nabbed for marijuana possession. His constantly shifting bank, credit card, and tax records showed he then roamed through Memphis, St. Louis, New Orleans, before dropping anchor in Pascagoula. Each stop filled with odd jobs—construction, service station attendant, janitor for a church, even the sanitation department in New Orleans. Garbage man. Been in his current location for just over three years. Jobs included a hand on a shrimp boat out of Biloxi, kitchen staff at two casinos, also in Biloxi, but mostly construction. Current employer listed as Bates Construction.

Six months ago, he had been popped for marijuana possession, but due to the small amount, the judge kicked the case. He rented an apartment in a run-down property next to a trailer park. The park had an extensive criminal record. Multiple police visits, arrests for possession, and dealing of meth and heroin. Brett's name not attached to any of the raids that Pancake found in the local PD database.

"Hard to imagine these two apples fell from the same tree," Pancake said. "Jason seemed to be a stand-up guy. Job, girlfriend, future. Brett a major loser."

"Who chose to live next to a known drug hot spot," Ray said.

"Bet he gets whatever his drug of choice is from there."

"Or deals himself."

"Let's check out the trailer park first," Pancake said. "Get the lay of the land."

Ray slowed as they approached. The road paved, but ratty. They were half a mile south of Highway 90 and east of Pascagoula proper. A sign indicated the entrance to the Shady Lane Trailer Park. Flat and dusty, a couple of trees that didn't appear all that healthy and offered zero shade. The dirt road that looped through the thirty or so trailers, most embedded on concrete block foundations, wasn't much of a lane. It was quiet except for an elderly woman in a sack dress watering pots of azaleas with a garden hose.

"Turn in here," Pancake said.

"Why?"

"I want to chat with that lady."

Ray slid the car up to her trailer. Unlike the others, it was clean and well kept, explosions of flowers from pots and planters lined up across the front.

Pancake lowered the window. "How you doing?"

She turned and smiled. "Fine. You fellows?" She directed the water toward another pot.

"Gorgeous flowers," Pancake said.

"I love them. Lots of work, but then I got the time." She laughed, followed by a deep smoker's cough.

"Mind if I ask a couple of questions?"

She folded the hose in one fist, crimping off the flow. "I'm busy Saturday night in case you were thinking of taking me dancing." Another deep laugh.

"I bet we'd have fun," Pancake said.

"Yes, we would. I was always partial to redheads. That's why I married one. 'Course he up and died a few years ago."

"I'm sorry."

She nodded but said nothing.

"You lived here long?"

"Nearly twenty years."

"Bet you know everyone around?"

"I do. 'Course it's changed a lot. Past few years."

"In what way?"

"Younger folks. Some of them not exactly my cup of tea." She looked up the dirt drive. "I'd move but can't afford to." She looked back at him. "And I love my place." She waved a hand toward her trailer. "I suspect I could take it with me but that ain't as easy as it sounds."

"I understand you've got a problem with drugs around here," Pancake said.

She stared at him, hesitated, then shuffled over to the water faucet, carefully bent over, widening her stance for balance, and twisted the metallic quail figure to shut off the flow. She walked to the truck, bent, looked inside toward Ray.

"Who are you guys?" she asked.

"This is Ray. I'm Pancake."

"Your mama named you that?"

"No, she chose Tommy. But that's what I'm called."

"I like it. My name's Rose. Rose Williamson."

"Nice to meet you."

She looked back up the dirt road. "But to answer your question, that's what's changed around here. You can smell that damned marijuana every night. It's like a putrid fog."

"Anyone dealing around here?"

"Some. Cops took away a few of them. I think there are still a couple. Over on the other side of the park. Don't know for sure, but we do get some late-night traffic, and they all head over that way."

That fit the profile. Buyers circling the supplier, most often after sunset. And this place being off the beaten path made it a prime location for dealing.

"What about the complex next door?" Ray asked. "Any issues with them?"

"Don't know many of them, but I 'spect it's the same as here. I see younger ones—by that I mean under forty or so—drive by all the time. I hear they got druggies and dealers over there, too." She looked toward her feet, then back up. "Maybe a month or two ago they had a big raid here, over there, too. Cops took a bunch of young guys in."

"Do you happen to know Brett Collins? Lives over there?"

Her brow furrowed, a slight headshake. "What's he look like?"

Pancake located the mug shot of Brett he had downloaded from the Pascagoula PD site and held it toward her. She squinted. "He does look familiar. Can't say for sure though."

"No real memory of him being over here? Maybe buying drugs?"

She examined the pic again. "Not that I recall."

"Thanks, Rose," Pancake said. "Love your flowers."

"Love your hair." She laughed, coughed, waved, and turned back to her work.

CHAPTER 29

SEAN AND ANOTHER guy were loading ten-foot two-by-fours onto the flat bed of a white delivery truck, *Watkins' Lumber Supply* block printed in black along the door. He looked our way as Nicole slid her SL into the lot and we climbed out. He said something to his work mate and walked toward us.

"What brings you guys by?" he asked.

"We were nearby and thought we would see how you're doing," Nicole said.

He shrugged. "Okay."

"This your stint onshore?" I asked.

"Sort of. The company felt uncomfortable with me going back out after everything. I guess they thought I might be distracted or something."

"A liability issue, I suspect."

"Except I was out there for two days because a couple of guys got sick. Just got back yesterday. Production trumps safety."

"Too often," I said.

"How's things with your investigation? Anything new?"

"Not really."

"That's what Chief Warren said. I saw her this morning at the coffee shop down the street."

"I think she's frustrated," Nicole said. "We are, too. Seems like everything is a dead end."

"It's looking more like a random thing," I said.

"Probably." He glanced back toward the truck he had been loading. Another guy had joined in to help.

"Made any decisions about the house yet?" Nicole asked.

"Mostly. I talked to a local realtor about selling. What it might be worth, how long it might take."

"So you've decided to sell?"

"I think so. It's more house and property than I need. Or want to maintain."

"Makes sense," Nicole said. "Unless you decide to remarry and have kids."

"No plans on that."

"We talked with Whitney," I said. "She seems nice."

"She is." He held my gaze for few seconds. "She told me you had dropped by, asked her some questions."

"We did."

"Why? She doesn't have anything to do with this."

"This is a small town. Everyone knows everyone else. She works at a popular place. Probably knows more about what goes on around here than most."

"Bars are gossipy," Nicole added. "We wanted her take on Emily and her friends."

"I guess that makes sense."

"She sure likes you. Said something about you guys moving in together." Nicole raised an eyebrow.

"She did?"

"See, bars are gossipy."

"We've talked about it. Which would be another reason to sell the house. Maybe get a bigger apartment. Or buy something of our own."

Nicole offered a soft laugh. "That is serious."

Sean shrugged. "I guess we'll see."

"We asked her about Jason. She said she didn't know him well, but he seemed like a nice guy."

"He was."

"I asked this before," I said, "but you had no issues with Emily seeing him?"

"And I told you no, I didn't. I thought they were good together. And I have Whitney."

"Whitney said the same thing," Nicole said. "Said that she and Emily got along well despite the tangled relationships."

"That's true," Sean said. "I remember the first time they were together in the same room. As far as I know anyway. I was nervous. Wasn't sure how it was going to go. It was at The Rib Shack. I was there, at the bar, talking with Whitney. Emily came in."

"That could've been uncomfortable."

"You've got that right. My first instinct was to run out the door." He smiled. "To avoid the fireworks. But it turned out to be okay. They actually sat and talked for quite a while. Between Whitney waiting tables." He glanced skyward as if recalling something. "What I remember most was when Emily got up to leave, she told me she liked Whitney and that she was a keeper. A keeper? Can you imagine?"

No, I couldn't. Not many of the triangles I stumbled into in my life were ever that pleasant. More ranting and raving. Some hair-pulling on one occasion. And that doesn't include Tammy. She became fissionable material when I strayed.

"Can I ask you about Charlie Martin?" I asked.

"Sure."

"Whitney said you felt he was jealous of Jason. That he loved Emily and considered Jason a rival."

Sean nodded. "That's true. At least, that's my take."

"Could be a motive," I said.

"I've asked myself that more than a few times since everything happened."

"And?"

"I can't see it. I know these things can get crazy and make people act completely out of character. Do some very bad things. But Charlie?" He shook his head. "I can't imagine."

"But you're not sure?" Nicole asked.

"How could I be? If you think about it logically, maybe he could do something to Jason. See him as a real threat to his happiness, or whatever. Someone who could make his life miserable. If Jason was out of the way, Charlie might think he could then have Emily. I can see all that. But Emily? I would have trouble believing that Charlie would do anything to her."

"Could be one of those if-I-can't-have-her-no-one can?"

"I suppose." He glanced back. The truck was now loaded. "I have a delivery to make."

"One more thing," I said. "Did Jason ever use drugs? Anything like that?"

Creases appeared in his forehead. "Not that I know. And if he did, he wouldn't've been with Emily. That I know for sure."

"That's what we hear," Nicole said.

"Believe it." He stared at his feet. "When Emily and I first met, I smoked a little weed from time to time. Kept it to myself. But after we dated for a few weeks, and I thought I knew her better, I offered her some." He shook his head, looked up at me. "Bad idea. She went ballistic. Nearly ended our relationship before it started."

"Apparently she got over it," Nicole said.

"Took a while. She wouldn't return my calls for a couple of weeks. Finally, we had a talk and I told her, promised her, I'd put all that aside if she'd keep seeing me."

"Did you? Put it aside."

"You bet."

"What about after you guys separated?" I asked. "Anything?"

Sean hesitated, his gaze moving away.

"We're not judging," I said. "Just asking."

"Yeah. Some. Not often."

"What?"

"Only weed. Nothing stronger."

"One more thing about Jason," I said. "Did you ever hear or suspect he might be using on the side? Without Emily knowing?"

"Chief Warren asked me the same thing, and I told her I had no idea."

"Emily ever say anything about that? That she had any suspicions?"

He shook his head. "Let's just say that if Jason was doing anything, it would have been away from Emily. Completely away. Just like she did with me, if she knew he was using anything, she'd put him on the road. So, no, she never told me she had thoughts along those lines." He looked at me. "You aren't thinking drugs had anything to do with their murders, are you?"

"We don't know what to think," I said. "Simply exploring every possibility."

"With Emily's stance on that, it would be the ultimate irony."

"Where do you get your stuff?" I asked.

"Here and there. It's not difficult to find."

"That's true. Do you know the Macks?"

Another hesitation. "I know of them."

"But you don't buy from them?"

"No."

"I understand anything drug related around here goes through them."

"That's the rumor. Which makes no sense to me. Why aren't they locked up somewhere?"

"Knowing and proving are two different things," I said.

"I guess that's true."

"I take it you don't know whether Jason had any dealings with them or not?"

"No. No one I know would. They aren't exactly part of normal society."

CHAPTER 30

JUST AS THE Shady Lane Trailer Park had neither shade nor a lane, the Cedar Oaks Apartments had neither cedars nor oaks. Made Pancake wonder if whoever named them had even bothered to visit. Seemed if they had they'd have come up with other names. But marketing is marketing.

Three tired buildings of eight units, stacked four up, four down, embraced a central courtyard. Mangy grass and scruffy shrubs. A couple of kid's swing sets. No pool. The units were dingy white with faded and chipped brown trim.

Brett Collins' unit was the lower corner unit nearest the road. Pancake rapped a knuckle on the door. Collins answered in boxers, a wife-beater tee shirt, hair disheveled, a half-empty bottle of beer in his hand. Looked like he had slept off one drunk and was beginning another.

"Brett Collins?" Pancake asked. He already knew it was. Giving the guy a chance to lie if he was so inclined.

"Who wants to know?"

Pancake introduced himself and Ray, told him they were investigators looking into the murder of his brother.

"Yeah, I heard about that. Our cousin called."

His concern seemed nonexistent.

"We have a few questions about Jason," Ray said. "Mind if we come in?"

Collins hesitated as if deciding what to do. Maybe he was feeling helpful, or maybe it was Pancake's size thirteen shoe already across the threshold, blocking the door, that proved the deciding factor, but finally, he said, "Sure." He stepped back. "Want a beer?"

"We're good," Pancake said.

"Have a seat." He raised the beer. "I need a refill." He headed into the open kitchen, dropped the bottle in the sink where the glass-on-glass clank suggested it wouldn't be lonely. He yanked open the fridge, twisted the cap from another beer.

Despite the fact that Collins looked like he needed a shower and maybe a good night's sleep, the place was fairly clean. Cheap furniture but in good repair. TV tuned to the local news, sound off. A police officer being interviewed in front of a convenience store that according to the crawl banner had been robbed. Pancake and Ray took the sofa, Collins a chair, facing them.

"We're sorry about your brother," Ray said.

"Yeah, well, he and I never really got along. Not even when we were kids." He took a slug of beer. "He's four years younger so even in school we ran in different circles."

"When did you last speak with him?" Pancake asked.

"Couple of years. Maybe three. I can't remember."

"So you didn't know the girl that he was dating? The one that got killed at the same time?"

"Sure didn't."

"What can you tell us about Jason?" Ray asked.

"Like what?"

"Anything. What was he like?"

Another sip of beer. "You might say he was the good one." He shrugged. "I was the wild one."

"How so?"

"Just that. Mom and Dad always liked him best. He took school seriously. Went to church with them. Played some sports. All that righteous stuff I didn't do."

"How'd you feel about that?" Ray asked. "The parents seeming to favor him?"

"You a shrink or something?"

"Just curious."

"Be curious about something else."

"I know that older brothers often feel more pressure to perform than do younger ones," Ray said. "Sometimes that leads to rebellion."

His head gave a quick bob as he tipped his beer toward Ray. "That's me. The rebel of the family."

"What about drugs?" Pancake asked.

"What about them?"

"We know your history."

His back straightened. Jaw set. "So you been digging in my life?"

"We wouldn't be very good investigators if we hadn't," Ray said.

Collins mulled that for a few seconds, then grinned. "I guess that's true." He worked the label on the bottle with a thumbnail. "Guess you know I spent a little time in lockup then?"

"We do. Drug related. But we're not interested in that. Not judging and not trying to hammer you about your life choices."

"I made a few dumb ones."

"We all do," Pancake said.

"You been locked up?"

Pancake tilted his head toward Ray. "Ray here had me and his son locked up once when we were kids."

"For what?"

"Doing stupid stuff."

Another slug of beer. "Stupid does rear its head, don't it?"

"Especially with teenage boys," Ray added.

He slapped a knee. "Wish you could've talked to my parents. Explained that to them."

"What about Jason?" Ray asked. "He ever do anything stupid?"

"Not much. Like I said, he was the good one."

"He ever use drugs?"

"Did that have anything to do with his death?"

"Maybe. We're not sure."

"We smoked a little weed. Jason rarely. Me, all the time."

"Anything harder?" Pancake asked.

"Coke a few times. I got him to try it. He didn't much like it." He shook his head. "Only person I ever met that didn't like a little marching powder."

"Anything else?"

"Not that I know."

"Would it surprise you if he used anything recently?"

"Actually, it would. But then I don't really know him anymore." He pushed his hair back. "Hell, I never really did."

"What about you?" Pancake asked. "You still use?"

"Every chance I get." He smiled.

"What?"

He shrugged.

"Weed? Coke? Meth?"

"Sure."

"I take it you have a local supplier?" Ray said.

"Ain't hard to come by around here. Half a dozen places here, and the trailer park next door, I could go knock on the door and get well real quick."

"What about over in Fairhope? Know anything about the scene over there?"

He shook his head. "Never been there in my life."

"You never visited your brother over there?" Pancake asked.

"Why would I? I didn't visit his room when we lived under the same roof." He sighed. "I know that sounds bad but it's the way it was." He caught Pancake's gaze. "Look, I'm sorry he died, or got killed, but it ain't something I'm going to cry over."

They left Brett to his beer and drugs and miserable little life. Once back on the highway, Pancake said, "I'd like to shoot him just on general principles."

"Don't think anyone would miss him."

Pancake grunted. "Want to go back?"

"Probably not."

"I wouldn't really shoot him. Maybe break something."

"We'll stop and grab you a burger," Ray said. "Let you work your anger out on that."

"That'll do."

CHAPTER 31

IT WAS THE camera that caught my eye. Across the street. Long lens, leveled at Nicole and me. The operator a young woman. Short, curly brown hair. Tan slacks, sleeveless white top, messenger bag over one shoulder.

At first, she looked like a tourist, taking street shots to show off downtown Fairhope to her friends back home. But her aim remained steady. No doubt we were the focus of her attention.

I had just gotten off the phone with Pancake. He and Ray were on Highway 90, north of Pascagoula, motoring back toward the hotel. Plans were to meet there and compare notes. Nicole and I were walking down Fairhope Avenue toward Mullins Bakery to grab some coffee and a bag of sweets for Pancake.

I stopped, touched Nicole's arm.

The woman saw me staring at her and lowered her camera. I waved. She waved back. Her head swiveled right and left as she darted across the street.

"Sorry," she said. She stuck a hand out. "Lauren Schultz."

I introduced Nicole and me. Handshakes followed.

"Aren't you the private investigators?" It wasn't really a question. "The ones looking into the recent murders?"

I hesitated. Not sure what the right answer was. Engage or not. But she had a pleasant smile. Seemed friendly enough. She didn't wait for my brain to sort it all out.

"I just chatted with Chief Warren," she said. "She told me about you."

"How'd you know it was us?" I asked.

"Tall and handsome; blond and gorgeous." She smiled. "See anybody else around here like that?"

"Jake is gorgeous," Nicole said. She bumped her hip against mine.

Lauren laughed. "I'm working on a story about the murders."

"Are you a reporter?" Nicole asked.

"Freelance journalist. I write articles mostly."

Interesting. My first thought was that Ray wouldn't be thrilled to see Longly Investigations in some bit of sensational journalism. My second was that she might know more than we did. Truth was, if she knew anything it would be more than we had.

"How about some coffee?" I asked.

"That would be nice."

We continued our walk.

"You write crime stories?" Nicole asked.

"Human interest. This'll be my first that involves a crime. I'm a little nervous about going there."

"Why?" Nicole asked.

"I don't know. I see those stories in the paper, online, and blasted on TV all the time. They always make me feel—what's the word? —vulnerable."

"You mean like the world's out of balance?" I said.

"Something like that. Not sure I want to get that close to it."

"Then why do it?" Nicole asked.

"I read about the murders. Here in such a pleasant and low-key town. My favorite town to visit, actually. It hooked me."

"Where are you from?" I asked.

"Mobile."

We entered the bakery. Allison looked up.

"You guys back already?" she asked.

"Need some coffee," I said. "And pick up something for Pancake."

She laughed. "He's my favorite customer. I can make rent based on his appetite alone."

I introduced her and Lauren, telling her that Lauren was writing an article on the murders.

"Allison was Emily Patterson's best friend," I said. "Emily worked here."

"I'm so sorry," Lauren said.

"It's been tough."

We ordered coffee. Allison waited on a take-out customer and then brought it to our table. She sat with us.

"What kind of stories do you write?" Nicole asked.

"Fluff." Lauren laughed. "I recently did one on Bellingrath Gardens and a fund-raiser onboard the USS *Alabama*. That was a hoot. Oh, and a fun story on area ghosts. My favorite was the one at the Pickens County Courthouse. The 'Lightning Portrait of Henry Wells,' as it's called."

I knew about that one. Not really a ghost but an odd story. The county seat of Pickens County was Carrollton. The story goes that in 1876 former slave Henry Wells torched the courthouse. It took two years to rebuild, after which Henry was arrested. The town had no jail so he was held in the attic of the courthouse. A single small window gave him a view of the world. A lynch mob gathered, and as Henry peered down on them through the window, a bolt of lightning struck the ground nearby. No one was injured, but the strike forever etched Henry's face in one of the windowpanes. It's still there a century and a half later. I've seen it. Pancake and I drove up once just to take a look.

I told Lauren about that adventure.

"It's amazing, isn't it?" she said. "His face is right there. Plain as day."

The conversation then turned to Lauren's story and why she found it so intriguing. She couldn't put it in words, just that it struck her as unacceptably tragic. Particularly since it happened here in such an idyllic locale. To her, it seemed unnatural.

I agreed. This town didn't have things like this in its history. Or, to my mind, its DNA. Unnatural seemed the right word.

Lauren went on. She made it clear that she didn't do crime coverage, too depressing, too violent was her take. But even though this had obviously been an act of extreme violence, she felt compelled to write about the town and the people affected by the murders.

"You'll end up digging into the crime," Nicole said. "Whether you want to or not. It's the only way you can get to the root of everyone's feelings. Their confusion and fear."

"I know." She spoke to her hands, now folded on the table before her. "That's why I debated even doing it. Thought about it for several days." She unfolded, refolded her hands. "It's outside my comfort zone but I guess I'll have to deal with that aspect of the story." She looked up. "I've always written about happy stuff. This is a big leap."

"Somehow I think you'll do just fine," I said.

"I hope so." She sighed. "It'll be a learning experience for sure."

"Maybe you'll even write a book about it," I said.

"I doubt that'll happen."

"That's what Truman Capote thought," I said. "He read about the Clutter family murders in the newspaper. Went to Kansas to write an article but once there became drawn into the story. Led to *In Cold Blood*."

"The most disturbing book I ever read," Lauren said. "I was in high school. We never locked our house. Never had to. But after that, I made sure every door and window was latched before going to bed." She smiled. "My parents thought I was crazy. But they didn't read the book."

I liked her. Her approach and transparent honesty. Her willingness to step outside of herself. Take on a challenge. I sensed Nicole and Allison felt the same vibe.

"What has your research turned up so far?" I asked.

"Not much that isn't in the papers. They were shot, left on a farm near here. Emily Patterson was going through a divorce and the other victim was a guy she was seeing. From my conversation with Chief Warren, there are no suspects." She fingered a curl near her left ear. "I suspect that makes the town nervous. Knowing whoever did this is still out there."

"Sure does," Allison said. "From what I see here, everyone is a little paranoid."

Lauren nodded. "That's the story I want to write. How this has affected the town." She smiled. "Anything you guys can tell me, anything that'll make it personal, I'd appreciate."

"I like that approach," Allison said. "Truth is, I've been waiting for—actually dreading— the press types to show up. From Mobile, or Montgomery, or wherever. Use this town's pain to sell their newspapers. Not to mention, this is the kind of story those TV magazine shows like to dig up. Then overdramatize." She shook her head. "If that's possible. But I don't want any of that. Don't want this town painted that way."

"I completely understand," Lauren said. "That's definitely not my intention."

Allison visibly relaxed. "Good. And if that's the case, I'll gladly help."

Lauren pulled a notepad from her purse. "Tell me about your friend. What was she like?"

Allison offered many memories of Emily, often through moist eyes and a constricted throat. She told of their friendship. How Emily had worked there. She was pleasant, reliable, and the customers loved her. How Allison helped her deal with her separation, and then her impending divorce, adding that Emily was grateful that it was all very smooth. No real contentions. No animosity.

As Allison spoke, I sensed she needed this. A catharsis of sorts. Talking openly and honestly about Emily. Saying things that probably invaded her dreams, or more likely kept her from sleep in the first place. Revealing her bond with her friend whom she'd never see again. Nicole's eyes glistened, and I felt tears push against the back of mine. In ten minutes, I learned who Emily had become. Made me wish I had known her. More importantly, that Pancake had.

I then related my history with Emily. Pancake's, too. How Emily's brother, a Marine on deployment, had hired us. How our investigation morphed from a simple divorce proceeding into a mysterious double murder.

Lauren mostly listened, scribbled notes.

Finally, silence reigned. Lauren scanned her notes. Flipping through her pages. She looked at me. "You have no idea who could have done this?"

I shook my head. "None."

"Not the husband?"

"He has an ironclad alibi."

"Maybe he hired someone to do it?" Lauren said.

"Haven't found anything to suggest that."

"Maybe the guy with her was the target?" Lauren said.

"We're looking into that, but so far we've got nothing."

Not exactly true. There was the drug angle. Not that it was panning out. I didn't feel comfortable talking with her about that. It was the one thing Warren wanted to keep in house. I didn't want to see that hit some article and have me attributed as the source. Warren would kill me. Maybe literally. Besides, it didn't seem fair to Jason's legacy if he was indeed completely innocent.

"Who have you talked to so far?" Nicole asked.

"The chief, and you guys. That's it. But I'm just getting started."

I told her about our chats with Sean and with Jason's former employer. I tossed in Charlie Martin.

"Emily was seeing two guys?" Lauren asked.

"That's right," Allison said. "One more serious than the other."

"And one of them was killed with her?"

Allison nodded. "The more serious one. Jason."

"And the other one?" Lauren asked. "How did he feel about being second fiddle?"

"Not happy," I said.

"Hmmm."

"But he doesn't seem the type that would do this," Nicole said.

Lauren tapped her pen against her pad. "Triangles are often dangerous. Make people do crazy things."

"I know," I said. "But I don't think that's the case here."

"Oh?"

"Talk to Charlie Martin. Make your own judgement."

"I will."

"See, you're a crime reporter already," Nicole said.

"Don't know about that. I feel more like a fish out of water."

"You're asking all the right questions," I said.

CHAPTER 32

"She's nice," Nicole said.

"She is."

"I think her article will be a good thing for the community."

"How so?" I asked

"She's sensitive. Seems more interested in the survivors, the community, than the gritty crime details."

We were in her SL zipping back toward the Grand Hotel. Exceeding the speed limit by a good thirty miles an hour.

"Bet she writes a book about it," I said.

"I don't think so."

"Want to bet?"

"What're the stakes?"

"The winner gets to have their way with the loser."

She swerved past a sedan, the two passengers not appearing happy with her *Top Gun* move.

"Not much of a bet," she said. "When did either of us deny the other?"

She had a point.

"I'll tell you what," she continued. "If I win, I get to have my way with you; and if you win, I'll have my way with you." She smiled. "How does that sound?"

"Deal."

Not waiting to see how the bet played out, she did exactly that. When we got back to the hotel, she literally pushed me onto the bed. Thirty minutes later, the bed covers were on the floor and I was exhausted. Not Nicole. She hopped out of bed.

"Get up." She gathered the top sheet and comforter, piled them on the bed.

"Why?"

"We have to meet Ray and Pancake in a half hour."

"They'll wait."

"No, they won't. Remember, we have Pancake's bear claws. Do you really want to risk his hypoglycemic wrath?"

She had another point.

Round two was in the shower. I swear, she was going to kill me. But everyone's got to die sometime, somehow. Right?

"You're late," Ray said as Nicole and I took the vacant chairs across from him and Pancake in the 1847 Bar.

"Nicole was primping," I said.

Pancake grunted. "I'm sure."

Nicole handed him the bag from Mullins Bakery. He ripped out one side and extracted a bear claw.

"I love you, darling."

Nicole laughed. "You love food. I'm merely your delivery service."

Ray and Pancake had drinks already. The waitress took our order. After she left, Ray asked, "Anything new come up today?"

"Allison had no useful info on Jason. Said she never suspected he was a user or anything like that. Had never heard of his brother."

"He never mentioned his brother?" Ray asked.

"Not to Allison."

"Not all that surprising," Pancake said. "They weren't exactly close."

"Oh?"

Ray told of their conversation with Brett. He and Jason hadn't talked in years. Were never close. Even as kids.

"Truth is," Pancake added, "Jason was probably lucky to be rid of his brother. Guy's a total loser."

"So, you're thinking Brett isn't a supplier for Jason?" Nicole asked.

"If Jason was a user," Ray said, "I'd doubt he was getting it from his brother. Or that his brother is involved in this in any way."

"Said he'd never been to Fairhope," Pancake said.

"Unless he's lying," I said.

"Don't think so." Ray took a sip of his bourbon. "My take is that he has trouble dealing with his own little world. He uses. Weed, meth, coke. The whole medicine chest. Does manual labor. Lives in a dumpy-ass apartment in a dumpy-ass part of town. Lots of drugs and dealers around. I don't see him as an itinerant dealer. Or hit man."

"Besides, his brother is someone he doesn't give two shits about," Pancake said.

"So you're trip was a bust?" I said.

"Not exactly," Ray said. "According to Brett, Jason and he smoked weed as kids. Jason used coke with him a few times. Long time ago, of course."

"Means he ain't exactly a virgin," Pancake added.

"You're saying the drugs found on him might have been his?" Nicole asked.

Ray shrugged, opened his palms. "Past users often become current users."

"Where do you think we stand on all this?" Nicole asked.

"Same place we were at the beginning. We have Sean Patterson, the aggrieved husband and the inheritor of Emily's property and cash, Charlie Martin, the jealous other guy, and the possible drug connection between Jason and maybe the Macks, or whoever."

Nicole nodded. "You still don't think there's any chance this could have a random thing? A stranger shows up, maybe to rob them, things go bad, Emily and Jason get shot?"

Ray shook his head. "Don't see it. Nothing was taken and the two were killed where they were found. Seems risky that a B&E artist would transport them to kill them. Why not just do it there?"

"I agree. Just thought I'd throw it out."

"We ran into a reporter today," I said.

Ray raised an eyebrow.

"Not a reporter," Nicole said. "She's working on an article about the case. But her focus is the damage to the town and its people."

"What'd you tell her?" Pancake asked.

"Nothing important. We sat with her and Allison at the bakery. Mainly we talked about Emily and what a great lady she was."

Pancake nodded. "She was. From what I remember."

"We figured she just might dig up some things that could be useful."

Ray shrugged. He wasn't convinced.

"What do you need for us to do?" I asked.

"Maybe go see Chief Warren again in the morning. See if she has anything new. Other than that, I'm not sure yet."

"So, we're off tonight?" Nicole asked.

Ray nodded. "Looks that way."

"Good. Jake has to pay off a bet."

"What bet?" Pancake asked.

"One we made today."

"Wait a minute," I said. "I haven't lost the bet yet."

"You will. And really? Does it make any difference?"

Actually, it didn't. I shook my head. "What about you and Pancake? What's next?"

Ray nodded toward the big guy. "We'll work it out. But I think we'll pay the Macks an official visit."

CHAPTER 33

BEFORE NICOLE HAD her way with me, again, we all had dinner at the Grand Hotel's Southern Roots restaurant. A wall of windows looked out over the water, now sparkling in the setting sun. The food was excellent, the drinks better. The bear claws didn't slow Pancake down a bit and he motored through a healthy portion of the menu.

Afterwards, Nicole and I went for a walk along the waterfront. A dirt and wood-slat path led past wonderful old homes to our left, the water and a series of wooden piers to our right. We held hands but said little. Nicole finally broke the silence.

"You're kind of fun," she said.

"What brought that on?"

"Nothing in particular. But you have to admit this place is romantic."

"It is that."

More walking, more silence.

"It's been nearly a year," she said.

Meaning the time we had been together.

"Seems longer."

"It does."

"I can't remember much about the time before," she said.

I stopped. Turned toward her. Kissed her. "You're amazing."

"We're amazing."

That, too.

"Maybe we should head back," she said.

"So you can make me pay off the bet I haven't lost yet?"

"Exactly."

We made it as far as the bar. Pancake was ensconced in one corner, laptop open. We veered that way and sat.

"What's up?"

"Digging around on the Macks."

"Anything interesting?" Nicole asked.

"Some."

A waitress appeared. Young, attractive. I noticed she smiled at Pancake. Stood near him. Looked at us. "Can I get you guys something?"

"Petron tequila," Nicole said. She wagged her head toward me. "He'll have the same."

So, it was going to be one of those nights. Lucky me.

"You okay or can I get you something else?" she asked Pancake.

"What'd you have in mind?" His eyebrows bounced.

"You're terrible." She swatted his shoulder. She looked at me. "Is he always like this?"

"Always," I said.

"I thought so." She tapped his shoulder. "I'll bring you another. You need it."

Pancake raised his empty glass. "Probably do."

"You dog," Nicole said after the waitress walked away.

"I learned from Jake."

Nicole ruffled my hair. "The top dog." Then to Pancake. "She likes you."

Pancake smiled. "Who doesn't?"

"Can we get back to what you found on the Macks?" I asked.

Pancake drained the drink before him. "The Macks own their house free and clear. And another piece of property they rent. Also, with no mortgage."

"Drug dealing is profitable," I said.

"Sure is. They have just under half a million in the bank."

I whistled.

"And two safe deposit boxes. Two different banks. Probably stuffed with cash."

"Avoiding taxes and scrutiny," I said.

"Their two sidekicks are natural-born losers. Jack Reed managed to finish high school. Reavis Whitt had to pick up a GED later. Worked a few odd jobs here and there but none of those in the past three years."

"Living off their dealing," Nicole said.

"Which'll give us leverage on them if need be. The Macks, too."

I knew what he meant. Ray had connections within connections within connections and could open up a can of worms for anyone who lived in an illegal shadow world. A simple phone call to a friend at one of the alphabet government agencies and someone's life could quickly get turned inside out.

"But, here's one interesting fact," Pancake said. "Reed worked for a couple of months over at Watkins' Lumber. Same place Sean works."

CHAPTER 34

"Mr. Watkins?" I said. Nicole and I stood in his office doorway.

"Oh. Hey. Come on in."

I had called earlier, asked if we could stop by. A couple of questions. Only take a few minutes.

Several stacks of what appeared to be invoices littered his desk. He held a page in each hand.

"I hope we're not interrupting," Nicole said.

"Not at all. Trying to get all these bills and receipts organized." He settled each page on a stack. "Accounting isn't my strong suit. Much rather deal with sawdust than paper. But it's the reward for being the boss." He waved a hand toward the two chairs that faced him. "Have a seat. What can I help you with?"

"A former employee," I said. "Jack Reed."

"He part of your investigation?" Watkins asked.

"We don't know. Let's just say his name came up."

"Don't surprise me none. I hear he's up to no good. Selling drugs is the word."

"I'd say the word is correct."

"He worked here briefly. Maybe three years ago."

"And?"

"Had to fire him. Was here only a couple of months. Wasn't very good. Not very interested. Lazy would be how I pegged him."

"Any problems?" Nicole asked. "Other than him being a slacker?"

He leaned forward, elbows on the edge of his desk, fingers laced. "I think he was stoned most of the time. Which would fit with his current employment, I suspect. Didn't seem to be able to follow even the simplest instructions." He shrugged. "Like I said, he wasn't very interested in the first place. But seemed to me he was on something."

"Uppers, downers?" Nicole asked.

Watkins offered a half smile. "Definitely not uppers. Maybe if he had been, he'd've been a better worker." He scratched one ear. "Let me tell you. One day I was standing in the drive, talking to a customer. Jack was leaving for the day. His truck rolled by. I smelled marijuana in his wake." He shrugged. "Fired him the next day."

"How'd he take that?" I asked.

"Didn't seemed concerned. Fact is, I think he was almost glad it happened. He just shrugged, asked when he could pick up his final check, and waved goodbye." Watkins opened his palms. "Never seen a man happy to be fired. But I don't think he was going to stay much longer anyway. Work was too hard for him. Who knows? Maybe he was already dealing by then."

"Probably."

"Regardless, he was making deliveries. I couldn't have some stoner driving one of my trucks around town. My liability would've been substantial."

"Did he work with Sean Patterson?" I asked.

"Sure. We're a small business. Everybody works with everybody else." He cocked his head. "Why?"

"Just wondering if they knew each other."

He leaned back in his chair, laced his fingers over his abdomen. "My impression is that they weren't friends or anything. But they knew each other. Sure."

"Not buddies though?" Nicole asked.

He frowned. "You thinking he or Sean had something to do with your case?"

"Sean has a pretty solid alibi," I said. "Reed we're not sure where, or if, he fits into any of this."

"I see."

"I can tell you we have no evidence of his involvement. But, like I said, his name did come up."

"Mind if I ask how?"

Let's see, I thought. Reed was a drug dealer. Jason had meth in his pocket when he caught his executioner's bullet. I wasn't going to reveal any of that. Rather, I said, "We're really grabbing for straws. Looking at anyone who knew Sean or Emily or Jason Collins."

"Got to admit, nothing about these murders makes much sense to me," Watkins said. "Emily Patterson was one of the nicest people you'd ever care to meet. I don't know much about Jason, but everything I ever heard is that he was a stand-up guy."

"Us, too," I said.

"Did Sean and Reed have any problems with each other?" Nicole asked. "Any disagreements?"

Watkins shook his head. "None that I saw."

"What about away from here?" I asked. "They ever talk about doing things together?"

He unlaced his fingers, rested his hands on the arms of his chair. "I'd be surprised if they ran in the same circles. Sean's a good guy. Smart. Hard worker. Reed ain't none of that."

CHAPTER 35

CHIEF BILLIE WARREN stepped from her SUV as Nicole turned into the lot of the Fairhope PD. She saw us and waited until we slid into a nearby slot and climbed out.

"Morning," she said. A slight nod.

"You, too," I said. "We were on our way to see you."

"About?" She crossed her arms over her chest.

"To see if you have anything new."

"Wish I did. This is getting more than a little frustrating."

"We've found a couple of things that might or might not be relevant," I said.

"Such as?"

"First off, Ray and Pancake tracked down Jason's brother, Brett, over in Pascagoula. Involved in drugs. Does manual labor. Not overly ambitious was Ray's take. Anyway, he said that he and Jason smoked weed and that Jason had used coke a few times that he knew of. Many years ago."

"Interesting. Not sure what it means though."

"Just that Jason has at least a remote history of using. Might make current use a more realistic possibility than we thought before."

Warren nodded but said nothing.

I went on. "Jack Reed worked at Watkins' Lumber a few years ago. With Sean Patterson."

Her chin came up. "That is interesting."

"Do you know of any other connection between the two?"

Warren shook her head. "No. And it might not mean anything."

"True," I said. "But I think that somehow this will all lead back to someone in the drug world. Whether Jason was using, or the drugs were planted, it all seems to close the same circle."

Warren uncrossed her arms. Propped one hand on the service weapon that clung to her right hip. "I've come to the same conclusion. I just don't know who to go after."

"Reed and his sidekick Whitt," I said.

"And the Macks," Nicole added. "Seems like they run the show."

Warren looked toward the PD building. "The problem I'm having with all this is the why." She looked back to me. "Why would someone in that world want to kill Emily and Jason? Sure, if Jason had a current habit, he could've owed them money, or threatened them with exposure, or something like that. Emily could simply be collateral damage. That might all sound copasetic, but we have no evidence connecting all those folks."

"Unless Jason was indeed a closet user and the Macks were his connection," Nicole said.

Warren nodded.

"Do you think the Macks or their crew are capable of this?" I asked. "I know they deal drugs, and aren't exactly stand-up citizens, but would they go all the way to executing someone?"

Warren seemed to consider that. "Anything's possible. If they were under significant threat, I think Clive and Reba would do just about anything. Self-preservation is a strong motivator." She shook her head. "Or maybe I'm just cynical."

"I think that's more realism than cynicism," I said.

"It's a lot to get your mind around," Warren said. "I'm not sure I buy it. We've found absolutely no evidence that Jason or Emily, or Sean, for that matter, were users to any significant degree. None of them were in debt. Or moved money around. Add to that that each of them was gainfully employed and weren't in the habit of missing work or unreliable in any way." She shook her head. "It just doesn't smell like a dealer-user conflict."

"I think we would agree with you," Nicole said. "Pancake looked into everyone's finances and he also didn't see any debts or moved money."

"Except for Sean," I said. "He transferred fifteen hundred into his checking account. But that seems to have been for some car repairs."

"Which he did," Nicole said. "Pancake has a copy of the invoice."

"I don't think I even want to know how you guys get your information," Warren said.

"Charm and hard work," I said.

"Yeah. That's what I thought."

CHAPTER 36

THE FAIRHOPE PD parking lot was apparently a popular gathering spot. After Nicole and I watched Chief Warren walk inside, a final wave over her shoulder, we stood beside Nicole's SL deciding where to go next. Ray and Pancake planned a visit to the Macks, but we had nothing on our plate. That changed when Lauren Schultz rolled into the lot and parked in the adjacent slot.

See? I told you it was a hot spot of activity.

Lauren bounced from her car. "Hey, guys."

"How's it going?" I asked.

"Amazingly well. Why're you here?"

"Just talked with Chief Warren."

"That's where I'm headed," Lauren said.

"Anything new?" Nicole asked.

"Lots actually. Interviewed a ton of people yesterday, including the mayor, several shop owners, coffee shop employees, bartenders, even the local vet. Everybody has been so great,"

"Good to hear," Nicole said.

"Everyone's shook up," Lauren said. "I can tell you that for sure. On a bit of an edge with the killer still out there." She glanced toward the PD's front door. "A few aren't thrilled with the pace of the investigation."

That was common. The populace always expected a resolution in an hour. Including commercials. Like TV. But some situations are infinitely more difficult to unravel. Like now. We had no viable suspects. A few maybes, but they all looked soft to me. Sean had an excellent alibi and I couldn't picture Charlie Martin standing behind Emily and Jason and pulling the trigger. And the drug world seemed like a stretch. Not impossible by any means, but I saw no clear motive for the Macks or their ilk. What niggled in the back of my brain was that we were missing something that was right in front of us. Something that would shift the winds in the right direction.

"I talked with Charlie Martin," Lauren continued. "Like you said, he seems fairly benign. Soft spoken, polite. But I did have a couple interesting conversations *about* him." She pulled her pad from her purse and flipped through several pages. "A guy named Phil Varney. Works over at Copeland's Nursery with Charlie. While Charlie and I were talking, this Phil guy was working nearby. Repotting some small plants, that sort of thing. But my impression was that he was more eavesdropping than working. I thought he was simply curious. But after Charlie and I finished, he followed me to my car. Told me a story."

"About Charlie?" Nicole asked.

She nodded. "One night, a couple of weeks before the murders, a group from work were at a local bar." She flipped a page. "Danny's Den. Downtown. Anyway, he and Charlie were drinking and chatting at the bar, and Phil mentioned he had seen Emily and Jason out somewhere the night before. He said Charlie got quiet, then angry. Said he wished someone would just shoot Jason. Get him out of the way."

"Really?" I asked. "He said that?"

"He did. Phil said he figured it was just blabbering and alcohol. Didn't think much of it. Until Jason was murdered."

"He tell Chief Warren this?"

She shook her head. "Thought about it but was afraid to say anything. Afraid Charlie was not the bad guy and he'd be pointing a finger." She closed her pad, returned it to her purse. "Said that since he worked with Charlie, it might make things uncomfortable."

"Then why now?" Nicole asked.

"It was eating at him."

"He chased you into the parking lot to tell you this?" I asked.

She smiled. "He said he talked to me because I looked nice. Someone he could trust." Her eyes brightened. "That's what he said."

"He's a good judge of people then," Nicole said.

"Did you believe him?" I asked. "This Phil guy? Didn't think he might be talking like he had Charlie's back but maybe had something else going on? Doing the exact opposite of what he said? Making trouble for Charlie?"

"It did cross my mind, but Phil said that a bartender at Danny's heard the conversation, too." She retrieved her pad once again. Flipped it open. "Lee Paulson. Because writers have to check and double-check everything, I went by and talked with him. He remembered it the same way."

"Interesting."

"You don't think Charlie did this, do you?"

I shrugged. "Do you?"

She considered that briefly. "What do I know? I'm just a girl with a pen."

"No, you're a reporter," Nicole said. "A writer. You interview people all the time. Probably can tell when they're being transparent and when they're hiding something."

"That's such a nice thing to say."

"I imagine it's true."

"Since you asked, no, I don't see him being that kind of person. Despite what he said. Both Phil and Lee said they thought it was simply the alcohol and the hurt talking. Didn't believe he meant it. And they, at least Phil, knows him well. So, no, I would doubt he's the one."

I agreed with her. But this little temper outburst at least showed that Charlie Martin was capable of anger. Enough to execute two people? One being the woman he supposedly loved? Didn't feel right. But to echo Lauren, what did I know?

"I think we'll drop by and talk to each of them," I said.

"Good. I'd love to get your take on them." She glanced at her watch. "I better get moving."

After Lauren disappeared through the PD's front doors, Nicole asked, "What now?"

"Let's go see Phil."

CHAPTER 37

"THE LEXUS IS gone," Pancake said. He rolled past the Macks' house.

Ray twisted in the passenger seat and looked over his shoulder. Only the white BMW X5 sat in the drive. "Hopefully Reba's gone and we can talk to Clive alone."

"You afraid of her?" Pancake chuckled.

"After what Chief Warren said, keeping her at bay might be wise. Sounds like she'd raise the temperature a couple of notches. I'd rather have a nice, calm chat with Clive."

"Divide and conquer is never a bad strategy."

Pancake flipped a U-turn where a gravel road spurred off to the right. "How do you want to play it?"

"Cool. Knock on the door. Be polite. Ask for his help."

"You don't want to kick a door down?"

"No."

"I never get to have fun," Pancake said.

"The day is young."

Clive Mack answered their knock. Barefoot, he wore baggy, well-worn jeans and a lime-green Flora-Bama tee shirt. The Flora-Bama was a bar, restaurant, music venue, and all-around purveyor of nightly chaos on the beach. Technically in Florida, but nudged, literally, right up against the Alabama line. Just a few miles on down the road from Jake's place.

Pancake introduced Ray and himself, finishing by complimenting Clive on his shirt. "Love that place."

"You know it?" Clive asked.

"We're from Gulf Shores. Know it all too well."

"What can I do for you?" Clive asked. His gaze scanned the world beyond Ray and Pancake as if he expected a posse or something. His paranoia evident.

"We're private investigators," Pancake said. "Looking into the murders of Emily Patterson and Jason Collins."

"What's that got to do with me?"

"Nothing. We need your help though. And would appreciate a few minutes of your time."

Clive hesitated. A veil of confusion descended over his face. "Help? With what?"

"Why don't we sit down?" Ray said. "We can explain what we need."

Another hesitation, followed by a quick nod.

Once settled in the living room, Ray and Pancake on a sofa, Clive in a chair, Ray said, "Clive, we know a good deal about you."

Clive sat up, back erect. "What's that mean?"

"We don't care what you do for a living," Pancake said. "But we know."

Clive started to stand, obviously preparing to ask them to leave, but Pancake waved him back into his chair.

"Relax. We aren't here to mess with your life. Not in any way. But your unique position might prove helpful."

The lines of confusion on Clive's face deepened.

"We're pretty much at a dead end with these murders," Ray said. "Chief Warren is, too. We're looking into a possible drug connection. Maybe an owed debt, something like that."

"I don't know anything about that," Clive said.

"I believe you," Pancake said. The lie rolled out easily. "But we know that you and your wife are plugged into that world and know what goes on around here."

"I'm afraid you're misinformed."

"Look, Clive," Ray said. "Let's not play that game. We're investigators. We know. A lot. That's what we do. Find out stuff." He opened his palms. "Once again, we aren't here to mess up your gig. We could care less. All we want to know is if you knew Jason Collins or Emily Patterson?"

Clive hesitated, as if considering how to handle this. He finally decided. "I'm not sure I want to talk about this."

Ray scooted forward on the sofa. "Clive, here are your options. We can sit here and have a nice chat. Like gentlemen. Or we can dig so deeply into your life you'll bleed. Excavate your supply lines and your dealers. Shine a spotlight on your entire operation. Maybe turn over everything we find to Chief Warren." Ray opened his palms. "Your call."

Clive's eyes narrowed. Pancake could feel Clive's internal pressure rise, then recede. His shoulders slackened. Obviously deciding that the best route was to have a casual chat.

"Emily sure. Sean not well but I know him. Reba actually went to school with Emily. She was a couple of years behind. But now? We only see them in passing from time to time."

"And Jason Collins?"

"Know who he is but that's about it."

"None of them were customers?"

"No. That's a fact."

"What about Jack Reed and Reavis Whitt?" Pancake asked. "Think they might've dealt with them?"

Pancake could almost hear Clive's wheels turning. Trying to sort out exactly how much they knew about his and Reba's business. He almost squirmed in his chair. He tightened one fist and released it, working his fingers as if they ached.

"No. They don't."

"You sure?"

He nodded. "I'd know."

"I think you would." Pancake offered a friendly smile.

"Do you know anyone else around here who might have sold Jason something?" Ray asked.

"Like what?"

"Let's say, for the sake of argument, meth. You aware of anyone else who peddles that around here?"

"Else?"

Pancake and Ray stared at him. Said nothing.

"Okay. Yeah, there are a couple of guys from Mobile that drop in here every now and then. I know they push meth and Oxy. Occasionally fentanyl."

"How do you feel about that? Them coming into your backyard?"

"I don't think on it much. They don't do a lot of business here."

"But business is business," Pancake said. "You aren't worried about them getting a foot in the door?"

Clive sighed. "Maybe a little."

"Maybe we can help you there," Ray said.

"Help me? I don't see how."

"We could have a chat with them. Maybe shake them up a little."

"I don't think these are the kind of guys you can rattle." Clive looked from Ray to Pancake. "Rumor is they're connected to the cartel out of Juarez."

Pancake smiled. "We like to shake the tree every now and then. No matter how big it is."

"Who are these guys?" Ray asked.

Clive said nothing. Obviously deciding how far to go. What to reveal. Probably thinking maybe he'd already said too much.

"It can only help you," Ray said.

"I honestly don't see how," Clive said.

"We dig into their lives. Make them uncomfortable. Maybe make them see the wisdom of not dealing in Fairhope. Maybe even connect them to a double murder and remove them from the board completely."

"There's really no downside for you," Pancake added.

Clive mulled things a beat. "White guy and a Mexican guy. Alex Talley and Santiago Cortez. They call him Sandman."

Pancake heard a car pull into the drive, a car door slam.

"We'll pay them a visit," Ray said.

"I don't know where they live. Or hang out. Really nothing much about them."

"We'll track them down," Pancake said.

The door swung open. Reba came in. Jeans, black AC/DC tee shirt, metal coffee mug in one hand, plastic grocery bag in the other.

"What's going on?" she asked.

Pancake stood. "Hello, Mrs. Mack. This is Ray and I'm Pancake."

A flash of confusion over Pancake's name, then she said, "And who are you?"

Reba wore hostility like a warm blanket. Seemed to be comfortable with it. Like it was her natural state.

"We're investigators," Ray said, standing. "Looking into the recent murders."

Her face darkened, eyes sparking. She placed the grocery bag on the floor. She looked at Clive. "Are you insane? Letting a couple of P.I.s in our home?" She turned on Ray. "Get out."

"Sorry we upset you," Pancake said. "We were just leaving."

She walked to the door and yanked it open. "Then get the hell out of my house."

They did. As the door slammed, they heard her say, "What the fuck is wrong with you?"

Once back in the truck, Pancake studied the house. "I'd say old Clive is in a world of swirl."

"I almost feel sorry for him," Ray said.

Pancake grunted. "Almost."

CHAPTER 38

JACK REED AND Reavis Whitt sat across from each other at the small dining table in their apartment. A metal tray mounded with rich, green, aromatic marijuana buds and a gallon zip-lock bag of crystalline meth sat between them. They busied themselves with packing the buds and powder into smaller plastic bags. Getting ready to hit the streets. Lay off their product and rake in the cash.

"I hate doing this shit," Whitt said. "It's tedious."

"But necessary."

"This'll help." Whitt snatched up a half-smoked joint from the nearby ashtray and fired it up. He took a couple of hits and passed it to Reed. Reed took a hit, dropped the remnant back into the ashtray.

"This even more so." Reed tugged open the meth bag, and with a small spoon lifted a dose to his nose. He snorted it, leaned back, waited for the rush. "Oh yeah."

Whitt took the spoon and followed suit. "Let's get this done."

An hour later they were nearing the finish line. A pile of small plastic bags now filled a large metal bowl.

Reed's phone sounded, vibrated on the table to his right. The caller ID read, "Macks." He punched the speaker button, asked, "What's up?"

"That's what I want to know."

Reba. Angry. Her voice carried heat.

Reed looked at Whitt, who now sat up straight.

"Is there a problem?" Reed asked.

"Is there?"

"Not on our end."

"Let me ask you," Reba said. "Did you sell anything to either Emily Patterson or Jason Collins?"

"No."

"You sure?"

"Of course I'm sure. We barely know them. We don't sell to people we don't know."

"You better not be fucking with me."

"Reba, what's this about?"

"A couple P.I. types came by. Asking questions about them."

Whitt's eyes widened. He mouthed "What the fuck?" to Reed.

"What do you mean, P.I. types?" Reed asked.

Reba huffed out a breath. "A couple of guys. Looking into their murders."

"What's that got to do with us?"

"That's what I'm asking. Have you two done anything that would bring this kind of shit down on us?"

"Of course not. We sell. We don't kill people."

Reba said nothing for a few seconds. The silence heavy and painful. "If they talk to you, don't say anything. Play dumb."

"Why would they talk to us?"

"Because they know about you," Reba said. "Rattled your names right off."

"Jesus."

"Jesus ain't going to help you here. Keeping your fucking mouth shut will. If they ask, you don't work for us. You don't deal. Got it?"

"But don't they already know that ain't the truth?" Reed asked.

"They suspect it. Can't really know it. Might be on a fishing expedition. So, don't tell them shit."

"Why would we say anything?"

"That's what I'm telling you. Don't. We don't need to give them any reason to sniff around."

"Look, Reba, we're cool. We don't know anything about any murders. I swear."

"You better hope for your sake you're telling the truth." She disconnected the call.

Whitt massaged his temples. "We are so fucked."

"No, we're not."

"What are we going to do?"

"Nothing," Reed said.

"Nothing?"

"Okay, maybe have a chat."

"You think that'll work?" Whitt asked.

Reed balled one fist. "If it does, it does. If it doesn't, it doesn't."

"It's the *doesn't* we better worry about."

CHAPTER 39

THE TRICK WAS to chat with Phil Varney without alerting Charlie Martin. Phil had waited until Lauren left, followed her into the parking lot, talked with her privately. Meant he didn't want Charlie knowing what was going down. That Phil was talking out of school. Maybe didn't want to strain their relationship. Or be seen as a snitch of sorts. Or did he consider Charlie dangerous? That he might retaliate in some way? Did he think Charlie was involved in the murders? I still didn't see that, but Phil knew him, worked with him every day. Regardless, a pinch of discretion here would be best.

Copeland's Nursery was a big place, but not enormous by any stretch. We couldn't simply stroll in and corner Phil without Charlie knowing. Maybe we could, but the risk would be considerable.

We got lucky though.

Nicole pulled into the lot of a patio furniture store across the street and parked aimed at Copeland's. "What do you think?" she asked.

"You distract Charlie and I'll chat with Phil."

"Or you can do the distracting."

"Somehow I think you'd be better at holding Charlie's attention than me."

"I feel like I'm being pimped out," she said.

"You are."

"That's me. A full-service chick."

"And you do it all so well."

"You're so romantic."

"I am," I said. "Now, let's get this done."

I popped open the passenger's door.

"Wait," Nicole said. She pointed. "We might've just caught a break."

A Copeland's truck slid by the side of the building, stopped at the street, then turned and disappeared up the road. Charlie Martin behind the wheel.

The same young lady we had seen a few days earlier was behind the counter. She yet again directed us "out back," this time saying that Phil Varney was tagging a new shipment of azaleas. We found him doing exactly that. Toward the rear of the shaded area, stooped over, clipping small yellow price tags on an assortment of healthy-looking red, pink, and white azaleas.

"Phil?" I said.

He straightened and turned. Tall and lanky. Shaggy brown hair that hung over his ears. Tennis shoes, shorts, and a wine-colored Copeland's Nursery golf shirt.

"Yes."

I introduced Nicole and me, told him who we were, and what we were doing, then said, "Mind if we ask a couple of questions?"

"About what?"

"Charlie Martin."

He looked past us, scanned the area. His shoulders seemed to drop as if he were trying to get smaller.

"He's not here," Nicole said. "Out on a delivery."

"I'm not sure I'm comfortable with this."

"We aren't trying to make trouble," I said.

He looked around again.

"We've already talked to Charlie," Nicole said. "A few days ago."

"And we think this is mostly a dead end," I added. "But we need to look into everything."

He sighed. "I suppose that's true."

"Lauren Schultz told us what you said. About Charlie getting angry and saying some things about Jason Collins."

"I told her that in confidence."

"Don't be angry with her," Nicole said. "We can be persuasive." She smiled. "Besides, she's doing a human-interest story. We're trying to investigate a double murder."

"Isn't that Chief Warren's job?"

"It is," I said. "We're actually helping her gather information."

"I see."

"Just tell us what happened, that night at the bar, and we'll be gone," Nicole said.

He did and it was just as Lauren had said. He and Charlie were having a few beers. Charlie was feeling no pain. Phil happened to mention he had seen Emily and Jason at a restaurant the night before. Charlie became morose—that's the word he used. Then angry. Didn't understand why Emily saw more in Jason than she did in him. And indeed, he had said that he wished "someone would shoot him." He concluded with, "Sounds bad, doesn't it?"

"Maybe," I said. "Or he was simply frustrated with the situation and needed to blow off steam. "

Phil nodded. "That's what it seemed like to me. I actually thought little of it. Until . . . until those murders happened."

"You never went to the police with this. Right?"

He shook his head. "I still didn't think it was much. Even afterwards. I just couldn't see Charlie being involved in any way. Still don't, for that matter."

"But you told Lauren."

He looked at his shoes, talked to them. "It kept nagging at me. What he had said. Woke me up a couple of times." He looked up. "Thought about going to the police, but then time had passed, and I thought—not sure what I thought. Like maybe they wouldn't believe me now." His gaze fell back toward his feet. "Or that me opening my mouth might get Charlie into some unwarranted trouble."

"Why Lauren?" Nicole asked. "Why did you open up to her?"

"I don't know. She seemed nice. I overheard her talking with Charlie. She seemed very sympathetic. Kind. I figured if I was ever going to tell the story that I better do it and quit hemming and hawing." He shrugged. "So I did."

"Let me ask you a couple of things," I said. "And feel free not to answer." That drew his attention back to me. "Do you know if Charlie uses any drugs? Even just marijuana? Anything?"

"Does beer and the occasional whiskey count?"

I smiled. "No. Those are fine."

"Then no. I think if he did, I'd know about it."

"You guys are good friends?" Nicole asked.

"Some. Not all that close. But we work together, end up in bars a couple of times a week. I think it would've come up."

"The other thing," I said. "Do you see any way Charlie could've been involved in these murders?"

"That's an easy one. No way. He's really a quiet, passive guy. That little angry outburst was out of character and I don't think it means squat."

"For what it's worth, we agree," Nicole said.

"Good." He glanced toward a woman, across the way, smiled, raised a finger, and mouthed, "Be right there." He looked back at me. "I better get back to work."

"Thanks for talking with us," Nicole said.

He nodded. Started to leave, hesitated. "I just don't want to be the one that gets Charlie in any trouble." He sighed. "If he is."

"Right now, we don't think he's the guy we're looking for," I said.

"And he'll never know we chatted," Nicole added.

"I'd appreciate that."

"One more thing," I said. "Lauren said a bartender overheard the conversation between you and Charlie."

He nodded. "Lee. Over at Danny's Den." Another sigh. "You going to talk with him?"

I nodded.

"His take might be little different than mine."

"Really?"

Another hesitation. "I'll let him tell you what he thinks."

CHAPTER 40

I BELIEVED PHIL Varney and, from the way he characterized it, agreed with his assessment of the conversation he had had with Charlie Martin. But, as Varney had eluded to, did bartender Lee Paulson have a different take on it? As an outsider, one who apparently eavesdropped on the conversation, did he hear it differently? Sense anything darker?

Danny's Den. A rustic-looking gray wooden structure, patterned after a rural cabin. A gallery extended the entire width of the building, shading two benches and four rocking chairs, offering a place where folks could wait outside for their tables.

My heart rate kicked up a notch as we walked from the parking lot toward the front door. For some reason, I found myself apprehensive about what we might uncover here. I was rooting for Charlie. I liked him. I didn't want to dig up anything that made me feel otherwise. Even more disturbing was the realization that this P.I. crap could be addicting. The chase. The anticipation. The unknown. It was like taking the mound for the first pitch of an away game.

I loved that, fingering the ball, locating the correct seam, staring down the first batter, but I hated this. Really, I did. Mainly because it meant Ray was right. Not that he wasn't often on point, but, as with any arm-wrestling match, I detested losing. Especially to Ray.

It was just after 11:00 a.m. Too early for the bulk of the lunch crowd. Which might give us a brief window to chat with Lee the bartender more privately. If he was here today.

The bar only hosted two patrons, a couple, far end, glasses of white wine before them. The bartender was a short, stocky guy, muscular arms, brightly colored sleeve-tattooing on the left, buzz-cut hair. His navy-blue tee shirt seemed a couple of sizes too small but showed off his devotion to the gym.

We took seats at the near end of the bar, as far away from the couple as possible.

"What can I get you?" the bartender asked. He swiped the polished-wood bar top before us with a towel.

"We're looking for Lee Paulson," I said.

"You found him."

I introduced Nicole and me. He glanced at me, but eyed Nicole with more interest. A lot more interest. His chest expanded and he smiled. She smiled back.

Work it, girl.

"Can we ask a couple of questions?" Nicole said.

"About what?"

"A conversation that occurred here a few weeks ago."

He laughed. "Really? How would I remember that? I hear a thousand conversations a day."

"I'm sure you do," Nicole said. "This one was between Charlie Martin and Phil Varney."

His smile collapsed. "I see." He looked back toward me. "Who are you guys?"

"Private investigators," I said. "We're looking into the recent murders."

"Seems like everybody is all of a sudden. Even had a reporter in here last night."

"Lauren Schultz," Nicole said. "We know her."

"Figures. That why you're here?"

"We've already talked with Charlie. Not about this, but we've talked to him. We also chatted with Phil just a little while ago. We wanted to get your take on the conversation."

"More or less what Phil told you, I suspect."

"He seemed to think you might feel differently about it. That maybe you heard more in it than he did."

He glanced down the bar. The woman waved a hand. "Just a sec," he said and headed that way.

After he refilled the couple's wine glasses, he returned. He braced his arms on the bar, leaning forward. His muscles flexed. "Like I told that reporter, I believe Charlie was simply running his yap. Most people in here do. Talk a lot of nonsense." He smiled. "Alcohol will do that."

"But you sensed something else, didn't you?" Nicole asked.

"I don't know Charlie all that well. Phil, either for that matter. Sort of over-the-bar acquaintances. They drop in from time to time. We chat. Small talk. Weather, that sort of thing. So any thoughts I might have on the subject probably aren't worth much."

"I disagree," I said. "I own a bar. Down in Gulf Shores. All my bartenders are amateur psychiatrists."

He nodded his agreement. "That's probably true."

"The point is, you meet people all day long. Talk with them. Listen to their stories. Their life victories and their tales of woe. You know people. I think your take is relevant."

"Maybe I should hang out a shingle," he said.

"You'd be better than most real shrinks," Nicole said.

The fingers of his right hand drummed the bar top. "I know Charlie had a thing for Emily and that she seemed to like Jason better."

"Did you know Emily and Jason?" I asked.

"Sure. They came in together from time to time."

"What about Emily and Charlie? They come in, too?"

"This is a small town. Everybody comes in here sooner or later."

"So, that's a yes?" I asked. "They came in as a couple, so to speak?"

"A time or two."

"Was Emily different around them?" Nicole asked. "Maybe favored one over the other?"

He nodded. "I think so. She and Jason seemed more of a couple. Her and Charlie?" A one-shoulder shrug. "I didn't see the sparks. At least not from her. But I could be wrong."

"From what we've heard, your take is correct."

"I do know Charlie wasn't happy about her and Jason. That was clear. He'd mentioned it before. Nothing big. More or less in passing. Making conversation. But, that night, when Phil mentioned seeing them out together, Charlie seemed to . . . not sure how to put it. Maybe went inside himself. Got quiet for a while. Phil apologized for even bringing it up. That's when Charlie said he wished someone would shoot Jason."

Another couple settled a few seats down. Lee excused himself and moved down that way. He took their order, mixed their drinks, two Bloody Marys, and then returned.

"Look," he said, "I probably over-read the entire thing. Like I said, I don't know Charlie all that well, but what I do know is that he seems like a decent guy. Truth be told, folks talk all kinds of shit over a bar." He looked at me. "You own a bar. I'm sure you've seen it a million times."

I had. And, more often than not, I, too, blew it off as drunk talk. Was that all this was? A morose Charlie yapping about things he couldn't control? Probably. Maybe.

CHAPTER 41

PANCAKE POINTED HIS truck north, past Daphne, toward I-10 and Mobile. Ray made a call. His phone on speaker. Took him less than a minute to get Special Agent in Charge Bruce Markham on the line. Markham was the director of the DEA's New Orleans Division office. His domain reached from Louisiana to Arkansas and included Alabama.

Pancake merged onto the interstate while Ray explained the situation, adding that his partner Tommy Jeffers was listening in. He made the over-the-phone introductions. Pancake knew of Markham but had never met him. He knew that Ray had known him for over two decades. Back to their military days.

"You say this is a murder investigation?" Markham asked.

"A bad one," Ray said. "Two young folks. Execution style."

"In Fairhope? That's a pretty quiet neighborhood."

"It is. But not for this couple." Ray explained his history with Emily Rhodes/Patterson.

"That's tough," Markham said. "What can I do for you?"

Ray detailed the crime scene, the meth found on Jason Collins, the style of the murders, the appearance of a drug deal gone bad, or revenge, or owed money, or whatever. How the victims were very low risk with no apparent bad habits or dark-alley connections.

"Any viable suspects?" Markham asked.

"None. We're working a possible love triangle that looks pretty weak, a husband with an ironclad alibi doing in his wife during a divorce, and a possible drug angle. So far we have zip."

"Ah, the life of a P.I."

"Glamorous," Ray said. "Just like on TV."

Ray then told of their chat with Clive and Reba Mack.

"Clive and Reba," Markham said. "I do hear their names more often than I'd like. If I had the manpower, I'd rattle their cage."

"Not yet," Ray said. "But I don't think we're quite through with them yet."

Markham chuckled. "Wouldn't want your crosshairs on me."

"They mentioned a couple of dealers. Over in Mobile. Guys named Santiago Cortez and Alex Talley."

"Oh, yeah. I know them."

"Tell me."

"Santiago. They call him Sandman, mainly because he deals in downers. Heroin, oxy, fentanyl. Also, meth and coke. He's full service. Talley's his partner. Not the sharpest knife in the drawer. Sandman definitely runs the crew."

"Crew?"

"He's got half a dozen guys that run with him. But he and Talley are at the top."

"Any evidence they might deal over in Fairhope?"

"Nothing direct. Wouldn't surprise me though. They reach over into Bay Minette and west to the University of South Alabama. Even down into your neck of the woods. Gulf Shores, Orange Beach, around there."

"So they might be doing business in Fairhope and environs?" Pancake asked.

"If so, I'd suspect it's small-time. I don't think the Macks would stand for it. And we have no ripples that a war is on the horizon."

"What else you got on them?"

"Other than armed and dangerous? Sandman is implicated in the murder of a small-time dealer in Mobile. Some guy tried to move in on his territory. Found himself dead in the Bay. Gunshot to the head."

Pancake flashed on Emily. And Jason.

Markham continued. "He has a loose connection with the Zetas. Through some cousin in Juarez, if I remember correctly. So the shooter in that deal might have been an import and not Sandman himself."

"Anything we can use for leverage in case we need it?" Ray asked.

"Other than me?"

"That should be enough. Just didn't want to unless you green-lighted it."

"It would be my pleasure. And I could use a little humor to help cut through all this paperwork."

"One more thing," Pancake said. "Do you know a couple of guys that seem to work for the Macks? Jack Reed and Reavis Whitt?"

"Sure. I think Reed got grabbed once. By the locals. Nothing big. Are they part of your murder investigation?"

"Maybe," Ray said. "Unfortunately, we're spinning our wheels. Everything we've found leads nowhere."

"Maybe Sandman can point you down the right path."

"We could use that."

"I'm here," Markham said. "Chained to my desk. In case you need to introduce me into the discussions."

"That's good to know."

"Sandman is stone cold. Watch your six."

CHAPTER 42

THE *TOP GUN* U-turn Nicole made gave me whiplash. Okay, maybe not really. No pain, but it was a shock to my delicate system. At least it happened before we stopped for coffee, which had been the plan. We were on Section Street in downtown Fairhope. Fortunately, there was little traffic, but I'm not sure she noticed.

"What are you doing?" I asked.

"Hot pursuit."

"What?"

"You didn't see them?"

I scanned the street, the sidewalks, the shops. "See who?"

"Those two guys who work for the Macks."

"What guys?"

She glanced at me, shook her head. "Do you not pay attention? Or is it a memory problem?"

Were those my only choices? If so, which was the right one? Reminded me of every test I ever took in college. I never did very well on those. Baseball, sure; exams, not my strong suit. I'm not sure she expected an answer anyway. Proved a moot point. Before I could make a stab at the answer, she continued.

"Remember the pictures Pancake and Ray took? At the Macks' house? The two guys?"

Oh. Those guys.

"Yeah, I remember," I said.

"There they are."

"Where?"

"Red truck. Half a block ahead."

Sure enough. A bright red pickup with a camper shell loped through the traffic ahead of us. "Are you sure?"

"I am."

"Why are we following them?"

"Pursuing." She smiled. "Hotly pursuing."

"We're only doing ten miles an hour."

"Semantics."

"But I must admit, everything you do is hot."

"You complaining?" she asked.

"Not even close."

She maneuvered around a car that had stopped, blinker on, prepping for a shot at parallel parking. As we slid by, I didn't see much confidence on the driver's face.

"Why are we following, sorry, pursuing, them?" I asked.

"To see what they're up to."

"Why?"

"Curiosity."

"Isn't that what killed the cat?"

We eased out of the commercial area. Traffic thinned.

"This isn't exactly the best car for stealth."

"Around here? Are you kidding?"

True. Fairhope was one of the wealthiest communities along the Gulf Coast. Mercedes were everywhere. Like the one that separated us from the pickup. It turned off, leaving us a hundred feet or so behind the truck.

"They're going to see us," I said.

"So? They don't know us. We're just tourists out for a drive."

She slowed, letting them get farther ahead.

"What were their names?" she asked.

"Reed and Whitt."

"See? You do pay attention." She patted my arm. "I'm so proud of you."

"Do I get a treat?"

"Later you can have all the treats you want."

"I'm going to hold you to that."

"I know."

The truck turned onto Highway 104. Nicole slowed then followed.

"Where are they going?" I asked.

"Fletcher's Farm is down this way."

"So is Emily's house."

Which is where they turned. Into the drive, stopping just behind Sean's Chevy.

"What the hell?" I asked.

"Curious," Nicole said. She continued a hundred yards past the house and turned onto a gravel road. Stopped. "Why would those two be visiting Sean?"

"Maybe they were just turning around."

"Didn't look that way."

She reversed onto the road, and we retraced our path. The pickup sat behind Sean's car. No sign of activity. House closed up. Nicole rolled on by.

"Maybe making a delivery," I said.

"If so, it puts Sean right in the middle of the drug world."

"We already know he uses. At least somewhat. And these guys are the major neighborhood candymen."

We backtracked to the intersection of Highway 104 and Section Road. Nicole continued across, then turned left into a dirt driveway.

It sloped down toward a house, its roof barely visible through a collection of trees. She jerked to a stop.

"Let's hang here for a few minutes," she said. "See if they come back by."

"We could get shot."

"By them?"

"The homeowner. He might take offense to us being in his drive."

"You worry too much," she said.

"Only about things like bullets."

"Just watch the intersection. I'll take care of the homeowner if he shows up."

"How?"

"Same way I do cops. Smile. Now pay attention."

The intersection wasn't very busy so there wasn't much to pay attention to. Except Nicole.

"Quit staring at me," she said.

"Not staring. Admiring."

"Oh. In that case, okay."

CHAPTER 43

"DON'T YOU THINK you're overreacting?"

Jack Reed considered that for a few seconds. "No. I don't."

"Me neither," Reavis Whitt added.

The two sat on wooden stools facing Sean across the kitchen breakfast bar. They were in Emily's old house. Now Sean's. Reed and Whitt had first gone by Sean's apartment, and when he wasn't there, came out this way. Found him packing things up, saying he'd finally decided to sell the place but needed to clean it up beforehand.

Sean flattened his palms against the counter's tiled surface, weight forward, shoulder hunched. "Tell me exactly what happened."

"Reba called. All pissed off. Said two P.I.s came by to talk to them. Asked Clive a bunch of questions. She threw them out."

Sean straightened, gave a half shrug. "I've talked to them, too."

"You did?" Reed asked. "When?"

"Couple of days ago. They seemed pretty harmless."

"That's not what Reba said. She told us they were tough-looking guys. One as big as a house."

A puzzled look spread across Sean's face. "Not the ones I talked to. It was a tall guy and really good-looking chick. Named Jake and Nicole."

Reed looked at him. "Them ain't the ones then."

"Maybe there're two sets of folks poking around?" Whitt said.

"Or maybe they're a whole team," Reed said.

"I need a beer." Sean walked to the the fridge, yanked it open. "You guys?"

"Sure," they said almost in unison.

Beers open, slugs taken by each. Sean placed his bottle on the counter.

"Back to Reba," Sean continued. "What'd they ask her?"

"They mostly talked to Clive, I think," Reed said. "Reba showed up and ran them off. But they knew what Reba and Clive did. The odd thing was they didn't seem to care none about their dealing. Wanted to know if they sold anything to Emily or Jason."

"They knew about us, too," Whitt said. "Me and Jack. Knew we worked with Clive and Reba. Reba said they might come talk to us. If they did, we should deny even knowing them."

Sean took a gulp of beer. "Makes sense."

Reed leaned his elbows on the bar. "You don't seem overly concerned. You don't see a problem here?"

Sean shook his head. "I don't. Not really."

"I wish I had your confidence."

"It was supposed to look like a drug deal. Right? Isn't that why you planted the meth?"

Reed shrugged.

"And left the bodies where they'd be easily found."

"Yeah, and I'm thinking maybe that wasn't too smart. Maybe me and Reavis should've done what we wanted to do in the first place."

Sean sighed. "Dumping them in a swamp over in Mississippi wouldn't've been smart. For me to get the accounts, the house, she had to be dead. Not simply missing. That could've taken years."

"I suppose."

"So, these P.I. types, and the cops, coming around and talking to Clive and Reba seems a logical follow-up, don't you think?" Sean asked.

Reed said nothing.

"They'll talk to everyone in town who has any connection with meth, that sort of thing. Come up empty. Then move on to assuming it was some outsider. Maybe from Mobile or Biloxi." Again, Sean braced himself on the counter. "I agree with Reba. You guys just play dumb and it'll all pass."

Reed glanced at Whitt. His gaze fell to the bar top. "Seems to me that this aggravation would deserve a little more money."

"Aggravation?" Sean asked. "What does that mean?"

"Just that me and Reavis are going to have to handle all this. For all of us. Take all the heat. All the questioning. Make it go away. Seems we should get paid something."

"You've been paid."

"Not for this," Whitt said. "We weren't counting on this."

"Sure you were," Sean said. "We planned it to look like a drug deal. You guys did exactly that. Why wouldn't you think the cops, or these guys, might come around and ask questions? It's part of the deal."

Reed considered that. Didn't like it. Said so, ending with, "Maybe another ten grand would be fair."

"Fair? Are you crazy? First off, you've been paid. Second, I don't have that kind of money."

"You will," Whitt said. He waved a hand. "Soon as you sell this place."

CHAPTER 44

ALEX TALLEY BENT over the trunk of a black Kia Optima, rummaging around as if looking for something. Jeans, no shirt, no shoes. Red baseball cap, turned backwards. He lifted a blanket, then a small cardboard box, dropping each back inside. He scratched his head, leaned in further, and then came out with a light-blue canvas kick bag.

Pancake watched through a pair of binoculars. He had parked at the far end of the parking lot, next to a blue van.

Talley slammed the trunk and walked back into the first-floor apartment he had exited only minutes earlier.

"How you want to handle this?" Pancake asked.

"Let's try to play nice," Ray said. "See if they'll be pliable. If not, we go at them hard."

Pancake lowered the glasses. "They'll be armed."

"I'd be surprised if they weren't." Ray popped open the center console and retrieved a pair of Glock nines. "We are, too." He handed one to Pancake.

The complex consisted of only three red-brick, two-story buildings that paralleled the tree-lined street like a trio of box cars. The sun-dappled parking lot virtually empty, most residents still at work. It was midafternoon.

Talley answered Pancake's knock. He had slipped on a gray tee shirt before donning his backwards cap again.

"We ain't buying," he said.

"We're not selling," Pancake said.

"What do you want?"

Pancake could see past him into a living room. Sandman sat on a sofa, cleaning a gun. Looked like a Heckler & Koch PV9. Partially disassembled. A good thing.

"We want to ask for your help."

Talley craned his neck, looking past Pancake, past Ray, as if he expected to see something in the parking lot. Maybe cops, or the SWAT team. "With what?"

"Who is it?" Sandman asked.

"Hey, Sandman," Pancake said. "We need a few minutes of your time." He glanced at Talley. "You, too, Alex."

"Who are you?"

"I'm Pancake. This is Ray."

Pancake pushed past him and entered the living room. "Thanks for talking with us."

"Whoa," Talley said. "You can't just barge in here."

"We wouldn't dare. But thanks for inviting us in."

"I didn't."

"Sure you did. You opened the door."

Sandman placed the disassembled weapon on the coffee table, but another gun appeared in his hand. Another PV9. He had swept it up from the sofa beside him. He leveled it at Pancake as he and Ray entered.

Sandman waved the muzzle toward the door. "I'd suggest you guys hit the road. Pronto."

Pancake smiled. "Nice weapon."

That seemed to confuse him. Guess he wasn't used to folks not reacting when he pointed a gun at them.

"I know how to use it," he said.

"I'm sure you do."

Pancake and Ray settled in the two chairs that faced him across a low coffee table. A can of gun oil, two stained rags, and the broken-down H&K lay on its surface. Along with two baggies of meth.

Talley remained standing but moved behind the sofa. Just to Sandman's left.

"Maybe I'll show you," Sandman said.

Now Ray smiled. "We'd rather you simply answer a few questions."

More confusion. "About what?"

"You guys do any business over in Fairhope?" Pancake asked.

"What business?" Sandman still held the gun aimed in their direction.

Pancake nodded toward the baggies. "You know. Meth, Oxy, coke. That sort of thing."

"Who the fuck are you?"

"We're private investigators," Ray said. "Looking into a couple of murders over in Fairhope."

"We don't know anything about any murders," Sandman said. "Not in Fairhope. Not anywhere."

"Then you won't mind answering our questions," Pancake said.

"The hell we will." He raised the gun, waved it from Pancake to Ray, centering it on his chest. "I suggest you get up and walk the fuck out that door. Before something bad happens."

Neither Ray nor Pancake moved. Or even flinched.

"I don't mean to dampen your enthusiasm," Ray said, "but this isn't the first time I've had a gun pointed at me."

Sandman seemed unsure what to do next. Probably weighing his options. Wondering why they weren't intimidated.

"Just talk with us," Pancake said. "Then we'll leave and your life can go on."

"Why should we do that?"

"You like your business?" Ray asked. "Want to keep it up and running? Stay out of jail?"

Sandman's eyes narrowed; his chin came up. Trying to act all macho. Gun in his hand. Probably feeling in charge. But Pancake saw the stress lines around his mouth, the micro-ticks in his facial muscles. Barely perceptible, but there.

"Don't get freaky," Ray said. "I'm going to get my phone." He eased it from his pocket. "I want to introduce you to someone."

"What the fuck you talking about?"

Ray raised a hand. He dialed a number, the phone on speaker. The answer came quickly. Bruce Markham.

"Ray, great to hear from you."

Markham was smooth. Knew what was what.

"I want to introduce you to a couple of folks. Alex Talley and Santiago 'Sandman' Cortez."

"I know them both. Quite well, actually. I've followed their careers for years."

Sandman and Talley each visibly recoiled. Pancake could almost hear the questions that rattled around inside their heads. *Who are these guys? How do they know so much? Who's the dude on the phone and how does he know them?*

"Bruce, why don't you introduce yourself," Ray said.

A soft chuckle. "Gladly. Hey, boys. This is Special Agent in Charge Bruce Markham. Division Director for the DEA."

Silence.

"Not much to say? No problem. I'll spell it out for you. I know who you are. I know who your suppliers are. I know everyone in your distribution network. I know where you live. I know where your money is hidden. I know every time you take a piss." Another chuckle. "The only reason I haven't already come down on your sorry asses is that you're small potatoes. Not worth my time and effort. So, answer Ray's questions. Don't lie or make up any shit. Cooperate. If not, I might move you to the top of my priority list. And that wouldn't go well for you. Any questions?"

More silence. Sandman paled. Tally wavered. Pancake feared he might faint and fall.

"Didn't think so."

"Thanks, Bruce," Ray said. "We'll chat later." He disconnected the call. He looked at Sandman. "Now, a couple of questions."

"Who the fuck are you guys?" Sandman asked.

"We might be your best friends," Ray said.

"Or your worst nightmare," Pancake added. "We could be that creature that hides under your bed, making sleep difficult."

"It's up to you which we are," Ray said.

"So put the fucking gun down and open your ears," Pancake said.

Sandman hesitated.

"Do as he says," Ray said.

Sandman looked his way. His eyes widened as he saw the gun Ray now held.

"Now," Ray added.

Sandman placed the gun on the table.

"And you," Pancake said to Talley. "Sit down. You make me nervous standing back there."

"You don't want him nervous," Ray said. "Makes him break things."

Talley sat next the Sandman.

"See," Ray said. "We can all sit and chat like adults."

"Back to the original question," Pancake said. "Do you guys deal in Fairhope?"

"Some," Sandman said. "Not much."

"Did you know Jason Collins?"

He shook his head.

"Emily Patterson?"

Another headshake.

"Who are they?" Talley asked.

"The two that got themselves killed," Ray said. "Executed might be a better word."

Talley looked at his partner, then back to Pancake. "We don't know anything about that."

"What about Clive and Reba Mack?" Ray asked. "You know them?"

Sandman's back stiffened. "I'm not comfortable talking about this."

Ray held up his phone. "Want to feel seriously uncomfortable?"

Sandman nodded. "Yeah. We know them."

"Thought you might. Tell us your relationship with them."

"We're competitors, I guess you'd say. But not really. We don't do much over there so we've never had any trouble with them."

"You don't supply them with anything?" Pancake asked.

"They have their own sources from what I understand."

"Doesn't that bother you? Losing all that business?"

"We do okay." He shrugged. "Why start a war over a small market." He actually smiled.

"What about a couple of guys who seem to work for them?" Pancake asked. "Jack Reed and Reavis Whitt?"

Now Sandman actually laughed. "Those two? They're losers. Too stupid to be in the business."

"What do you mean?"

"You ever met them?"

"Not yet."

"Well, when you do, you'll see. A couple of redneck mother-fuckers."

"They actually came to us," Talley said. "When was that?" He glanced at Sandman. "Six, eight months ago?" Sandman gave him a hard look. Tally apparently missed it and went on. "Wanted to work with us. Be our guys in that area."

What was that look? Sandman was obviously upset. Maybe he simply didn't want Talley mouthing off about their business. Or tying them in any way to Reed and Whitt. Was there a connection?

Sandman did recover nicely though. Had to give him that. "We blew them off," Sandman said. "Too cocky. Full of themselves. Didn't seem to understand discretion. Could've posed a problem for us. Would've required too much babysitting."

Pancake understood. Drug dealers liked the shadows, not the sunlight. Back alleys, dark barrooms, side roads. Off the radar. Low profile. Not that some didn't go all Tony Montana. Dress flashy, drive expensive cars, live in gaudy houses, throw around wads of money. He didn't see that in these two. So anyone who didn't understand the wisdom of staying low to the ground wouldn't mesh with their business model, so to speak.

"Sound like a smart business decision," Pancake said.

"Exactly."

"Just so we're clear," Ray said. "You don't have a business relationship with the Macks? Or deal with their two boys? You don't know Emily Patterson or Jason Collins? You don't know anything about who might have murdered them? Is that about right?"

"That's it."

Ray stood. "You boys have a nice day."

Sandman stood. "What about the guy you talked to? The DEA guy?"

"What about him?"

"Are we going to hear from him? Is he going to cause us any trouble?"

"Eventually, yes. It's always that way. Sooner or later you'll do something stupid, ping the DEA radar, and they'll come sniffing around. But right here, right now? You're cool as far as we're concerned."

CHAPTER 45

"WHAT DO YOU think?" Nicole asked. "Wait a little longer?"

We had loitered in the driveway for nearly a half hour. At least we hadn't been shot. Or shooed away by the homeowner. We had a direct view of the entire intersection and up Highway 104. So far, no sign of Reed's red truck. Were they still at Sean's? Had they gone out the other way? On down 104? Maybe making deliveries or whatever drug dealers do.

"I don't know. Maybe drive back by and see if they're still there?" I said.

"Better than sitting here. My butt's going to sleep."

"Want me to massage it?"

"Pervert." She smiled. "And I mean that in the best way."

My cell chimed. Tammy.

I wondered what she wanted this time. It was a game I played with myself. Stupid but there it was. She called in fits and spurts. Several times for a couple of weeks then nothing for a while. That's actually when I was most worried. Not about Tammy per se but more about whatever crises were building. Tammy always had a crisis brewing, mostly in her imagination, but when it erupted, somehow I was considered the go-to solution. The game was trying to decide exactly what calamity would be next. A fool's errand. No one could fathom Tammy's brain.

I punched the speaker button.

"Congratulations, Jake," Tammy said.

"Thanks. For what?"

"Walter's in Montgomery for the next two days."

"Okay. Why do I need to know that?"

"Because it's your fault."

Of course it was. Why wouldn't it be?

On she went. "You killed off that simple little divorce case so Walter had to take a bigger one. He has to be up there for two days."

Killed off was an interesting turn of phrase. I started to point that out, but decided not to push my luck.

"Okay."

"Is that all you can say? Okay? You never understand."

This one I was having more than the usual dose of trouble deciphering.

"What am I supposed to understand?" I asked.

A huff of frustration followed. "Walter's gone. I'm here by myself. Rattling around this big old house."

The big old house was on The Point. Around a curve from where Nicole lived in her uncle Charles' house. Tammy's hovel was big, not old, actually very modern, and cost more than my net worth. The good news was I deciphered the reason for the call. Tammy was lonesome. Bored. I was sympathetic. Really, I was, so I said, "Maybe you should have bought a smaller house."

"You mean like that dump you live in?"

Dump? I liked my house. On the sand in Gulf Shores, it was nice. Not The Point nice, but good for me. And there was less rattling-around space.

"But that suits you," Tammy continued. "You couldn't live in this neighborhood."

Not that I would, but I had to ask anyway. "Why?"

She snorted. "You couldn't afford it. Besides, we don't let just anyone live here. We have standards."

"I'd say your community filter is a little porous."

"What does that mean?"

"Nothing. So, why are you calling me?"

"I don't have anything to do. I thought you might have some ideas."

Bingo. Bored.

"You could go bowling. Or miniature golf. Maybe turn off the TV and read a book. That would be a new experience."

"You're an ass." She hung up.

"My day is now complete," Nicole said.

"Let's go do a drive-by," I said.

Nicole cranked the engine.

"Hold it," I said.

Reed's truck swerved through the intersection, turned back toward town. We followed. At a distance. Shielded by a car and a panel truck. Reed and Whitt seemed in no hurry. More likely obeying all the traffic laws because they were carrying. Wouldn't do to get pulled over with a bag of meth in your glove box. Ah, the trials and tribulations of drug dealers.

Their first stop was the lot of Garnet's Furniture. Reed pulled into a space along the side of the building, away from the front windows that were splashed with red and yellow paint announcing "Big Sale" and "All Items Reduced." Whitt rode shotgun, a cell phone to his ear. We parked, well away, sandwiched between two cars.

Two minutes later, a young man, tan slacks, light blue golf shirt, came through the front door. His head swiveled as he scanned the lot. He turned toward the side lot and walked with forced casualness toward the truck. His efforts to go unnoticed were almost comical. Hands in his pockets, smile on his face. I expected him to start whistling. He approached the driver-side window. The exchange was made.

"Free enterprise," I said.

The man headed back toward the store. I snapped a couple of pictures with my iPhone.

The truck backed from the space and climbed back on the road toward downtown. A cigarette hung from Reed's mouth; elbow jacked out the window. Casual, cool.

Reed pulled to the curb near a busy intersection. A young woman, twenties, climbed in the front, Whitt sliding over to give her room. We followed. A spin around the block and the woman was deposited at the same corner. I grabbed her image, too.

"Clever," Nicole said.

"I got to say, they're smart enough to not have a stream of folks coming to their place. That sort of thing attracts attention."

"But it also means they're carrying. A simple traffic stop could do them in."

"According to Warren they've tried but these guys are just full of dumb luck."

"Maybe we should call Warren. Tell her what's happening."

"I'd love to, but right now, I think we should simply follow them. See who they see. Their visit to Sean changes things. Makes me think there's something else going on. As Pancake would say— something feels off kilter."

She smiled at me. "You're becoming a true P.I. Right before my eyes."

"Drive."

She did.

Next stop the parking lot at the Fairhope Municipal Pier. An oval of angled slots around a pleasant, park-like central area, fountain in the middle. Reed pulled in next to a white Toyota minivan. Nicole rolled on around the circle, parked across the way. A brunette sat behind the wheel of the Toyota. Twenties, dark, round sunglasses covering half her face. Sleeveless yellow top, large gold hoop earrings. A child in the back, strapped in a car seat.

"You've got to be kidding," Nicole said.

Whitt jumped from the truck, circled the minivan. The driver's window descended. The transaction completed, he jumped back in the truck and they were off. I captured images of the entire deal.

Now I seriously considered calling Warren. I mulled it while Nicole followed Reed back through downtown, and then to an apartment complex on the north side. The Evergreen Apartments. Not great, not ramshackle. Lots of evergreens. Nicole didn't turn into the lot but rather continued past, pulling to the opposite-side curb a half block away. I twisted in the seat, looked back over my shoulder. Reed and Whitt stepped from the truck. Reed's head swiveled as he scanned the area. On alert. He and Whitt then disappeared inside a first-floor unit.

CHAPTER 46

THE BEST RESTAURANT in the Grand Hotel was Southern Roots. A sweeping panorama of windows looked out over the water, calm tonight. Stars began making their appearance in the darkening sky. Three high-backed, semicircular booths, meshed together in a quad, dominated the center of the room. We settled at the one facing the view. Nicole, Warren, and I enveloped by the bank seat, Ray and Pancake in chairs opposite us.

"Haven't been here in a while," Chief Warren said.

"It's not that far," Ray said.

"Yeah, but they don't pay me enough. Maybe I should consider P.I. work."

"You'd be good at it," Ray said.

"That a job offer?"

Ray shrugged. "Could be."

"Truth is, I love my job. Most of the time. Not so much right now with all this going on."

"Our job has those same moments," Pancake said. "This situation would qualify on all counts."

We had invited Warren down to Point Clear, only a handful of miles south of Fairhope, for dinner. Sort of a thanks for allowing us inside her case. And so we could go over everything we had uncovered.

Earlier, while Nicole and I were in the shower, doing what seems to always happen when we climb under the spray together—I'm not complaining, mind you—she asked me, "What do you make of Reed and Whitt visiting Sean?"

This was taking multitasking too far. I told her that. She said, "You're doing fine."

"Fine? Just fine?"

"Okay, stupendous. Now answer the question."

A war broke out in my brain. One voice saying, pay attention to what you're doing; the other chiming in that answering the question was the only real option. She wouldn't relent, would keep at it until I did the relenting. Okay, okay, I tried to put my body on autopilot—actually not that difficult given the circumstances—and said, "It raises some intriguing questions."

There. That was a good answer. Now, back to business.

"You mean like maybe Sean and those two were involved in Emily's murder?"

Not more questions. Maybe if I ignored her, her questions anyway, and concentrated on the other parts.

Didn't work. Apparently, she was also on autopilot and focused on the newly minted trio of co-conspirators. If that's what they were.

"What do you think? Is that possible?"

I knew the answer to that one. "Possible."

"Which means we need to know more about Reed and Whitt."

"Maybe Warren can help with that."

"I guess we'll know soon."

That seemed to satisfy her curiosity. At least it stopped her interrogation, and I could get back to the business at hand.

We were the last to reach the table. Fifteen minutes late.

"Glad you could join us," Pancake said. He bounced an eyebrow.

"We were talking about the case," Nicole said. Straight faced, not a hint of a smile. "Lost track of time."

That was true. Not completely, but mostly.

Pancake knew better. He said, "Yeah, right."

Drinks were ordered. We all had bourbon, Warren a beer. Said she allowed herself only one a day.

"So, what's new?" she asked. Getting right to it.

"Jake and Nicole have something interesting," Ray said. He nodded toward us.

I told her of us stumbling on Reed and Whitt. Following them to Sean's house.

"Really?"

I nodded. "Any relationship between them that you know of?"

She seemed to consider that. "No. Maybe Sean buys from them?"

"Could be," Nicole said. "We followed them on their rounds after they left Sean's. They made several deliveries before heading back to their apartment."

I told her of the places they had stopped and who they saw, concluding with, "Sold something to a woman with a baby in the car."

Warren sighed. "People. Who can understand them?"

"Jake took pictures," Nicole said. "Of everyone they hooked up with."

"Let's see," Warren said.

I brought the images up on my iPhone and passed it to her. She swiped through them.

"That's Raymond Hopp," Warren said. "Works over at Andrew Garnett's store."

"That was taken in the parking lot," Nicole said.

"I'm sure Andrew would love to know that." More swipes. "Don't know this girl. Downtown street corner." Another swipe. "Jesus." She swiped a couple of more, shaking her head. "Lillian Fowler. With her youngest." She stared at one of the images. "She has two in grammar school, and this one's a year old." She passed the phone back to me. "She has a history of using, but I thought she was clean now."

"Bad habits seem to recycle," I said.

"Sure do," Warren said. "Can you send me those?"

"What's your email?"

Our waitress returned. We ordered dinner while I sent Warren the images.

After the waitress left, I asked Warren, "You're thinking that Reed and Whitt dropping by to see Sean was simply them doing business?"

"Most likely. But it does raise some interesting questions."

"Like maybe Sean and them are involved in the murders?" Pancake asked.

"There's no evidence of that. And Sean has a solid alibi."

"Unless he hired them," Nicole said. She nodded toward me. "Jake believes there was more than one killer. That the whole scenario, the control, the transportation to where they were shot, that a single person couldn't have easily done that."

"I agree," Warren said. "Seems a pair, or more, would be most likely. Reed and Whitt are losers. No doubt. But murderers? I'm not sure they have the smarts or the *cajones* for that."

"Don't have to be too smart to commit a murder," I said.

"Getting away with it is where the brains come in," Warren said.

"What about the Macks?" Nicole asked. "Could they be the ones who set it up? For Sean? Maybe got Reed and Whitt to do the deed?"

Warren folded her hands on the table. "The Macks do hold sway over those two. But I don't know of any connection between them and Sean." She shrugged. "Of course, I didn't know of one between him and Reed and Whitt."

"So, it's possible?" I asked.

"Anything's possible. But this doesn't seem to be in the Macks' wheelhouse. They're business folks if nothing else. Illegal business. But the way I read them is that they wouldn't do anything to jeopardize their income. This could surely do that."

"They like to keep a low profile?" Pancake asked.

"Very low."

"Maybe Reed and Whitt freelanced it," I said.

"Money makes folks do all kinds of things." Ray took a sip of bourbon. "We visited that pair of miscreants over in Mobile. Sandman and Talley. A couple of real beauties. I left with the impression that they did some work with Reed and Whitt."

"Interesting," Warren said. "Not sure the Macks would stand for that."

"If they knew," Pancake said. "But I agree with Ray. Sandman said they had approached him. Wanted to be their dealers in the Fairhope area. Sandman said he passed. Didn't think they were reliable. But I'm not sure that's the truth. Why would Sandman turn his back on a new market? The profit potential is real, and it wouldn't really cost him anything. So Reed and Whitt just might be part of Sandman's crew."

"That means Reed and Whitt would be double-dipping, so to speak," Warren said. "The kind of thing that could spark a range war."

"But how does that bounce back to the murders of Emily and Jason?" Ray asked. "Why would those two, or the Macks for that matter, want them killed? Makes no sense."

"The only people that truly profit from this are Sean and Charlie Martin," I said.

"Charlie?" Warren asked. "That one I don't see."

I told her of our conversations with coworker Phil Varney and bartender Lee Paulson. Of Charlie's anger with Jason and Emily being so close. Of his feelings of jealousy.

"Broken hearts make folks say a lot of stupid stuff," Warren said.

"And do even stupider stuff," Pancake said.

"So, what? Charlie got pissed. Took a gun. Marched Emily and Jason out in a field, and shot them?" She shook her head. "Jason maybe. But from what I hear, not Emily."

"I agree," I said. "I think he's a long shot. But Sean had a lot to gain. The other half of their money, Emily's savings, plus the house. It adds up to an adult number."

"Which means he could afford to hire Reed and Whitt to do it."

"No evidence he moved any money around," Pancake said. "A little to fix his car, which he did. Came to just about the fifteen hundred he transferred. I don't think that'd be enough for a double hit anyway."

Warren nodded. "Even a couple of imbeciles like Reed and Whitt would probably demand more."

"But he stands to come into a pile of cash," I said. "Particularly after he sells the house."

"How much are we talking abut here?" Nicole asked. "What would it take to have two people killed?"

Pancake shrugged. "Five, ten grand, or more, I'd imagine."

"Maybe he put aside a little here and a little there?" Nicole said. "Planned this for a year or more?"

"Or he hasn't paid them yet?" I said.

"Maybe that's why they stopped by today," Pancake said. "Pick up the cash."

"Or maybe remind Sean he owed them," I added.

Warren sat up straight, twisted her torso one way and then the other as if working out a kink. "I'm sensing all roads lead back to Reed and Whitt. Might be time to have a sit-down with them. Sean, too."

"I agree," Ray said. "If they're in bed together, maybe we can peel one of them off. Incentivize someone to turn on the others."

"How would you do that?" I asked.

Ray opened one palm. "Pressure comes in an abundance of flavors."

Warren nodded. "I have to admit that at first I was skeptical. But I like the way you guys work."

Ray smiled. "That feeling goes both ways."

CHAPTER 47

"You sure about this?" Whitt asked.

"Don't really see no other way," Reed replied.

"He ain't going to say nothing. He can't. He's in this up to his pecker."

"But he didn't do it," Reed said. "We did."

Whitt didn't seem to have a reply for that. Reed knew he wouldn't. How could he? That was the truth of it.

They had again driven by Sean's apartment finding it dark and quiet.

"He's probably still out at the house," Reed said. "Probably going to stay the night."

"Unless he's out at a bar somewhere."

"Maybe. Let's just hope he's home."

It was 9:00 p.m. Little traffic, few people on the streets, as they motored through downtown, heading north on Section Street. After leaving the business district behind, Reed pulled into a service station.

"What're we doing here?" Whitt asked. "You got a nearly full tank."

"Grab the gas can out of the back and fill it up."

"Why?"

"We ain't going to leave behind no evidence. At his apartment that wouldn't be too wise, but out there middle of nowhere, no one'll see nothing until the whole place is ashes."

Whitt filled the can, paid, climbed back in the truck.

Five minutes later, they rolled past Fly Creek Marina, its sparsely lit main building and boat slips barely visible through the trees.

"Why don't we turn in there?" Whitt said, pointing to the road that spurred off in that direction. "Drop into Sunset Pointe. Grab something to eat."

"Are you insane? We got business to take care of."

"I'm hungry."

Reed lit a cigarette with a cheap plastic lighter. "You're just trying to delay this deal."

"I'm not either."

"We'll get something later. After we're done."

"It'll be closed then."

"It ain't the only place in town."

They rode quietly for a half mile, then Whitt said, "We should buy a boat sometime."

Reed gave him a look. "What on earth for?"

"You know. Go out in the Gulf. Motor around. Maybe do some fishing."

"You ever fished in your life?"

"No. But I might want to."

"I swear, you come up with the dumbest ideas I ever heard of."

"Ain't no dumber than what we're doing."

"Except we don't have a choice here."

Reed turned onto Highway 104 toward Emily's old house.

"You sure this is necessary?" Whitt asked. "Maybe we should lean on him harder. Make him see that talking wouldn't be healthy."

"That might convince him to keep it to himself," Reed said. "Or it might not. He just might get pressured into talking. Offered some deal for giving us up. Who knows? He might even grow a conscience. Get all guilty inside." He glanced at Whitt. "I'd feel better if none of that was possible."

"I know. I just don't like it."

"You willing to bet your life on him shutting his yap? Willing to risk spending your life up in Kilby or some such? Or sitting in the electric chair?"

"I reckon not."

"Me neither."

Reed slowed as they rolled past Sean's home. A corner lamp dimly lit the living room. The flicker of the TV danced against the windows.

"He's there," Reed said. "Watching TV."

He continued on, reaching Fletcher's Farm. Quiet. The couple obviously down for the night. He spun a U-turn.

"How we going to do this?" Whitt asked.

"I figure we'll park along that little old dirt road near his place. That way if anyone happens to drive by, they won't see my truck sitting there."

"Then what?"

"We knock on the door," Reed said. "Say we need to talk a bit more. Once inside, I'll distract him. You shoot him in the head."

"Why me?"

"Because I did the other two. This one's on you."

Whitt said nothing.

"Then we dump the gas and burn the place down. Clean and simple."

CHAPTER 48

"THANKS FOR THE grub," Warren said. "Not often I get to eat the fancy stuff."

"Our pleasure," Ray said.

She patted her stomach. "I'll need to spend a little extra time at the gym tomorrow."

I held one of the Grand Hotel's massive front doors open for everyone and we exited. The clear night held a slight chill, a breeze sliding off Mobile Bay. We walked up the tree-lined drive to where Warren had parked.

Warren took out a wad of keys. Jangling as she located the one to her black and white SUV. "Looks like we have a plan worked out. A chat with Sean and then Reed and Whitt."

"Might I suggest something?" Ray asked.

"Sure."

"Let us take a run at Reed and Whitt."

Warren looked at him but said nothing.

"We can speak their language."

Pancake grunted, said, "Loud and clear."

"And not run the risk of police intimidation," Ray added.

"But that's the fun part of the job." Warren smiled. "But I see the wisdom in what you're saying." She raised an eyebrow. "Just don't go overboard."

Now, Ray smiled. "Wouldn't dream of it."

"Yeah, right." She nudged Pancake with an elbow. "With this guy around I suspect the intimidation factor alone will be enough."

"Me?" Pancake said. Mock shock on his face. "I'm a teddy bear. Ray's much more dangerous."

That was actually true. Pancake could tear you up, maybe even bring down an entire building, but Ray? Ray had been trained by the best of the best. I don't think even he knew his full capabilities.

Warren's phone buzzed. She answered, walking a few steps away.

What I heard was, "What?" and "You're kidding?" and "I'm on the way."

She disconnected the call and turned back toward us.

"What is it?" I asked.

"That was Burt Moody. Sean's house is on fire."

"We'll follow you," Ray said.

Warren hesitated briefly, then nodded. "Okay, but I'm going to light it up. Try to keep up."

I looked at Nicole. She smiled. Like the big bad wolf.

With the ease and efficiency of a Formula 1 driver, Nicole followed Warren as we bounced over to Highway 98/Greene Road and turned north. This would bypass downtown, make the trip up to Sean's faster. And attract less attention. Nicole hung on Warren's bumper. A little too close for me. I knew better than to say anything. Rather, I held on and mentally uttered a few prayers. Pancake and Ray did their best to keep up, the headlights from Pancake's truck gyrating behind us.

When we squeezed a left turn onto Highway 104, I could smell smoke. Engine, brakes, tires? No, this was the acrid odor of burning wood.

Emily's place—I still considered it hers for some reason—came into view. Two firetrucks sat in the front yard. Thick sprays of water arched over the remains of the structure from two hoses wrestled into position by a pair of firemen. The flames had been beaten down. Smoke curled skyward from where the left front corner of the roof had collapsed, leaving a defect, and from the two front windows that appeared to have shattered. Though blackened, the walls still stood.

Moody, hands shoved in his pockets, loitered next to who I recognized as Carl Fletcher, watching us as we climbed from our vehicles. We walked that way.

"Burt." Warren nodded to Moody, then to Fletcher. "Carl? What brings you here?"

"Carl discovered the fire," Moody said.

Fletcher gave a quick head nod. "I smelled the smoke. I guess the wind was just right to push it down toward my place."

He pointed to the smoldering remains of the home. Indeed, the smoke trailed to the east, toward Fletcher's Farm.

"Seemed strong so I knew it was nearby," Fletcher continued. "Walked out on my porch and saw the glow beyond the trees." He scratched an ear. "Didn't know what it was so I slipped on some clothes and drove over. Found the house in flames. Called nine-one-one."

"See anybody?" Warren asked.

"No. I got as close as I could, while I waited for the fire crew to get here. Tried to see if anyone was in there. It was burning pretty hot. Yelled a few times. Didn't get any response."

Warren scanned the area. She pointed toward the metallic gray Chevy sedan near the garage. "Isn't that Sean's car?"

"It is," I said.

Warren turned toward the ashes. "You suppose he's in there?"

"God, I hope not," Nicole said.

Warren gave a wave to one of the firemen. He was near the truck closest to the smoke, talking with a younger-looking guy. The man acknowledged her wave and headed our way. Warren introduced us to the fire chief, Rory Fleetwood.

"Looks like we managed to save a good deal of it," Fleetwood said. "Thanks to Carl." He nodded toward Fletcher. "Not that it'll be habitable anytime soon. Probably not ever."

"Anyone been inside yet?" Warren asked.

"Nope. Been too hot."

"That's Sean Patterson's car," she said, pointing in that direction.

Fleetwood looked at her. "I didn't think anyone lived here. Not since . . . not since the murders."

"Apparently he's been prepping it to sell. Guess he could be here this late. Maybe even stay over some nights."

Fleetwood sighed. "We got it mostly under control. Should be able to go look around soon."

It was another thirty minutes before Fleetwood slipped on his hard hat, and he and another fireman disappeared through the damaged front door. We waited. Not long.

The grim look on Fleetwood's face as he waved us over from his perch on the front porch was evident even in the dark.

"We've got two bodies," he said.

"Two?" I asked.

"They're actually pretty well preserved."

That was a surprise, given the fact that everything else seemed blackened.

"One is Sean Patterson. The other guy I don't know." He looked at Warren. "Pretty obvious they both were shot."

Warren took in a deep breath and puffed it out. "When can I go in and take a look?"

"Now. My guys say the floor is sound and the walls are amazingly stable." He pointed to one of the front windows. "Looks to me like these front windows popped late in the whole deal. The guy who started this wasn't smart enough to open the windows. Feed the fire. So it burned a lot slower than it could have."

"So this is definitely arson?" Warren asked.

"Oh yeah. Started in the living room where the bodies are. Fire seemed to move toward the back of the house where there was an open window. Helped preserve the bodies. Arson? You bet. You'll smell the gasoline as soon as you get inside."

We moved through the door.

"Just watch your step," Fleetwood said, following us.

The inside smelled of charred wood, and yes, gasoline. The sofa was charred but still upright. As was the coffee table before it. Two bodies lay beyond, toward the dining room. Both were charred, but neither severely damaged. That made no sense to me, but then I'm not an expert in charred bodies. Barbecued ribs is about as close as I get. But Chief Fleetwood was correct. They were damaged, but definitely recognizable.

Sean Patterson lay on his back. Clothes burned to black threads, flesh charred. A single entry wound clearly visible through the singed hair on the left side of his head.

The other body lay chest down, face twisted toward me. Reavis Whitt. No doubt.

CHAPTER 49

"What's the plan?" Ray asked Warren.

"Knock on his door," she said. "See if he's home and what he has to say."

The finding of Reavis Whitt's body along with Sean Patterson's in the relic of Emily's old house pointed the finger directly at Jack Reed. He and Whitt were partners in crime and both knew Sean. Nicole and I had seen that firsthand. Just hours earlier. So, when the first name that came out of Warren's mouth was Jack Reed, it seemed logical.

Did this mean Reed was in some cabal with Whitt and Sean? A murder for hire? And now Reed was getting rid of all the witnesses? That was Ray's take. Warren's, too.

We were parked at the far end of the Evergreen Apartments lot, a good hundred and fifty feet from Reed's apartment. Pancake had already determined that Reed lived in the apartment Nicole and I had seen him and Whitt enter earlier. Whitt two doors down.

"He'll be armed," Pancake said.

Warren nodded. "He sells drugs. Meth and guns go hand in hand. So, I suspect he is."

"Maybe with the murder weapon," Ray said.

"That'd be nice."

It would? Personally, I'd prefer it if he wasn't armed. Sure, finding the proverbial smoking gun would be helpful, even solve the entire case, but I envisioned the smoke twisting up from a muzzle pointed in our direction.

Warren pulled her service weapon. A Glock nine. She ejected the clip, slammed it back in place, reseated it at her hip.

"Here's how it'll go. Burt and I'll make contact. You guys lay back. If this doesn't go well, I don't want any citizens involved."

"We'll provide backup though," Ray said.

"I won't say no to that."

We passed Whitt's place, dark, and neared Reed's apartment. No light through the curtained window, no sound. Warren and Moody flanked the door. Ray and Pancake to one side, each with a weapon hanging at their sides. Nicole and I stood near a tree, twenty feet away, and out of the line of fire. Nicole wasn't happy with that. Said she would Krav Maga the dude if he made a false move. I told her that the line between bravery and stupidity was thin. She punched my ribs. Hard.

No answer to Warren's knock. She rapped the doorframe louder, said, "Police department. Mr. Reed, if you're in there, make yourself known."

Silence. Then movement, light pushed against the drapes. The door cracked open. Reed. Rubbing one eye with a balled fist.

"What's going on?" he asked.

"Need to ask a couple of questions."

"What time is it?"

"Early," Warren said. "Or late. Depends on your perspective."

He looked at Moody, then seemed to notice Ray and Pancake, finally Nicole and me. "What's this about?"

"Maybe we should talk inside."

He hesitated, debating, then stepped back. We all entered.

Reed examined each of us, finally resting his gaze on Chief Warren. "So, what is this? A party?"

"Something like that," Warren said. When Reed lowered his gaze to the floor, avoiding eye contact, Warren said, "Look at me." His head came up. "Where've you been the last few hours?"

"Here. Asleep."

"What time did you go to bed?"

"Early. Eight or thereabouts."

"That does sound early," she said. "Guy like you. Seems to me most of your business would take place in the dark of night."

"What does that—" He caught himself, changed directions. "I ain't been sleeping well lately. I was tired. Trying to catch up on my beauty sleep." He smiled.

"Sounds like a guilty conscience to me," Pancake said.

Reed's smile evaporated. "Who the hell are you?"

"One of the backup singers."

That seemed to confuse him. Questions behind his eyes, brow knitted. What I didn't see was any hint of fatigue. Or that he had been asleep. No redness to his eyes, no puffiness, no excessive blinking, hair revealing no disarray. As if he almost expected us and had worked out his story.

"Where's your buddy Reavis Whitt?" Warren asked.

"Not my week to keep up with him."

"Listen, Jack, you can be an ass, and I can make this very difficult. Or you can answer my questions and maybe, just maybe, we'll go away."

"My guess is that this time of night he's sleeping, too," Reed nodded toward one wall. "He lives just down the way."

"I know. But that isn't where he is."

"Then you know more than I do."

"When did you last see him?" Warren asked.

"This afternoon."

"Where?"

"We had some business to take care of. We were all over."

"Maybe Garnet's Furniture? Down by the pier?"

He stared at her.

"Maybe out at Sean Patterson's place?"

"I told you, I've been here. Asleep."

"Interesting that you'd go there," Warren said. "I was talking about earlier today."

Lines of worry dug into Reed's face. That look you get when you screw up. Like when your mom catches you in a lie. Of course, this was worse than that. By a mile.

Warren continued. "Did you and Reavis drop by and see Sean earlier? This afternoon?"

"Why would we?"

She took a step toward him, capturing his attention. I imagined her gym-pumped arms and balled fists looked like sledgehammers about now.

"So, if I had a couple of witnesses who put you guys there, you'd hold to that line of thinking?"

"No, wait a minute." He snapped his fingers. "We did go by. Just for a minute." He shrugged. "I forgot."

"Convenient." She waited a beat. "Why were you there?"

"Just chatting."

"He a customer of yours?"

Another stare. More tension lines.

"Didn't think you'd want to talk about that." She sighed.

"Yeah. We do a little business with him. Went to collect some money."

There it was. Tell half the truth. Cop to a minor crime to cover a bigger one. Seem all honest and forthcoming. Even I knew that ploy and I wasn't a cop. Or a P.I.

"Money for what?" Warren asked.

A look settled over his face. One that said he'd just stepped in it. Maybe fell in it. He was grinding to come up with something, anything, that sounded reasonable. Finally, he said, "I don't really know but I think he owed Reavis a few bucks."

Actually, an excellent recovery. One that required no proof and allowed no follow-up. If such a debt existed, which I didn't believe for a minute, the two parties to said debt were dead. Reed only had to play dumb.

"Mind if we take a look around?" Warren asked.

"Look for what?"

"Something. Anything."

"I do mind."

"I can get a warrant."

"You do that. But I ain't going to just let you wander around my place. Plant some shit."

Warren nodded. "Yeah, we do that all the time."

"Wouldn't surprise me none."

"So to be clear," Warren said, "you and Whitt saw Sean this afternoon, to collect a debt, but you didn't go out there tonight?"

"No."

"And you don't know where Whitt is?"

"He said he might hit a couple of bars. Maybe you should go sniff around a few of those. Or you might find him in bed."

Warren twisted her neck as if working out a kink. "He isn't at any of those places. He's in a body bag headed to the coroner's office."

"What?"

His innocent expression wasn't even close to convincing. I now had no doubt that our earlier thoughts were correct. Reed was the shooter. For Sean and Whitt. Maybe for Emily and Jason. The question was, why? What was in it for him? Some dispute among the three might account for Sean and Whitt. Drugs, money, and guns leave behind dead bodies all the time. But Emily? Why? If he did do her and Jason, were tonight's killings an attempt to eliminate witnesses? If so, it brought Sean right back into the picture. Alibi or not. What before had been simply confusing was now a writhing snake pit. And the list of people who knew the truth was dwindling by the minute.

"We found him in the middle of a house fire. Along with Sean Patterson." Warren took a deep breath, let it out slowly. "But I'm sure you know nothing about that."

"I don't."

"You better pray I can't put you there. But as stupid as you are, I'm sure that'll happen before long."

CHAPTER 50

WE LOITERED OUTSIDE Whitt's apartment. Pancake suggested we simply kick the door down. Wasn't like Whitt would complain. Being dead and all. Warren nixed the idea. Not the smart approach. She needed to make sure any evidence inside found its way into a courtroom. Not against Whitt, that was a done deal, but maybe to help put Reed away for the rest of his life. I guessed she felt even dead guys had Fourth Amendment rights. Really?

Instead, she called a friendly judge—maybe not so friendly for being awakened—to get a verbal warrant. With Whitt being a homicide victim, that was an easy ask. She also tried to get one for Reed's apartment. Boy, would I love to see his face when she waved that at him. But the judge declined. Apparently, he said she had no real evidence against him and therefore had no probable cause. Disappointing but understandable.

She dispatched Moody to grab a key from the manager. I followed him.

"I like Reed for all of this," Moody said.

"I do, too," I agreed.

"Definitely for Sean and Whitt. That's easy. But I can even see him for Emily and Jason. Just not sure why."

"Maybe Sean hired him?" I said. "He's the one with a motive here."

"Not anymore."

We turned around the back of the building and moved across an open courtyard that was enveloped by the other buildings in the complex. A few trees and couple of seating clusters. Nothing special.

"The problem is, we found no wads of money taken from his accounts," I said.

"How do you know that?"

"We have ways."

"I bet."

"Pancake," I said. "He handles firewalls like he did defensive linemen and linebackers."

"From the looks of him, even a concrete wall wouldn't slow him down."

"True. What's the going rate for a contract murder around here?"

"Don't know. We've never had that kind of thing in our domain. I do remember one. Over in Mobile. Maybe four or five years ago. I think a guy paid twenty K to have his business partner whacked."

"Sean took out fifteen hundred but he used that to repair his car. Other than that, nothing to raise suspicion."

The manager lived in unit number one, corner of the building farthest from the road. He wasn't happy. Maybe seventy, hair disheveled, bathrobe, scowl. He listened as Moody told him that he needed into Reavis Whitt's apartment.

"You try knocking on the door?" His unshaven chin jutted toward us.

"He won't answer," Moody said. "He's dead."

The old man wavered, took a step back. "What are you talking about?"

"He was murdered."

"Here?"

"No. We need to search his place. See if we can find any clues as to who might've done it."

The man hesitated, nodded. He turned toward the wall just inside the door. A peg board with several wads of keys suspended by small hooks. A pair of car keys with a small red Swiss Army knife attached. A half a dozen larger loops with a dozen keys each. Probably one for each unit. He grabbed a single key attached to a six-inch strip of translucent plastic, "Master" in black block letters. He handed it to Moody.

"This here's the master. Opens all the units."

"Thanks."

"Be sure to bring it back."

"Will do."

"Any idea how long you'll be?"

Moody shrugged. "As long as it takes."

The manager nodded. "Just drop it in my mailbox when you're done." He pointed to the gold metallic flip-top next the the door. He closed the door.

Inside, Whitt's place was neater than I had suspected. Sparsely furnished, but all seemed in order. A water bong, a small bag of marijuana, and a yellow plastic dinner plate sat on a wooden coffee table. On the plate a straw, a razor blade, and a few grains of white powder.

"Meth or coke," Warren said.

One bedroom, one bath, small kitchenette. No sign of a struggle. Not that one was expected. The chaos went down at Emily's house. The bed was unmade, the mirrored closet slider open. Clothes neatly hung, a pair of jeans and a green tee shirt wadded on the floor. Next to them sat a cardboard banker's box. Top off, leaning against the back wall. Inside, disarrayed papers and a smaller metal box, open, empty.

"Probably where he kept his drug money," Ray said.

Warren nodded. "He, or somebody, emptied it."

"Reed," Ray said.

"That'd be my guess."

"You know he killed them?" Ray said.

"I know." She sighed. "The problem will be proving it."

"Are you still thinking this is related to drugs and bad deals?" Nicole asked.

Warren closed and opened her left fist a couple of times. "Maybe. I can see Reed, Whitt, and Sean getting into it. Sean the customer, the other two dealers. Money gets sideways, ill will enters, and shit happens. What I don't see is how Emily and Jason fit in here."

"Maybe there are connections we don't see yet."

Warren looked at Nicole. "Could be."

"Are we sure the two events are connected?" I asked. "Couldn't each murder be more random than that?"

"Possible," Warren said. "But I don't believe that. We don't get this stuff around here. When it happens twice. One on the tail of the other." She shrugged. "They're connected until proven otherwise."

"A murder for hire would snug the pieces together," Pancake said. "We just don't have the money trail yet."

"What now?" I asked.

"Time to rattle the cages," Warren said. "Stir up the natives. I think I'll drop by and see what the Macks are up to."

"You think they're involved in this?" I asked.

"I think Reed and the late Reavis Whitt don't do do-wah-diddy without Clive and Reba knowing about it. Especially if it's got anything to do with their livelihood. So if I believe, and I do, that Reed and Whitt had something to do with the original two killings, the Macks are likely in there somehow."

"Me and Pancake will head back to Mobile," Ray said. "Have another chat with Sandman. His connection to Reed and Whitt is deeper than he wanted us to believe. Time to explain things to him."

"Explain ain't exactly the right word," Pancake said. "Last time we were polite. I'm about done with cordiality."

"If you get in trouble over there, give me a call," Warren said. "I know the chief."

"Won't be any trouble," Pancake said.

CHAPTER 51

WE FOLLOWED WARREN and Moody to the Macks' place. I was surprised she let us. We asked, she hesitated, but finally agreed.

"Witnesses might be good," she said. "So they can't accuse Burt and me of harassment. Or brutality if it comes to that."

I had second thoughts on the way. I think it was Warren's use of the word "brutality" that creeped in my head.

"This could go badly," I said.

"How so?" Nicole asked.

"They're drug dealers. Cops knock on their door in the middle of the night. They have guns. Little things like that."

She smiled. "Don't worry. I'll protect you."

"You?"

"I know Krav Maga."

Just enough to be dangerous, I thought. Didn't say it though. I knew better.

Turned out, the Macks were night owls. Watching TV. Clive with a beer, Reba a glass of white wine, the aroma of marijuana in the air. Your typical home movie night.

After Clive answered the door, invited us in, reluctantly, we gathered in the living room. We stood, facing Clive. Reba never moved from her place on the sofa, but the hostility in her face radiated throughout the room.

"What the hell do you want?" she asked.

"Sorry to bother you," Warren said. "Just a couple of questions."

"Couldn't it wait until sunup?"

"Not really."

"You'd rather push your badge around, I suppose," Reba said.

"Something like that." Warren crossed her arms over her chest. Muscles bulged. "What do you know about what went down out at Sean's Patterson's place tonight?"

"What are you talking about?" Clive asked.

"I take it you two have been here all night?"

"Yeah, we have," Reba said.

"All night?"

Reba now looked a little confused. Maybe even a hint of concern. Badass only goes so far when the law is standing in your living room. Especially when the law looked like she could whip your ass without breaking a sweat.

"We grabbed dinner," Clive said. "Over at The Rib Shack. Got back here about six thirty. Ain't been nowhere since."

Warren nodded.

"You can check if you want," Reba said. "Lots of folks saw us over there."

Clive took a slug of beer. "What's going on?"

"Somebody killed Sean Patterson. Your boy Reavis Whitt, too. Torched the house."

Reba actually recoiled. A hint of fear entered her face. Interesting. Was she that good an actress or was she truly shocked? Did they really know nothing about it?

"What about Jack Reed?" Warren asked. "You see him tonight?"

"Why would we?" Reba asked.

Warren massaged the back of her neck. Her bicep looked like a tumor. "Okay. Let's not play games. Reed and Whitt work for you. Deal for you. The whole world knows that. So cut the crap. Did you see him tonight or not?"

"No."

"You don't think Jack did this, do you?" Clive asked.

"He's right near the top of my list."

Now, Clive looked confused. "No way. He and Reavis are like brothers. He'd never."

"And Sean? He a customer of yours?"

"Not that we know," Clive said.

Reba shot him a look. One that said he shouldn't be offering any information.

"Look," Clive said. "We have no idea what Jack and Reavis do. Who they see. Who they do business with."

Warren smiled. "You expect me to believe that? It's your business. And neither of you strike me as the type to leave anything to chance."

"Well, we don't know anything about any of this," Reba said.

"Okay, I'll play. Let's say, for the sake of argument, you're totally innocent. Who would do this? Anyone trying to muscle in on your business? Anyone who would want Reavis Whitt gone? Or Sean?"

"No." Clive glanced at Reba. "We don't have any of those problems."

"In your business you don't have to go looking for trouble. It'll find you."

"We ain't got no problems," Clive said. "And we don't know shit about any of this."

"You know a couple of guys from Mobile?" Warren asked. "In your line of work. Alex Talley and a dude they call Sandman?"

Reba hesitated, considering. "Yeah. We know of them. Don't really know them."

"That a fact?"

"It is. They stay over there; we hang around here."

"Any chance Jack Reed works for them?"

Another hesitation. Reba shook her head. "No. He doesn't."

"You sure? We have reason to believe otherwise."

Nothing. Neither Clive nor Reba responded. You could almost hear their collective mental wheels turning. Finally, Reba spoke.

"He better not be," she said.

"Maybe you should have a chat with him."

She drained her wineglass. "Maybe I will."

Outside, Warren stood in the open door of her SUV. "That went well," she said.

"I'd say you got their attention." I looked back toward the house. "Wouldn't want to be in Jack Reed's shoes."

Warren nodded. "Better than a body bag." She tapped the roof of the vehicle. "Hope Ray and Pancake find something we can use. Shake the tree without knocking it down."

"Pancake likes knocking things down," Nicole said. "It's a hobby for him."

Warren jangled the keys she held. "I hope I don't hear from them again tonight." She sighed. "Drop by the office in the morning and we'll go over everything."

She climbed in and she and Moody drove away.

When we got back to the hotel, I didn't see Pancake's truck. I considered calling and checking in. Thought better of it. I didn't want to interrupt whatever they were doing. I had a mental image of Pancake tying someone in a knot. Literally.

We went to our room where I stretched out on the bed, while Nicole washed her face. I needed to think about things. An idea was rummaging around in my brain. Not sure how it fit yet, but it was beginning to take shape.

When she came out of the bathroom, she wore one of the hotel's plush robes. "What are you doing?" she asked.

"Thinking."

"Don't hurt yourself."

"Funny. Actually, I'm coming up with an idea about how all this might fit together."

"Like how?"

"Let me ponder it some more."

"Well, I'm going to save you from all that painful rumination."

"Oh, really?"

"Really." She dropped the robe, exposing, well, everything. "I'm going to turn your brain to oatmeal."

And so she did.

CHAPTER 52

PANCAKE SAT ON the edge of the mattress, canting it decidedly in his direction. Sandman, sleeping facedown, head beneath the pillow, one arm draped over the top, stirred but didn't awaken. Ray flipped on the bedside lamp. Still no reaction.

"Hey," Pancake said. He followed it with a not so gentle kidney punch.

Sandman jerked, rolled from beneath the pillow. His now wide-open, glassy eyes reflected the light.

"What the . . . ?"

"How you doing?" Pancake asked. "Comfy?"

Sandman's gaze jerked left toward the bedside table.

Ray held up the Glock he had scooped up. "Looking for this?"

Confusion didn't quite cover the expression on Sandman's face. He tried to sit up. Pancake flattened a palm against his chest and pressed him into the mattress.

"What the hell are you doing?" Sandman asked.

"Trying to decide what to do with this," Ray said. He ejected the clip, popped out the chambered round, deftly catching it in midflight. "Maybe take it over to Fairhope. Hand it off the Chief Warren. See if she can match it to the bullets the coroner extracted from a couple of corpses."

"Who the hell do you think you are?" Sandman now somewhere between indignant and scared.

"Me?" Pancake said. "I'm the one who's going to shove your sternum against your spine. Flatten your heart like a pancake." He smiled. "No pun intended."

"How'd you get in here?"

"Your security's a bit flimsy."

"What do you want?"

"Just a few questions," Ray said.

"Like hell. Get the fuck out of here."

Pancake increased the pressure on Sandman's chest. "You don't listen very well, do you?"

"You can't break in here and threaten me."

"Want to call the cops?" Ray asked. He picked up the cell phone from the table. "I can punch in nine-one-one for you."

"Or I can punch your lungs into mush," Pancake added. "Totally your call."

Sandman's adrenalin-expanded pupils now blackened his eyes. Sweat peppered his face. His gaze gyrated around the room, looking for some way to escape.

"Now, listen up," Ray said. "Answer our questions and we might walk away without doing you any damage."

"Not too much anyway," Pancake said.

Sandman looked from Pancake to Ray.

"We asked the last time we were here, but I'm not convinced you were being entirely truthful," Ray said. "So we're giving you a chance to set the record straight." He took a step forward and looked down at Sandman. "If you lie, it'll be the most painful decision you've ever made. Understand?"

Sandman nodded. His breathing was short, raspy.

"You know anything about a couple of double murders over in Fairhope?"

"What are you taking about?"

"A young couple," Pancake said. "Executed a few days ago. Out in a rural area."

"Like I told you before, I don't know nothing about that. Didn't even know them."

"One of them wasn't a customer of yours?"

"No."

"The meth we found at the scene wasn't yours?"

"I don't go over that way."

"What about your boy Jack Reed?" Ray asked. "Or Reavis Whitt?"

"I told you that, too. They aren't part of my crew."

Ray nodded. "Let me tell you what I think. You signed them on to make an inroad into that area. Move in on the Macks' territory. A bit of a spat broke out, and you hired Reed and Whitt to make waves for them. Maybe even frame them for the murders."

Sandman again tried to sit up. Pancake, palm still flat against his chest, applied more of his body weight.

"Look, okay, I did have them move some product over there. Not much. It was more or less an experiment. See if it was worth looking in that direction. But I don't know anything about the rest of it."

Pancake studied him. Fear and desperation etched his face. He sensed Sandman was telling the truth. So far. "What about Sean Patterson? You know him?"

He shook his head. "Who is he?"

"He's the one who got a bullet in his head. Along with Reavis Whitt. Got his house torched."

"What?" His eyes glistened. He looked as if he might cry. "Whitt was killed?"

"Just a few hours ago."

Sandman gulped some air. "I don't know anything about it."

"We think Jack Reed was the shooter. Started the fire." Ray examined the Glock again. "What we want to know is if you paid him to do it."

"Of course not. Why would I?"

"That's what we're asking."

"I didn't. Makes no sense. Why would I want to get involved in something that doesn't affect me? Something like this? No way."

"What about Jack Reed? Would he?"

"I barely know him. And that's the truth."

"He sells for you," Pancake said.

"Not much. And about now I wish I'd never met him."

Pancake chuckled. "I imagine so."

"This is your one chance," Ray said. "You screw this up, and we'll be back. And next time we really won't play nice."

Sandman was now in full panic mode.

Ray continued. "Just so we're clear. You know nothing about the murders? You didn't hire Reed or Whitt to do anything stupid?"

"No."

"And you know nothing of the murders of Sean Patterson and Reavis Whitt?"

"I don't. I swear."

"Hope you're being truthful," Pancake said. "I truly do."

"I am."

Ray nodded. He tossed the clip and the bullet into the nearby wastebasket, the gun on the bed.

Pancake stood. "Have a nice evening."

They left.

Pancake pulled from the curb. "I believe him."

"Me, too,"

"Puts the crosshairs squarely on Jack Reed."

"It does do that."

CHAPTER 53

"So, you're thinking the oh-so-wonderful Mr. Sandman and his sidekick Talley are free and clear on this?" Warren asked.

Ten-fifteen a.m. Warren and the four of us gathered around the Fairhope PD conference table.

"Don't know for sure about Talley," Ray said. "Didn't talk to him. Doesn't really matter. Sandman runs the show. But, yes, I do believe he's clean on this one."

"We had a pleasant chat with him last night," Pancake said.

Warren smiled. "Bet *pleasant* isn't the best word."

"Not so much for him," Pancake said. "He was afraid of Ray."

"I think that was you."

"You had the gun."

"I did," Ray said. "But you had you."

"Well, there is that."

Ray gave us a sketch of their visit. "Sandman did give up that Reed and Whitt had done some dealing for him over here."

"Really?" Warren asked. "I don't think the Macks would take that lightly." Her brow furrowed. "You don't think this could be the beginning of a range war between them and Sandman, do you?"

Ray shook his head. "I don't. We walked away thinking he didn't know anything about the murders."

"Wouldn't be in his best interest to meddle over here," Pancake said. "Not on that level anyway. Sure, he tested the waters with Reed and Whitt, but he's got no real motive for bringing this kind of grief into his world."

"So we can slide him off the front burner?" Warren asked.

"That'd be my take," Ray said. "What about the Macks?"

"Same thing. I don't think they'd do this. Again, too much grief." Warren looked at me.

"I agree. Looked to me like Sean and Whitt getting killed spooked them."

Warren sighed. "That leaves Jack Reed as the last man standing."

"You're going to love this." It was Moody. He entered carrying a laptop. "You know I stopped by all the service stations between here and the Patterson house?"

"And?" Warren asked.

"Well, none of them remember Reed and Whitt pumping gas there last night. No receipts or anything like that. But the one up there just north of town?" He held up the computer. "Golden."

"Let's see it."

Moody settled the laptop on the table and flipped it open. The screen churned to life. "This was recorded around 8:00 p.m. last night. An hour before Carl Fletcher called in the fire."

According to Moody, the footage came from the station's single security camera. Fortunately, it covered the two pumps out front. Grainy but good enough. Reed's red truck pulled up. Whitt climbed out, disappeared from the angle. Probably went inside to pay. He returned, grabbed a gas can from the back, lifted a pump nozzle, filled the can. He replaced the nozzle and climbed in the truck. They drove away.

"Good job," Warren said. "I think we just found our accelerant."

"And good evidence that Reed and Whitt were together last night," Ray said. "Around the time of the murders."

"But it doesn't put Reed at the murder scene," Warren said. "Not tight enough to go cuff him."

"True," Ray said.

Warren tapped a finger on the table. "What I don't see is his motive. For Jason and Emily for sure. It doesn't make sense."

"Maybe Jason and Sean owed him money," Moody said. "Maybe they made some waves. He pressed them to pay, they responded by threatening exposure."

"So Reed and Whitt killed Emily and Jason?" Nicole asked. "Because Jason was going to rat them out? Then Reed did Sean and Whitt for the same reason? And to eliminate any witnesses? Is that what you're saying?"

"Wouldn't be the first time a rat nest ended in an internal war," Warren said. "But why would Reed kill Whitt? He was Reed's buddy."

"He seemed like a weak sister to me," Pancake said. "Maybe Reed couldn't trust him anymore. If he and Reed did Emily and Jason, and then Sean, Whitt had the keys to the jailhouse. Could've walked in here and sold Reed out for a deal."

"He didn't," Warren said.

"But Reed could've feared he was wobbling in that direction."

Warren considered that. "I've never heard of any strife on the home front." She looked at Moody. "You?"

"Nope. Every time I've had the pleasure of chatting with them, they seemed solid."

"Still," Warren said, "we do come back to Reed as the last straw in the drink."

"What is it?" Ray asked me. "You look like you have something to say."

"I was thinking last night."

"Bet that hurt," Pancake said.

"Do you and Nicole use the same writers?" I asked.

Pancake shrugged. "Is what it is."

"Thinking about what?" Ray asked.

"I don't have this completely worked out," I said. I looked at Nicole. "I might've if Nicole hadn't distracted me."

"I want to hear this," Pancake said.

"It wasn't difficult," she said. "Jake doesn't function well when confronted with a naked woman."

"Not what you said last night," I said.

She raised an eyebrow. "I should've qualified that. His brain doesn't function well."

"Story of his life," Ray said.

I looked at Warren, who was clearly amused. "I could blame it on bad parenting, but my mom was cool."

"So, where did all these mental gymnastics lead you?" Ray asked.

"Looking at all the players in this Greek tragedy, I kept coming back to the same question. Who stands to gain from the murder of Emily and Jason? That's where I think this all started. The answer was always Sean. Let's say Emily was the real target. Jason was merely in the wrong place at the wrong time. What would Sean gain? A free divorce. Emily's money. The house, which is a pretty good chunk of change."

"But Sean's dead," Pancake said.

"He didn't know that would be his fate when he started the ball rolling. He knows Reed and knew Whitt. Through drug deals if nothing else. Maybe more. What if he hired them to kill Emily?"

"Would they do that?" Ray asked Warren.

"I wouldn't put much past Jack Reed. His moral compass is a little bent. Whitt? He's a follower. Whatever Jack says, he'll go with it."

"Where'd Sean get the money for this?" Ray asked.

"I looked into his world," Pancake said. "He didn't make any moves that would suggest that."

Ray nodded. "Something like that would take a few thousand. Ten or so, I'd guess."

"I'll get to that," I said. "So Reed and Whitt do Emily and Jason. Maybe with all the scrutiny that followed, Reed got nervous. Worried that you—" I nodded toward Warren—"or us, might connect the dots back to him. Who knew of the plan? Who was part of it? Reed, Whitt, and Sean. Maybe Reed was cleaning house."

"A secret among three folks can only be kept if two of them are dead," Pancake said.

"Back to the money to do all this," Warren said. "Where'd Sean come up with it? And hide the fact that he had it?"

"We talked about this," Pancake said. "Sean was coming into money. Maybe he was going to pay after he sold the house?"

"Then why would Reed kill him?" Nicole asked.

Warren sighed. "I don't think he would."

"That's not what I'm thinking anyway," I said.

"Okay," Ray said. "Let's have it."

"It's tricky. And I'm not sure Sean is smart enough to have rigged this whole enterprise. But I read about a case a few years ago. It was on the net. Up in the Midwest somewhere. Indiana, Illinois, I forget the details. A guy wanted to off his business partner. Take over the entire deal without the expense of a buyout. He hired a hit man. Knew that if he moved any of his money around, he'd have a lot of explaining to do. So, he arranged a robbery of the business. The gunman came in, walked with around twenty grand if I remember correctly. That paid for the hit."

Warren stiffened. "The robbery over at Watkins' Lumber?"

"Exactly."

"Sean worked there," Pancake said. "And was there the night of the robbery."

I nodded. "He and the bookkeeper. Around closing time."

"The perfect time," Ray said.

"And don't forget," Pancake said. "Reed worked there briefly."

"With Sean," Nicole added.

"Could be where they first hooked up," I said. "As user-supplier and ultimately as co-conspirators in murder. Regardless, Fred Watkins said they took eighteen thousand in cash from the safe."

Pancake gave a grunt. "Definitely enough for a double murder."

"Jesus," Warren said. "That would surely tie things up with bright yellow ribbon." She glanced at Moody. "If we can prove it."

Moody smiled. "Track the money."

"Without spooking Reed," Warren said. "I want him nice and comfortable."

"Maybe making him uncomfortable would be better," Ray said. "Folks, particularly those that aren't all that bright, when placed under a bit of pressure, make mistakes. I think Reed might fall into that category."

Warren considered that, stared at her hands, now flattened on the table, right index finger lightly tapping its surface. She looked up. "What do you have in mind?"

"Pancake and I'll drop by. Reiterate our condolences on Whitt's death. Let him know Sandman tossed him under the bus on his double crossing the Macks. See how he reacts."

"That's it? A nice civil chat?"

Ray smiled. "More or less."

"It's the *more* I'm worried about."

Pancake jumped in. "Can't hurt to have a little talk. Shake him up. Make him think he has a way out. Offer up a chance to put this off on someone else."

"Like who?" Warren asked.

"The Macks. Sandman. Whoever else might pop up."

Warren held his gaze for a beat. "How are you going to do that?"

"We have ways." Pancake smiled. "Who knows? Maybe he'll screw up. Say something stupid. Once he thinks he has a way out and thinks we're onboard with considering others, who knows what he'll say?"

Warren hesitated, finally said, "Okay. But try to play nice."

"We'll do our best," Pancake said.

"Nicole and I'll go by Watkins' Lumber and see the bookkeeper," I said. "What was her name? "

"Becky Woodley," Nicole said.

How does she remember this stuff? The name that rattled in my brain was Debbie. Not even close. "Yeah, her."

"Are you guys trying to do our job?" Warren asked.

"Just helping," Ray said. "You and Burt showing up with badges might make everyone nervous. We can go in at a lower temperature. Like we're curious, even helping, not threatening."

"Okay. Give it a shot," Warren said. "I'm going to lean on the judge. Try to convince him to give me a warrant on Reed."

"Hopefully he'll stammer out something to us that'll help you there," Pancake said.

Ray looked at me. "Good thought on the robbery. It never crossed my mind."

Ray said that? That I had actually figured out something before him? Of course, the fact that I just might be wrong hung out there. But still . . .

"Wouldn't have crossed mine either," I said. "Except I saw that story and it stuck with me for some reason."

"Because it's clever," Warren said. "In a criminal sort of way."

"When did you come up with this anyway?" Nicole asked.

"Last night."

"And here I thought you were paying attention." She smiled. "I need to up my game."

"Before, and after."

"That's why you weren't snoring."

"I don't snore."

"You wish."

CHAPTER 54

NICOLE AND I swung by Mullins Bakery to grab some coffee. Just after 10:00 a.m. We had skipped breakfast and everything in the display case before us beckoned. Truth was, I wasn't very hungry. Apparently, Nicole felt the same as we both declined Allison's offer of food.

While Allison poured a pair of go cups, she asked about Sean's murder, saying, "Everybody's talking about it. What? Four people now? Do you think all these are connected?"

I played it vague, not wanting to reveal the investigation's new angle. Said that we were still at square one. As far as we knew, Chief Warren was also. In other words, I lied, ending with, "We honestly don't know."

"Will this ever end?" Allison asked.

"Sooner or later," I said. "The thing about criminals is that they always make mistakes. Or open their mouths. Think it's all behind them so it's okay to talk about their deeds."

"But murderers? If you got away with it, why on earth would you tell anyone?"

I added some cream to my coffee. "I read an article by a homicide detective. From Atlanta, I think. He said that a cop's greatest advantage was that criminals were stupid."

"Let's hope." She asked if we wanted anything to eat. No, coffee was fine. I pulled cash from my pocket, but she refused, saying, "It's on the house." I put a five in the tip jar.

Allison looked past us. "Here's my favorite customer."

I turned. Pancake came in.

"Why am I not surprised?" Nicole said.

"Because you know me too well, darling," Pancake said.

"Where's Ray?" I asked.

He jerked his head over his shoulder. "In the truck. Making some calls."

"What would be your pleasure today?" Allison asked him.

"Everything. If I had the time. But I'll settle for a couple of those ham and cheese croissants, three chocolate donuts, and a bear claw. Make that two of them."

"You got it." She began filling a white paper bag.

"Add a bran muffin. I better get something for Ray."

Allison waved the tongs she held over the display case. "I might be able to make rent this month."

"Just trying to help the local economy."

"Here you go." She handed him the bag.

Nicole and I hit the street. Our next stop was Watkins' Lumber. As usual, it was busy. Workers loaded two trucks out front. Inside, a dozen customers stalked the aisles for wood, tools, and gadgets. We found Fred Watkins out back. Supervising two guys who were loading lumber onto another flatbed truck.

"Mr. Watkins?"

He turned, nodded.

"We wanted to say we're sorry to hear about Sean," Nicole said.

"Quite a shock," he said. "Still hard to believe. I mean, first his wife. Now him. Sometimes this planet doesn't make sense."

A worker walked up. Handed him a clipboard. Watkins signed the top page and returned it.

He looked at us. "You been working with Chief Warren? Right?"

"We have."

"She have any suspects yet?"

I shook my head. "Not really."

"What can I do for you?"

"We wanted to talk to Becky Woodley," Nicole said.

Confusion slid over his face. "Why?"

"About the robbery. She and Sean were the only ones here at the time. Right?"

"That's right." His eyes narrowed slightly. "What does that have to do with anything?"

"Maybe nothing," I said. "But Sean was robbed. Then murdered. It's simply something that needs looking at."

"You saying the robbery and his murder are connected in some way?"

"We have no evidence of that. None at all." Not exactly the truth, but that would work for now. "We have to look under every rock."

I was getting pretty good at this deceit thing. First Allison, now Watkins. Wasn't sure how I felt about that. Nicole gave me an expressionless glance, but I saw a slight smile in her eyes. Like a proud mother.

"So why talk to Becky?" Watkins asked.

"She saw the robbers. Masked, but she saw them. Maybe she'll remember something that'll help track them down."

"Then maybe we'll know if they had anything to do with Sean's murder or not," Nicole said.

"Guess that makes sense. Becky isn't here yet. She had some stuff to do." He glanced at his black sports watch. "Should be here in an hour or so."

We thanked him and left. Nicole said she was hungry. I swear Pancake rubbed off on her more every day.

"We should've gotten something over at the bakery," I said.

"I wasn't hungry then."

I suggested The Rib Shack. Nicole said Whitney might be there and maybe we could get her take on things. I replied that with Sean's murder she might have taken the day off. Certainly wouldn't blame her.

Whitney was there. Behind the bar, standing across from Lauren Schultz, seated on a barstool. Lauren had her notebook open, taking notes, Whitney talking, hands orchestrating whatever she was saying.

"Whitney, Lauren," I said as we walked up.

"Hey," Lauren said. "What's up?"

"Same old," I said. Then to Whitney, "How're you doing?"

"Been better."

"We're so sorry," Nicole said.

"Thanks."

"Actually, we didn't expect to see you here."

"Better to work than sit home and let the wheels spin." Her eyes moistened.

"I understand," I said.

"We were just talking about it," Lauren said. "It's awful." She placed her pen on the bar top. "Any idea who could've done it?"

"No. But we're working on it. Chief Warren is also. We just left her office."

"Do you have any thoughts on it?" Nicole asked Whitney.

Whitney gave a headshake. "I wish. I've been racking my brain." She knuckled the corner of one eye. "Nothing. No one."

"What about Reavis Whitt?" I asked. "He and Sean friends?"

I sensed tension rise in her. Her shoulders elevated slightly, lines in her face hardened. "No. Not at all."

"Why was he there? At Sean's?"

"I don't know."

"Maybe delivering something?" I asked.

Her lips tightened. "Maybe." She sniffed. "Look, Sean used marijuana sometimes. I did, too. Not often. He always got it from Reavis. So, probably that's why he was there."

"But you're not sure?" Nicole asked.

"No. In fact, he just got some a couple of weeks ago." Her gaze dropped; she studied the bar top. "Like I said, we didn't use it much. Seemed like we had plenty."

"Maybe he was there for something else?" I asked.

She looked up at me. "Can't imagine what. They weren't friends."

"What about Jack Reed?"

More tension. "What about him? You mean were he and Sean friends?"

I nodded.

"Sean didn't like him. Said he had a mean streak. Never liked being around him."

"But was he? Around him at times?"

"Not that I ever saw. Truth is, I've never actually met Jack. Seen him in here before. Not often. All I know is that Sean said he would be with Reavis sometimes when he made a buy and that he didn't like the guy."

Good instincts was my first thought. My second was too bad he didn't keep his distance from Jack Reed's world. Unless, of course, he was part of Reed's world. In which case, karma is a bitch.

CHAPTER 55

"WHAT DO YOU want?" Jack Reed asked as he opened his apartment door.

"A couple of questions," Pancake said.

"I'm done talking to you guys."

"Problem is, we ain't finished talking with you."

Reed tried to close the door. Pancake stopped it cold with his forearm. Pushed it into Reed, walking him back.

"Don't mind if we do," Pancake said. He continued inside, Ray following. "Neighborly of you to invite us in."

"I didn't."

Pancake grunted. "Could've sworn I heard you ask us to come on in, grab a seat, chat a while."

"You can't come here and harass me. I have rights. Leave or I'll call the cops."

"Go ahead. It'd be the waste of a dime though. I suspect they're going to get around to dropping by before too long."

"Might even be on the way," Ray added. "Chief Warren is thorough if nothing else."

Pancake moved forward. Reed backpedaled into his living room. Pancake and Ray sat on the sofa.

"Take a load off," Pancake said. "Let's have a talk."

Reed hesitated, obviously weighing his options. Apparently finding none that made sense, he eased into the chair opposite them.

"Just to make sure we heard you correctly yesterday," Pancake said, "you know nothing about the murders last night?"

"I told you I didn't."

"And nothing about the earlier ones?" Ray said. "Emily Patterson and Jason Collins?"

"Why're you asking about things you already know?"

Ray smiled. "We don't really know anything."

"We do suspect a lot though," Pancake said.

"The only thing we know is what you told us." Ray leaned forward, resting his elbows on his knees. "But why should we believe anything you say?"

Reed's chin jutted forward. "Because it's the truth."

"You hear that?" Ray asked. "Old Jack Reed is speaking the truth."

"Is he now?" Pancake said. "Is that the truth, Jack? The whole truth and nothing but the truth so help you God?"

Reed's composure was fraying. His gaze couldn't find a comfortable landing place. "I ain't lied about nothing."

"That a fact?" Pancake stabbed him with a glare. "Or do you sometimes shade things? Maybe not tell the entire truth? Maybe simply fucking lie through your teeth?"

"I'm not. I told you everything I know."

"We're nice guys," Ray said. "Until we're not. I'd prefer we sit here and converse like gentlemen. Like adults. But if you keep lying, I might just turn Pancake loose on your sorry ass."

"I don't want to break all your ribs," Pancake said. "Maybe puncture a lung, or trash a kidney. But then again, I just might enjoy it."

Reed glanced toward the entrance. Probably calculating if he could make it.

"Wouldn't try that," Pancake said.

"Here's the question," Ray said. "You know a guy over in Mobile they call Sandman?"

Reed stiffened.

"And let me remind you, you're under oath here."

"I know of him."

"You do any dealing for him?"

Reed hesitated. Pancake thought he looked like his brain might explode. Asking himself what to say, what not to say. Lie or let it out. Pancake balled his fists, relaxed them. Giving him a little incentive.

"Some. Not much."

"Good answer," Ray said. "You see, we paid him a visit. Lucky for you, that's exactly what Sandman said." Ray smiled. "See? Telling the truth isn't that hard."

"You think he's the one that did this? Killed Reavis?" Reed asked.

"Do you?"

"Maybe."

Pancake liked that this was moving along according to plan. Give the bad guy an out. Make him think the heat is off him. Get him talking. Let him spill his guts. Make a mistake.

"He the violent type?" Pancake asked.

"Wouldn't surprise me none. I mean, I understand he has some connection with one of the cartels."

"We know."

Reed actually smiled, getting into it now. Grabbing the rope that might pull him to safety. "Maybe he and his crew decided Reavis and me might rat him out or something. Or maybe he wanted to move his own guys in. Cut us out. And the best way to do that would be if we was gone. So he sent some guys over. Thought it'd be me and Reavis, not Reavis and Sean."

"You believe that?" Ray asked.

"It'd explain everything, wouldn't it?"

Pancake nodded. "It would. Except when we left him all snuggled up in his bed, shit in his pants, we felt he was telling us the truth when he said he didn't know anything about all this. Said it wouldn't be in his best interest."

"You believe him?" Reed asked. "A big-time drug dealer with the cartel behind him?"

"We do," Pancake said, thinking it time to toss another lifeline. "What about the Macks? I mean, if it wasn't Sandman's guys, could they have done this?"

Reed rocked back and forth as if his whole body was nodding in agreement. He clutched the offered line firmly. "Sure. Absolutely. They can be ruthless. Especially Reba. That woman is a danger. A menace to the community."

Ray looked at Pancake. "Maybe we should take a another look at them?"

"I would," Reed said. "Wouldn't surprise me none if they tried to get rid of me and Reavis."

"Why would they do that?" Pancake asked.

That stumped him. For a few seconds anyway. Then it was as if a light went on. Like a man in quicksand seeing his salvation coming. He spoke fast, his body rocking even faster. Almost like a kid riding a hobby horse. "Maybe they found out we was doing some work with Sandman. Took their revenge. Wanted to send him a message not to come on their turf." He looked at Pancake expectedly. "Something like that?"

Pancake nodded. "Makes some sense. Of course, that doesn't explain the murders of Emily and Jason."

Reed had that deer-in-the-headlights look.

"But you don't know anything about that." Pancake stood. Looked down at Reed. Figured he'd toss one more boulder in the pond. "You understand how security cameras work, don't you?"

"What?"

"Have a nice evening."

He and Ray left.

"He's the guy," Pancake said as they walked to his truck.

"Sure is. Not much doubt." Ray opened the passenger door.

"One more thing," Pancake said.

He unlocked and opened the metal tool bin welded into the bed of his truck, tugged out one of the duffels inside, rummaged around. He lifted a magnetic GPS tracking device. He held it up.

"A slight modification to his pickup."

CHAPTER 56

"Thanks for seeing us," I said to Becky Woodley.

"Mr. Watkins said you wanted to ask about the robbery."

"That's right. Can you take us through it?"

"I told the police everything I know," Becky said. "Which isn't much."

"We'd like to hear it again. Maybe you'll remember something else."

Invoices littered her desktop. She gathered them into a neat stack and set them aside. "What do you want to know?"

"Tell us what happened. Step by step."

"The scariest thing I've ever been involved in." She sighed. "I honestly thought they'd kill us."

"Just relax," Nicole said. "Tell us what you remember."

She closed her eyes, as if trying to picture things.

"It was a Saturday. Closing time. Actually a few minutes past. Mr. Watkins had to leave early so he asked if Sean and I would close up."

"That happen often?"

"Sometimes. He's a busy man. Seems to work all the time. Too much if you ask me."

"Which explains his success," Nicole said.

"I guess that's true. Anyway, we were about done. Everything locked up. Sean was going to walk me to my car. That's when they came in. Two of them. One tall, the other shorter. Stockier. They had on ski masks. The tall one had a gun. They made us lie on the floor. Me right here—" she pointed to the the area beside her desk. "Sean over there." Behind where Nicole and I sat. "One of them, the tall one, went to the safe." She pointed to it. "He tried to open it but it was already locked. He got angry. Stuck the muzzle of his gun against my face." Her fingers trembled as she touched her right cheek. "It was cold and hard. He said he'd kill me if I didn't open it."

"So you did," I said.

"Of course. Wouldn't you?"

"I would. No doubt."

"Took three tries. I was shaking so badly. My fingers felt numb, almost dead. Wouldn't do what I wanted them to do. My eyes wouldn't even focus. That made him even more angry." She stopped, looked toward the safe. "He rapped the gun barrel against my head. Said I better quit stalling. I told him I wasn't. I was just scared. I finally got it open. He pushed me to the floor again. Took the money. It was in a bank bag."

"Did he rummage around in there?" I asked. "To see what was what?"

She stared at me and hesitated before she spoke. "You know, he didn't. I didn't think of it before, but he seemed to know what he wanted."

He did, I thought. Sean had told him.

"They wrapped us with duct tape. Ankles, wrists, even over our mouths. Then they left."

"You guys did manage to get away," Nicole said. "How long did that take?"

"Nearly an hour. We scooted toward each other. Then Sean worked my hands free. It wasn't easy. They'd put a half a dozen wraps around our wrists."

"Tell me about the guys," I said. "You said one was taller and the other stockier. What else did you notice?"

"You mean besides the gun? They wore all black. Tee shirts. The masks were similar, but one was black, the other dark gray. The tall one had lighter eyes. Either blue or green. I can't remember. They both wore plain athletic shoes."

"Did you see what brand?"

She shook her head. "No logos that I saw. The shoes were black. One of them had white laces. The shorter guy."

"You have no idea who they were. Right?" Nicole asked.

She sighed. "No. And I've thought about it. A lot."

"What about Sean?" I asked. "Did he seem to know them?"

"He said he didn't. Told Chief Warren that, too."

"Any interactions between them and Sean? Other than him being tied up like you were?"

"Not really. Except maybe one thing. I hadn't given it much thought, but now that you mention it. While I was trying to open the safe, I heard the other guy say something to him. More a whisper. I couldn't hear what was said." She looked at me. "I figured he was threatening him to stay put and not make trouble. That sort of thing."

"Maybe so," I said.

"Wait a minute. You aren't suggesting Sean was in on this, are you?"

I held her gaze but didn't respond.

She leaned forward. Buried her face in her hands for a few seconds, then looked up. "I don't believe that." Her lower lip quivered. "I can't believe that."

"Do you know Jack Reed or Reavis Whitt?"

Her eyes widened. "The guy who was killed with Sean?"

I nodded. "And his partner in crime."

Her breathing became deeper, more rapid. Tears welled in her eyes. "I've never met either of them. Never even heard of them." Her gaze slanted downward. "I don't believe this."

"Let me show you something," Nicole said.

She pulled her iPad from her purse and brought up the photos Ray had made at the Macks'. He had sent them to her. She walked around the desk and laid the device before Becky. She flipped through several pictures.

"Could these two be the guys who robbed you?"

"That's Clive and Reba Mack."

"Focus on the guys they're talking to. Could they be them?"

Becky swiped back and forth, carefully examining each image.

"They look to be the right size. I couldn't see their faces. Or their hair."

Nicole opened up Ray's video and began playing it. They watched as the pair said goodbye to the Macks and walked to their truck.

Becky's head and shoulders sagged. "They walk the same way. The shorter one sort of marched around the room. Like that. The tall one had a slouch to him. Like that." She pointed to the screen.

"You're saying these could be the guys?" Nicole asked.

She sniffed, nodded. "I guess so." She looked up. "I can't be sure."

"She did very well," Nicole said as we walked out to her car.

"Amazingly so. Excellent recall of the entire situation."

"Something like that does make an impression."

"That'll last forever."

I had read an article on this once. Yes, I do read. And sometimes remember. Pancake had given it to me. Said I could use the help. He's funny. Really, he is. It was on how memories are made, stored, and recalled. Pancake read that kind of stuff all the time. One part talked about people in stressful or traumatic situations and how they process the details of the events. In such situations, a car wreck was the example given, the brain kicks into high gear. Gathers information very rapidly. Massive amounts. Then later, some subjects could recall even the most minute details. Often in slow motion. Things like seeing the cracks in the windshield appear very slowly like a creeping snowflake pattern and collisions that were more like deadened thumps rather than violent impacts. Others remember only chaos and can't call up any details. Just noise and blurs of light.

My experience with that was the night Nicole and I jumped in the Gulf from the back of Victor Borkov's massive yacht. It was either that or ride an iron ring to the bottom. I remember it was frantic, me throwing baseballs at Borkov's two thugs and the wind whipping and the waves churning, and us flying off the back of the yacht. Then, everything slowed. The fall seemed to take forever. Almost as if we were flying, not falling. When we hit the water, everything sped up again. The hard impact and its coldness seemed to flip a switch, turning the Gulf into a high-speed washing machine.

Once we climbed into Nicole's car, I called Ray. Told him that Becky had more or less ID'd Reed and Whitt as the robbers. Not completely, but close. Enough that I felt we were on the right track. Ray said he and Pancake would meet us at the hotel.

I then called Chief Warren. Told her the same thing. She said she was prepping a warrant for Reed's place. The judge hadn't signed off on it yet, but she was working him. Said she'd call later.

CHAPTER 57

LATE AFTERNOON HAD begun to melt toward evening, the shadows long and muted, when Chief Billie Warren reached the Evergreen Apartments. It had taken a while to get the warrant. The judge, who she'd known for many years, wavered. Said that even with the wobbly ID provided by Becky Woodley and the fact that Jack Reed had a rather convenient but uncorroborated alibi, he still wasn't sure she had enough probable cause. She reminded him that four citizens had been brutally murdered and a structure had been torched. She added that Jack Reed wasn't likely to register a complaint given his history and current livelihood. As for him getting any evidence dismissed for unlawful search and seizure in a future trial, she said she didn't give one hoot. All she wanted was to take a dangerous and armed thug off the street. The judge finally relented. After making her reword the application two more times. Aggravating, time consuming, but in the end, it worked.

Now she gathered the troops in the parking lot down the way from Jack Reed's unit. The troops consisted of Burt Moody, three uniformed officers, and a crime scene tech.

"I don't see his truck anywhere," Moody said. "You think he's out somewhere?"

"Would make things easier," Warren said. "Not have to deal with him while we do our search." She scanned the faces of the three eager officers. "I want everyone to walk away from this in good order. Got it?" A couple of head nods. "We have to assume that he's in there, that he's armed, that he might resist. First order is to protect yourself, and each other." She looked from face to face. "You've been trained in this. You know what to do. Any questions?"

A few headshakes but no one spoke.

"Let's go."

Warren rapped on the door, announced herself. Asked for Reed to come out. Nothing. The place was dark. Obviously, he wasn't home. Everyone reholstered their weapons.

"Want to kick in the door?" Moody asked.

"No," Warren said. "I want you to go get a key from the manager."

"He won't be happy."

"We're not here to please the natives."

"Just saying, he's a surly guy."

Warren pulled the warrant from her pocket, unfolded it, and handed it to Moody. "Wave this in his face. That should do the trick."

Five minutes later, the door was open and they were inside. More shouting for Reed, more silence in response. Each room was cleared. Warren had the uniforms wait outside while she, Moody, and the tech searched.

In the living room, a few grains of what appeared to be meth dotted the coffee table. A bong sat on the floor by the sofa, and a single 9 mm shell lay on the carpet, near the front curtain.

The kitchen was messy. A pot with what looked like the remnants of canned soup and a bowl and spoon sat in the sink. Milk, cheese, bread, mayo, mustard, salsa, and three beers in the fridge. Cereal and canned soup in the cabinets. And a small bag of marijuana, mostly stems and seeds, in one drawer.

The bedroom told the tale. The bed was unmade, sheet and blanket mostly on the floor. Another 9 mm round on the carpet. A partially smoked joint in a yellow Cohiba ashtray on the bedside table. The closet was empty except for a few hangers, and on the floor, sneakers that had seen better days, a pair of dirty blue socks, a stained and frayed white tee shirt. A small duffel held nothing of interest.

"I don't see any clothes," Moody said, stating the obvious.

Warren walked over to the three-drawer chest and pulled open each. Two mismatched pairs of socks, some underwear, another ratty tee shirt, a red baseball cap with an Atlanta Braves logo, and a few coins were the sum total.

"He's flown," Warren said.

"Looks that way." She pulled her phone, then looked at Moody. "Get an APB out on his truck. Include Mississippi in case he heads that way."

"Got it."

She dialed.

CHAPTER 58

EARLIER, AFTER WE returned to the Grand Hotel, Nicole and I explored the brick pathways that wound through the wonderfully landscaped grounds, beneath Spanish moss–draped trees. We played with the very guest-friendly cats, nodded to other strollers, and ultimately ended up at the end of the pier, beneath the gazebo. We leaned on the railing and watched as the sun began its descent flaming the western sky.

"I love this place," she said.

"What's not to love?"

"Can we come back sometime under better circumstances?"

"Absolutely."

"I'm going to hold you to that."

"You can hold anything you want."

She laced her fingers with mine. "I love that about you."

"It goes both ways."

"Speaking of which, how about a shower before dinner?"

"Good idea,"

It was. We had one of those showers that Nicole loves. Me, too. Afterward, I lay on the bed, while Nicole brushed her hair.

"Sure looks like your idea was correct," Nicole said. "Sean planning the robbery to pay for the murder."

"Sure does."

"That was very clever of you. Coming up with Sean's entire cabal."

"I like that word. Cabal. Sounds so sinister."

"It is. And it was."

She spun toward me. She wore only the hotel bathrobe. It parted just enough to give me an idea.

"Come here," I said, patting the bed next to me.

She did. Curled in my arm.

"I guess our work is done here," she said.

I slid my hand beneath the robe and down her back. "Not even close."

"I mean the case. It's all up to Chief Warren now."

"Which means we don't have any distractions. And can enjoy our last night here."

She rolled on top of me. "Sounds like a plan."

My cell buzzed. I considered ignoring it, but Nicole scooped it up from the bedside table, handed it to me. I said a silent prayer that it wasn't Tammy. About now would be her kind of timing. It wasn't. It was Ray.

"Reed's in the wind," he said.

"Oh?"

"Warren executed the warrant on his apartment. He cleared out. Meet us in the lobby in five. We're going to meet her at the station."

After we dressed and scurried downstairs, we found Pancake near the door, working his phone, Ray waiting impatiently.

"Warren asked for our help finding him?" I asked.

"We offered. She called to let us know he was gone. Said she has an APB out. I told her that we know where he is. She couldn't re-fuse that."

"Pancake?"

Ray nodded. "He put a GPS tracker on Reed's truck."

"Of course he did."

Fifteen minutes later, we were in Warren's office.

"Okay, where is he?" Warren asked.

Ray nodded to Pancake. He turned his phone toward her. "Here."

I looked over her shoulder. A satellite picture. Rural area. Single house, nearby barn. Red dot in the middle of the screen.

"It's his uncle's place," Pancake said. "Guy named Kenneth Reed. You know him?"

"Never heard of him."

"It's up just north of Daphne. Off Wilson Road."

"How'd you do this?" Warren asked.

"Placed a GPS tracker on his truck when we visited earlier," Pancake said.

Warren looked at him. "Clever. And something I couldn't have done without another warrant."

"We do have a bit more leeway."

Warren turned to Moody. "See if we have anything on this Kenneth Reed."

"You don't," Pancake said. "He's a farmer. Same acreage for over twenty years. No criminal record. Not even a speeding ticket."

"Not sure I want to know how you uncovered that."

Pancake shrugged. "It's what we do."

"Apparently. But how'd you do all this so fast?"

"Only took about ten minutes." He smiled. "If you know which rabbit holes to peek in."

"Okay. I'll call the chief up there. Maybe the sheriff. Get some city and county backup and pay him a visit."

"Bringing in the cavalry could create a dicey situation," Ray said. "Maybe a standoff. Could get messy."

"Don't see any way to avoid that."

"Might I make a suggestion?" Pancake said.

"Suggest away."

He jerked his head toward the door. "Step into my office."

Warren looked confused but joined the parade as we all followed Pancake to his truck. He popped open the toolbox, lifted out a bag, zipped it open. Warren's eyes widened as he pulled out equipment.

"Where'd you get all this stuff?"

"Ray's toy closet. We have night vision, thermal scanners, shotgun mics, and these." He lifted a nasty-looking weapon, held it up. "Heckler & Koch HK419 assault rifle. Just in case."

"Looks like overkill to me," Warren said.

"It is," Pancake said. "Unless it's needed." He hefted the weapon. "If it's good enough for the Delta Force guys, it's good enough for us."

Concern fell over Warren's face. "This isn't exactly a war we're going to."

"Funny thing about wars," Ray said. "No one ever sees them coming until they're all over them."

Warren said nothing.

Ray continued. "The best way to prevent a war is to have overwhelming superiority in information, mobility, and firepower. Seems to make folks much more polite."

The worry creases in Warren's forehead deepened. "I don't know about this."

"Look," Ray said. "We can get in there. See who's at the property. Maybe get to Reed, both Reeds, before they even know. End this quietly and quickly."

"And if it gets crazy?"

"That's what this if for." Pancake nodded toward the rifle.

Warren considered it. Looked at Pancake, Ray. "I take it you guys have done this kind of thing before."

"I could tell you a few stories," Ray said. "Some of them anyway."

"Military?"

Ray gave a quick nod. "You might say that."

"Can't say I'm not more than a little curious."

"Later." Ray smiled. "Over a beer. But right now we need to take Jack Reed off the streets."

She hesitated, nodded. "Okay. But I hope I don't regret this."

"Always better to ask for forgiveness than permission," Pancake said.

And we were off.

Nicole followed Pancake's truck, which followed Warren and Moody in Warren's SUV. Made her crazy to bring up the rear. They were moving way too slow for her blood.

My cell buzzed. This time it was Tammy. Her timing was a thing of beauty. And aggravation. I answered.

"I'm a little busy, Tammy."

"Walter's stay was extended. Another two days."

I guessed she missed the busy part.

"Good for him," I said.

"What does that mean?"

"Business must be good. More money for you."

"Yeah, I get that."

Of course she did. Money and Tammy were one and the same. Her main joy. Maybe even reason to exist.

"But what am I supposed to do? Here all by myself?"

"Go online," I said. "Buy some shit."

"Why do you have to be this way?"

"Bad parenting."

"That's a given. But I could use a little sympathy."

"I'll send some your way."

"You're such an ass."

"I think we established that long ago."

"Are you in a car?" Tammy asked. "Sounds like you're in a car."

"Nicole and I are headed to a shoot-out."

That stopped her for a couple of seconds.

"I hope nothing happens to her."

"What about me? Don't I get a little sympathy?"

A sharp laugh. "They can shoot you in the ass for all I care."

"They just might."

"Since you're all ass, it should be easy."

"Goodbye, Tammy."

"Don't you hang up."

"Why not?"

"What about me?"

"Wash your hair. Do your nails. Wait, I got it, go buy one of those puzzles. One with flowers or beach scenes. Maybe a cat. Try to get all the pieces to fit without using scissors. That should occupy you until Walter gets back."

"Asshole." She hung up.

"I love her calls," Nicole said.

"I know you do."

CHAPTER 59

KENNETH REED'S FARM clung to the north edge of Wilson Road. Couple of miles above and east of Daphne. The farmhouse faced down a gentle slope a good two hundred yards from the road. The grounds that fronted it were plowed and ready for winter planting. Pancake's map showed that a pair of dirt roads bent off the blacktop and flanked the field's east and west edges. The closest, left of the house, edged the furrowed soil, clearly visible from the house along its entire journey. It terminated near a barn, just behind the house. The other wound through trees, which protected it from view. We chose the later. Lights off, we crept up the rutted road until we were a hundred yards from Uncle Kenneth's home.

It was nearing 9:00 p.m. Dark, the sky mostly clear, the moon nearly full. Its glow silvered the trees around us.

We gathered near Pancake's truck. He looped a massive pair of binoculars around his neck.

"What are those?" Moody asked.

"Pretty cool toy," Pancake said. "Gives me night vision and infrared heat signatures."

Moody whistled. "Bet those were cheap."

"Not bad. No more than a couple of mortgage payments."

"More military-grade stuff?" Warren asked.

"Sort of," Pancake said. "Most of this stuff is a generation or two old but they work just fine for our needs."

"Where do you get this kind of thing?" Moody asked. "I don't see anything like this online."

"It's there," Pancake said. "Even on Amazon. Maybe not exactly this, but some pretty cool stuff." Pancake adjusted the neck strap. "We get most of our toys through friends."

"Some friends you have," Warren said.

"The best," Ray said.

Boy were they, I thought. That night. The one where Nicole and I leapt into the raging Gulf from Victor Borkov's yacht. It was Ray and his friends who came to the rescue. With some nasty toys. Riddled Borkov and his crew with automatic weapon fire.

"What's the plan?" Warren asked.

"You guys stay here," Pancake said. "I'll go take a gander." He headed into the trees.

I followed. He heard me and turned. "What are you doing?"

"Keeping you out of trouble."

He grunted, shook his head, moved on. He squatted near the tree line. I settled beside him. The house was single-story, white clapboard. Interior light fell through the front and side windows. Pancake raised the binocs, made a couple of adjustments.

"Don't see anyone inside." Another adjustment. "Let's make a thermal scan." He did. Then, "I see you."

"They in there?" I asked.

"Yeah. Both in the living room." He scanned the surrounding area. "Pretty open. Not a lot of cover. Barn just beyond the house." He lowered the glasses. "We need to get closer."

We returned to the group.

"They're both in there," Pancake said.

"Anyone else?" Ray asked.

"Only two heat signatures. Both in what I suspect is the living room. Let's move on up the road and get closer. See if we can get eyes and ears on them."

He reached into the toolbox and pulled out another piece of equipment. He handed it to me. A pair of headphones and a pistol-gripped wand-like gadget.

"Shotgun mic," Pancake said. "I made a few modifications. Moved the processor into the grip, attached it to the mic. All one piece now. Easier to use. Simply point at your target, press the trigger to activate the mic, and listen."

"Amazing," Moody said.

"Okay. Let's saddle up," Pancake said.

He pulled out a Glock and stuffed it in his pants. Ray hung the HK assault rifle over one shoulder. Warren and Moody each checked their service weapons. I felt naked.

"Do I get a gun?" Nicole asked.

Pancake smiled. "Only if you promise to shoot Jake if he screws up."

"Deal."

I didn't bother to ask for a weapon. Would've been a waste of time.

"You guys don't need guns," Ray said. "Too dangerous."

As we walked up the road, Ray explained the situation and for some reason it made sense. He said four people with guns was more than enough. We'd be coming from different directions and a cross-fire situation, or worse, a circular firing squad, could result. Made sensing what was down range at all times an absolute necessity. Otherwise friendly fire could be devastating. Said that sort of attention to detail required skill and experience. The point being that Nicole and me didn't. Like I said, it made sense.

Not that I didn't understand down range. But for me it meant firing a split-fingered fastball over the catcher's head—down range as it were. Nothing good ever followed. Could simply be embarrassment. I mean, really, a major league pitcher chucking one into the sixth row? Or it could advance any base runners, even let a guy on third score. A wild pitch letting in the tying, or leading, or God forbid the winning run was a pitcher's worst nightmare. That and giving up six hits in the first inning. Been there, done that.

Bottom line? I didn't get a gun. Fortunately, neither did Nicole. I felt much safer.

CHAPTER 60

SOON WE WERE level with the house, its lights barely visible through the sparse stand of trees. Fortunately, the wispy clouds that lolled in from the west muted the nearly full moon. We congregated in the deeper shadows, several feet back from the tree line.

Pancake lifted the binoculars. "They aren't in the living room anymore." He scanned the house, the property. "Reed's truck is out back, near the barn. There's a tractor there, but I don't see any other vehicles."

"There." I pointed.

The two men returned to the living room, from this distance clearly visible through the side window. Reed paced back and forth while Kenneth dropped onto the sofa. Reed stopped his movement, looked at his uncle, making a point, arms waving. He started pacing again.

"Take a listen," Pancake said to me.

I slipped on the head phones, aimed the mic at the window. The voices popped into focus, amazingly sharp. Uncle Kenneth's raspy voice made it easy to determine who was talking.

This is what I heard:

KENNETH: "I don't like it."

REED: "I don't have much of a choice."

KENNETH: "Sooner or later they'll come by and talk to me. What am I going to say?"

REED: "Nothing. Say you haven't seen me in weeks. I'll be in New Orleans by then. Gone and soon forgotten."

KENNETH: "I don't think they'll just quit. Not with what you did."

REED: "I got friends in New Orleans. I can disappear."

KENNETH: "You sure?"

REED: "Yeah. Look, I'm sorry to drag you into this. It's not fair. But I needed somewhere to hide and figure this out."

KENNETH: "You know I'll do what I can."

REED: "I think I should leave tonight. Right now."

KENNETH: "Not in the morning?"

REED: "What if they show up beforehand? That would put you in a pickle. Besides, probably better to travel at night."

KENNETH: "If that's want you want. I'll help you get ready."

I turned toward Pancake and the others. "The uncle isn't happy with him but says he'll help. Reed says he's going to leave right now. Go to New Orleans and try to disappear. Was going to wait until morning, but he's scared."

"Okay," Ray said. "Let's move." He looked at Warren. "You and Moody take the front. Pancake and I the back. Wait until he comes out and heads for his truck."

"What about us?" Nicole asked.

"Stay here."

She frowned. "Yeah, like that's going to happen."

Seemed like a plan to me. Why get in the middle of something that could turn bad in a minute? I said so.

"You stay here and watch the cars," Nicole said. "I'm going with Ray and Pancake."

"Maybe we should simply knock on the door?" Warren said. "Give him a chance to give up."

"He won't," Ray said. "He's beyond that. Best if we get him out of the house. You two can make sure Uncle Kenneth doesn't pick up a shotgun or something and make things more difficult."

"Okay." Warren nodded. "I agree."

And just like that it was decided.

CHAPTER 61

I WATCHED AS Warren and Moody, staying low, darted from the trees and slanted toward the front corner of the house. Nicole and I followed Pancake and Ray up the tree line, across an open area, and past the rear of the house, giving it a wide berth. We reached the barn and settled along its rear wall. Reed's truck was thirty feet away. The back of the house was dark. We waited.

Not for long. Reed came out the back door, followed by his uncle. Each carried a duffel bag.

Then things happened fast.

Ray and Pancake stepped from behind the barn. I peeked around its edge, Nicole clutching my shoulder, looking past me. Ray leveled the rifle toward the two men.

"Reed," he shouted. "On the ground."

Reed froze. Dropped the duffel. His uncle stood transfixed. Then, he also dropped the bag he held; his arms jumped toward the sky.

"Now," Ray said.

The gun came from nowhere. Reed got off two shots. One hit the edge of the barn just above my head, spraying splinters. The other struck Pancake in his left arm. Reed dove behind his truck. Ray opened up, spraying the Ford. Headlamps and the windshield shattered; bullets thumped into the truck's metal. Then, the rattle of gunfire stopped. The sudden silence seemed to suck the oxygen from the air.

Pancake staggered back around the corner. One hand clapped over his arm, blood seeping between his fingers. "Goddamn it," he said.

"Let me see," Nicole said.

"It's a scratch."

"You're bleeding."

"I'll rub some dirt on it. It'll be fine."

It didn't look fine. The bullet had frayed the sleeve of his shirt, blood soaking it downstream. Looked almost black in the moonlight.

Before Nicole or I could argue, he moved forward to where Ray knelt. He dropped to one knee.

I stole a quick glance around the corner, above their heads. Reed had taken refuge behind the truck. Uncle Kenneth still stood with his hands in the air.

"Get down," Ray shouted.

Kenneth dropped to the ground, facedown, arms spread as if flying.

"Reed," Ray said. "Give it up. Don't make this any worse."

Warren and Moody scurried around the front corner of the house, guns raised.

"Put your hands up," Warren ordered.

Reed didn't hesitate. He darted toward the barn. Warren and Moody fired several rounds. I could hear the bullets strike wood.

I felt Nicole move and turned. She ran along the back side of the barn. What the hell? I followed. I caught her at the corner.

"What are you doing?"

"He shot Pancake. I'm going to kill the son-of-a-bitch."

"What?"

I heard a pair of gunshots. From the front of the barn.

"Reed," Warren shouted. "You've got nowhere to go. Come on out. Make it easy on everyone."

I heard a shuffling sound. Somewhere around the corner, along the side of the barn. Nicole did, too. We peered around the corner. Reed. Running toward us. Gun in hand. I grabbed Nicole, pulled her back. Reed veered to his left, chugged toward a stand of trees at least a hundred yards away.

I clutched Nicole's arm. She would have none of that. She jerked free and took off. On a straight line that would intercept Reed.

My first instinct was to yell, tell her to get down. But that would only alert Reed. And right now, he hadn't seen her. His only glance back was over his left shoulder, toward the front of the barn. Where Warren and Moody were.

I sprinted after Nicole. My brain screamed prayer after prayer that Reed wouldn't turn and start firing. There was no place to hide and nothing but our meager Krav Maga classes to defend us. Not much against a handgun.

I saw several loose fist-sized rocks on the ground. I scooped a pair up. Not much better than Krav Maga but better than empty hands.

Nicole closed on Reed; I closed on her. I tried to move faster, get her down, but it was like one of those dreams where no matter how hard you try you can't get away, or reach the person you're trying to save. It seemed things began to slow down.

Nicole was still twenty yards away when Reed sensed her approach, his head swiveling that way. Shock caused him to stumble. He quickly recovered and swung the gun her way.

I let loose a perfect fastball. Absolutely perfect. Maybe one of the best of my life. And missed. It whizzed by his head, just nipping his ear. But it redirected his attention toward me for a second. Now, he angled the muzzle in my direction. He fired just as I let loose the other rock. The bullet whined past my left ear. So close I could almost feel it. Fortunately, the rock caught him in the right cheek. He staggered, again recovered.

Too slow. Nicole was on him. She slammed the heel of her right hand into his nose. Blood erupted. The gun loosened in his hand. She chopped her forearm across his. The weapon thudded to the ground. She spun and kicked him in the ribs. A gush of air escaped. He wobbled, but didn't go down. He unleashed a wide left hook. Caught Nicole square on her cheek. She went down.

I tackled him. Football was never my game, but Pancake would've been proud. We rolled and slugged and I swore he tried to bite me. I took a couple of shots, but managed to land a few of my own.

This went on for what seemed hours but more likely only a few seconds. I heard Warren's voice. Shouting, coming closer. Reed grabbed me by the throat. His mangled nose dripped blood over my face. I slammed a fist into his jaw.

Then the gun appeared.

I don't know how he got it. We must have rolled over it in our struggles. He squeezed my throat as he raised up, the gun's black muzzle hole lifting toward my face.

Then, pop. His head jerked sideways. He shuddered and collapsed to one side.

Pancake walked up, his gun dangling at his side. "Motherfucker."

CHAPTER 62

BACK IN FAIRHOPE, at the ER, Pancake was top priority. He was taken into their trauma cubicle. Nicole and I were placed in a room just down the hall. After the doctor finished with Pancake, he examined us. Ordered X-rays, and when they returned, neither of us had any fractures. Me bruised ribs, Nicole a facial contusion. We'd live, just be sore for a while.

We pulled back the curtain and entered Pancake's cubicle. He was in his element. Two nurses fussing over him. Him smiling, soaking it all in. Calling each "darling."

The doctor had determined that the bullet had passed through and had hit "nothing important." He had cleaned and dressed the wound and X-rayed the arm. Offered Pancake some morphine for pain, but Pancake allowed that pain meds were for wimps.

"I'll have some whiskey later," he said.

So Pancake.

The doctor left.

"The doctor said you should stay overnight," one of the nurses said.

"For you I would, darling. But I better mosey on home."

"Probably not the smartest thing," she said.

"Probably not." He smiled. "But why don't you go home with me?"

She looked at Nicole and me. "Is he always like this?"

"This is nothing," Nicole said. "Wait until he really gets going."

"There everyone is."

I turned. Lauren Shultz.

"Lauren?" I said. "What are you doing here?"

She laughed. "Chasing the story."

"How did you know?"

She raised an eyebrow. "I have my sources. Besides, I didn't want to miss the party."

Warren walked in. She saw Lauren. "Well, if it isn't the press."

"That would be me."

"If you found your way here on a night like this one has been," Warren said, "I suspect you're going to be one hell of a crime reporter."

Lauren beamed. "Speaking of which, I'd like to come by and talk with you."

Warren nodded. "My office. Tomorrow morning. Or should I say, later this morning."

"I'll be there."

Warren looked at Pancake. "You okay?"

"Fine. Just a scratch. Nothing a couple of bourbons and a mess of Jake's ribs won't patch up."

"Sounds like some pretty good medicine to me."

"Everything okay up on the farm?" I asked Warren.

"Mostly. I called in the sheriff. Wasn't happy with us storming into his turf, but after I rolled out the story, I think he was relieved we hadn't dragged him into it. But he still wants to have a sit-down with each of you." She looked at Pancake. "Especially you and Ray."

"No problem," Pancake said

"I smoothed the path. Made it clear that you and Ray, hell, all of us, did what was needed."

"And Uncle Kenneth?" Nicole asked.

"The sheriff didn't take him in or anything. Said he wasn't yet sure how to handle him, or if any laws were actually broken on his part. Said that he and Kenneth would sit down and have a talk about things."

Ray walked in. "All good?"

"Seems that way," Warren said. "I was just telling Pancake the sheriff up there wants to have a chat with you guys."

Ray nodded. "We can do that."

"I've got to say," Warren said, "it's been a pleasure, of sorts, working with you." She waved a hand. "All of you."

"We appreciate you letting us inside," Ray said. "You didn't have to do that."

Warren gave a quick nod. "In return, you owe me a beer and a few war stories."

"Done deal."

CHAPTER 63

WE WERE BACK in Gulf Shores. Three days later. Pancake's arm was heeling and he had indeed been treating it with bourbon and ribs. And everything else on Captain Rocky's menu. Someday I'll have to send him a bill. I'll probably forget to though.

Speaking of ribs. Mine were still sore, but at least I could breathe normally. Coughing, and oh Lord sneezing, were still an adventure. Nicole showed little sympathy and no mercy, saying that if I focused a little more, I could ignore my ribs during sex. My ribs thought otherwise. But I soldiered on. It's what I do.

Nicole's bruising got worse the first couple of days but was now beginning to recede. She covered it somewhat with makeup—something I'd never seen her wear. Didn't need it. Maybe a swipe of blush and a touch of lipstick every now and then, but nothing else. The swelling gave her a slightly lopsided appearance, but she wore it well. As beautiful as always.

Nicole and I were hanging at Captain Rocky's, drinking whiskey with Pancake, when my cell rang. It was Daniel. I had tried to reach him the day after the big shoot-out, but he was on patrol. Out of reach.

"What's up?" he asked.

I put the phone on speaker. "I'm sitting here at my bar with Nicole and Pancake. Where are you?"

"Can't say."

"I understand. I called to let you know we got the guys who did it."

I told him the story. A thumbnail anyway. Giving him what we knew about Reed and Whitt. About Sean's involvement, the robbery to pay for it.

"So, in the end, it was all about money?" Daniel asked.

"Looks that way."

"I guess you never really know anyone, do you?" Daniel asked.

"There's truth in that."

"I can't thank you enough," he said.

"We had to earn our buck."

"I'd say you did. And then some."

"Pancake'll never tell you this but I will." Pancake frowned, but I waved him away. "We're heading back up to Fairhope in a few days. To place the head marker Pancake bought for Emily."

"Really? I can't believe you'd do that."

"It's Emily," Pancake replied. "Enough said."

I hate to hear a Marine cry. But that's what he did.